Praise for Scott Sherman's *First You Fall*

"This is a gem of a novel. I read it in one day, recommended it to a bunch of friends, and, for the first time in my reading life, received back unanimous agreement with my own enthusiasm. The story's got characters you care about, a mystery worth solving, and a pitch-perfect sense of humor. (Each time I recall the hero's climb up a tree outside a certain bedroom window I start laughing.) *First You Fall* exemplifies that rare bird: light reading that is never lite."

—Drewey Wayne Gunn, author of *The Gay Male Sleuth in Print and Film*

"Spending time with Scott Sherman's reluctant detective, Kevin Connor, is like being with a lovable best friend. He's cute, adorable, sexy, the ultimate naughty-but-nice boy next door. Balancing a career as a hustler, volunteer work, an ex-boyfriend or two, a bevy of admirers, a murdered best friend, an intrusive mother, and a horde of suspects is no problem for sweet but smart Kevvy. *First You Fall* is an endlessly enjoyable read, with plenty of laugh-out-loud moments. Sherman is particularly adept at making his quirky cast of characters sing out loud, oftentimes with nothing more than a word or two. Enjoy this book. I think the author wants you to."

—Anthony Bidulka, author of the Russell Quant mystery series

"*First You Fall* is a hoot, particularly in the interaction between the hero and his mother. It's also a solid, carefully-constructed mystery. I love the way in which Kevin's physical attributes—he's small, blond, and cute—work into the story and determine the way he operates, as both a hustler and a detective. He's a resourceful, determined sleuth, and I hope we'll see a lot more of him in the future."

—Neil S. Plakcy, author of the Hawaiian Mahu mystery series

"I love Kevin Connor! Even though I don't have the right pieces for him to love me back, and even though he's a fictional character, I'd gladly pay Kevin for a few hours of his . . . time. From the first page I was giggling and oohing over Sherman's boy-toy hero. Then I was gasping at the book's sneaky twists and turns. Then grimacing at the gross bits and back to oohing at the love story! With murder, romance, and plenty of hot sex between cute guys, *First You Fall* is a quick, fast-paced, fun read that I heartily recommend."

—Megan Hart, author of *Tempted*

FIRST YOU FALL

A Kevin Connor Mystery

Scott Sherman

Manufactured in the United States of America

This trade paperback original is published by Alyson Books
245 West 17th Street, New York, NY 10011

Distribution in the United Kingdom by Turnaround Publisher Services Ltd.
Unit 3, Olympia Trading Estate, Coburg Road, Wood Green
London N22 6TZ England

First Edition: June 2008

08 09 10 11 12 13 14 15 16 17 a 10 9 8 7 6 5 4 3 2

ISBN: 1-59350-059-9
ISBN-13: 978-1-59350-059-7

Library of Congress Cataloging-in-Publication data are on file.

Cover design by Victor Mingovits

One day, I'll write books I can dedicate to my parents and children; this isn't one of them. Kids, if you're reading this, put it down till you're twenty-one.

So, Marty, this is for you. It's not necessarily the kind of thing you'd like, but then again, neither was I when we first met. Sixteen years later, we're still together. I hope the book grows on you, too. I love you.

FIRST YOU FALL

CHAPTER 1

A Date, A Death, A Return from the Dead

EIGHT O'CLOCK ON a hot and humid summer night in The Astor, a pricey hotel on New York's Central Park West. The paintings were original oils, the furniture heavy mahogany, and the sheets had a thread count three times higher than my hourly rate. Not that I'd gotten to sample them.

Well, not this time at least.

A strange hotel room with a stranger. So far, it was a pretty usual night for me. I figured I'd finish up work, stop off at home to change, and then meet my friend Freddy at a club.

What I didn't know was that before the night was over I'd be embraced by a homeless woman, I'd ignore a call I really shouldn't have, that a man I loved would turn up dead, and that a man I considered dead would come back to life.

Now, those things *were* unusual.

They were also just the start . . .

The room smelled like expensive soap, probably because I just used so much of it. The air conditioning was too cold on my naked body, but, in my line of work, I've put up with worse.

"So, Kevin," my client, asked, sitting in an overstuffed easy chair and watching me get dressed, "what's a nice boy like you doing in a business like this?"

It wasn't the first time I've been asked that question. OK, it wasn't the hundredth, either. But when you're twenty-three years old, clean-cut, and reasonably intelligent, people are always surprised to discover you're a male prostitute.

Why, my client wondered, would a guy like me make his living like this? Well, you'd think the three hundred dollars he paid just to watch me take a shower would have given him a clue.

"I'm a people person," I told him, pulling on my underwear. "And all the jobs at the Gap were filled."

My client chuckled. I had forgotten his name, but he was an out-of-towner, and this would probably be the only time we got together. Local clients often want to see you more than once, but travelers like a new guy every time.

"I enjoyed watching you," he said. I figured as much when he shot a load so hard that, even over the roar of the shower, I could hear it hit the shower door. I wouldn't have thought such vandalism would be acceptable in a hotel like the Astor.

"You're really cute," he said.

I get "cute" a lot. At five foot three and one hundred twenty-five pounds, with blond hair that I keep short on the sides and floppy on the top, it's hard to be called anything else. My face fits the bill, too, with a slightly broad nose, thick lips, and cheeks that turn red at the slightest chill or embarrassment.

Rent boys have to keep fit, so I work out four times a week. Luckily, I have a fast metabolism, so I can pretty much eat what I want. Years of high school gymnastics have made me limber and strong.

I also have a nice dick. It's not huge—just an inch or two above the American average—but on a little guy like me, it's impressive.

The whole thing makes a nice package. I don't mean to sound conceited, but in my line of business, you have to know your product. I work at my looks because they're my living. My body is nice, but that's because I exercise to maintain it. I keep my hair long in front because it's such a good flirting aid.

I'm the archetypal little brother, the boy next door, Dennis the

Menace all grown up and gone gay. I'm, well, cute, and that's what sells the tickets.

"Thanks," I told my client. Gary? Larry? Something like that.

"So, really," he asked, "how did you get into this?"

I figured I'd never see this guy again, so why be coy? Dressed now in baggy Abercrombie cargo shorts and a tight CK T-shirt, I sat on his lap.

Guys love it when I sit in their lap.

"It's not that interesting a story," I said. "I was a sophomore in college and went to a bar. This incredible looking guy came up and asked me to dance. I wound up going back to his place and the next morning, he says 'You're really cute, and a great lay. I know a way you can get paid for both.'

"Then, he told me about Mrs. Cherry—you know, the guy you talked to on the phone?"

"Mrs. Cherry's a guy?" my client asked.

"Yeah, a drag queen. Or a transvestite. I'm not sure which. Anyway, I was a psychology major at the time, with a minor in English. I knew I wanted to go to graduate school, but I couldn't afford it. And psychology majors aren't generally big money-makers.

"So, I called Mrs. Cherry, went for an audition, and, well, here I am."

My client tousled my hair. Yeah, I get a lot of that.

"Do you like your work?" he asked.

This could be a tricky question. Some tricks get off on your not liking it—they want to feel like they're defiling you or something. But, you can usually tell those guys right off the bat. They're creepy in other ways, too. This guy seemed normal.

"Yeah, I do. I've been fooling around with guys since I was fifteen years old. Mrs. Cherry handles the business end of things really well—everyone is referred by someone she knows or by a former client. That makes it pretty safe. It's not like I'm walking the streets or anything. So, yeah, I like it."

"Yes, but doesn't your, um, work make it hard to have a regular relationship?"

The truth was, I didn't want a regular relationship. The last time I was in love was with Tony Rinaldi. I was sixteen, he was nineteen. I knew it was love because of that squishy feeling I got in my stomach whenever I saw him in the neighborhood, playing stickball or hanging with my older sister. I had been watching him for years, getting close just to breathe in the way he smelled in the summer, green and fresh like newly mowed grass. Tony was six feet of smooth Italian pony boy deliciousness, lanky muscles, dark eyes, and ebony hair that he wore in a sleek Caesar.

When I finally seduced him, it was like fireworks and Ecstasy and the best ice cream sundae of your life, all mashed together. We spent two months screwing everywhere we could. Tony's kisses were so ravenous it was as if he was trying to inhale me. He did everything in bed. He even let me fuck him (although only once, claiming that for such a little fellow, I sure could hurt a guy).

It was after that when, sticky with sex and sweat, he pulled me close and told me that he loved me. I had known for a while, but it was still the greatest thing I'd ever heard.

It was also the first time he called me "Kevvy," a nickname no one else had ever called me. It was almost as good as when he said he loved me.

Two weeks later, I came home to an e-mail that stopped my heart. "It has to be over between us. I'm going to college this fall, and I think it's best we don't see each other again. I hope someday we can be friends. Just friends. Take care. Your friend, Tony."

Had that e-mail contained the word "friend" one more time, I would have printed it out and used the paper to set his house on fire.

Since then, falling in love hasn't really been my thing. I didn't need any more squishy stomachs, thank you. I had friends, friends with privileges, and tricks. Maybe I'd love again someday, but I didn't need romantic love to make me feel complete.

Of course I didn't go into all this with some guy whose name I couldn't even recall. "I'm really concentrating on getting into a graduate school, and on my volunteer work," I told him. "I also help out at the local AIDS meal charity." Both of these statements were not only true, but they were the kind of things that make clients give you bigger tips.

Clients like when you spend extra time like this talking after the shooting is over. It's rude to fuck and run. No one wants to feel hustled—even by a hustler.

We spoke for a while more, and then my client announced that he had to get some work done. He had already paid for my time through Mrs. Cherry with his credit card, but as I was walking out the door, he slipped an extra hundred into my jeans.

"You were great," he said, shaking my hand as if we had just negotiated a very important business deal.

"Thanks,"—I remembered!—"Jerry. Feel free to ask for me again if you come back to New York." I flung my backpack over my shoulder.

"Well," Jerry said sheepishly, "I usually like a new guy . . ."

Figures. Now I'd have to forget his name again.

There was nothing forgettable about the furnace outside. New York in August is like a hot day in Hell. Even at 9:00 P.M., the air was wet and heavy.

I was supposed to meet my best friend, Freddy, at a bar at around midnight. That gave me enough time to drop off a book I had borrowed from my friend Allen Harrington on the way home.

Allen and I had met under odd circumstances. A year ago, he had called Mrs. Cherry looking for some companionship. He had asked for a blond, blue-eyed guy, and I fit the bill. But when I knocked on the door, the good-looking, distinguished gentleman of about sixty looked disappointed.

"Oh no," he said, "you won't do at all."

Now, as a professional, I don't take this kind of thing personally. People want what they want, and for me to be hurt by rejection would be like the subway complaining every time someone takes a bus. Different strokes for different folks.

Still, a flicker of annoyance must have passed my face, because Allen immediately looked chagrined.

"But where are my manners?" he asked. "Forgive me. Come in, let's have a drink. And of course, I will pay you for your time. But let me explain."

I walked in and sat at a table where two wineglasses sat with an open bottle of Merlot. I didn't know much about furniture at the time (Allen would eventually teach me more), but this place was obviously posh. Expensive looking paintings, vases displayed on marble columns, and thick wool carpets made everything seem rich and comfortable.

Turns out Allen liked his guys blond and blue-eyed, which I fit. But he also wanted them taller, more muscular, and more mature. "It's really my fault," he explained. "I should have been more specific with that woman on the phone. Mrs. Cherry, wasn't it? A lovely lady, even if, as I suspect, she has a penis.

"Besides," he continued, "you look like you're what, sixteen?"

I do look a lot younger than I am. "I'm perfectly legal," I assured him. I put my head down and regarded him through my bangs. "Are you sure," I said, rubbing my finger along the rim of the wineglass from which I had been sipping "that I can't interest you in anything? How about a massage?"

I had seen the wineglass trick used by my favorite actress ever, Barbra Streisand, in *On a Clear Day,* when she tries to seduce a handsome young man by rubbing her glass with her finger, then across her lips, and down to her bosom. I didn't have the tits for that last gesture, but you have to work with what you got.

Apparently, the move was familiar to Allen, too. "Did you by any chance get that affectation from a Barbra Streisand movie?" he asked me. "*Nuts?*"

Nuts, of course, was Barbra's seminal film in which she plays a prostitute accused of murdering her john. She also played a hooker in *For Pete's Sake* and *the Owl and the Pussycat.* Those movies, along with *Pretty Woman,* and about a hundred Falcon videos, were pretty much all the training I had for my job.

I was excited that Allen made a Barbra reference, even if he got the film wrong. I corrected him gently.

"That's right," Allen said, "you know, some people find her a little overbearing, but I think she's marvelous."

We started talking about our favorite Barbra scenes. Allen couldn't believe I liked *The Mirror Has Two Faces,* but I could watch Babs in a fire drill. We went on for hours. It turned out that we both were huge movie fans.

And thus a friendship began. Allen tried to pay me for my time that night, but I refused to take his money. After all, we hadn't fooled around, and I enjoyed the evening as much as he did.

Since then, we'd get together about once a month for dinner or a show. While he always insisted on picking up the check, I never let him pay me as an escort.

Hustlers need friends, too.

I even recommended Randy Bostinick to him. Randy was another hustler Mrs. Cherry represented. He looked like an older, bigger, butcher version of me, with a body that could only be shaped by back-breaking workouts, steroids, and the appetite-suppressing powers of crystal meth. Randy's figure is flawless; his biceps are cantaloupes, only tastier, his tits rival Dolly Parton's, and his abs are so defined they look like a topographical map of a place you'd need a Land Rover to navigate.

Once, Mrs. Cherry talked me into doing a boy/boy scene with Randy at a gay bachelor party (well, now that we're getting "married," don't we have the right to enjoy the same rites of debauchery as everyone else?), and I have to say that just touching his chest was an erotic highlight of my life. The chemistry between us was so hot that we both walked out of there with over a thousand dollars in our hands. Now that's what I call a good night's work.

Allen Harrington was an interesting man. A self-made millionaire in real estate, Allen was married for most of his adult life, with two sons to show for it. In middle age, while his children were still young, Allen came out of the closet with a bang when he realized that he had spent the last five years in love with his best friend. They finally got together, and Allen realized that the love of another man was what he'd been longing for.

The friend died of cancer three years after Allen's divorce became final.

In the process of his coming out, Allen's wife came to despise him. So did his sons.

"Losing my boys is the greatest sorrow of my life," Allen confided over dinner at the Four Seasons. "I haven't seen or spoken to them in years. When I did, they were full of venom towards my 'lifestyle.' My older son, Michael, was particularly convinced that I had 'chosen' to be this way, and that I could change if I really wanted to. He even offered to help me, whatever that meant. My younger one, Paul, well, he was always a follower, and he just went along with Michael's and my ex-wife's bitterness.

"Not surprisingly, Paul married a girl whose bitchiness makes even my ex-wife's seem minor league. It's sad how children are doomed to repeat the mistakes of their parents, isn't it?"

Allen figured he'd hear from the boys again when they started having children. "Grandchildren tend to bring families together," he told me. "Plus, I don't think they'll want to stay away from my inheritance forever. I've already told them they're out of my will until they come around."

"Well, they're idiots to give up a great dad like you," I told him. "I can't believe your kids rejected you just because you're gay."

"Well, even if I left their mother for another woman, I'm sure they would have had issues. But I don't forgive them. I'm their father and to be honest, I raised them to have better manners than this.

"I've made many mistakes in my life," Allen told me. "I let the expectations and prejudices of other people make me deny the best parts of me. That's what's so great about your generation. You don't have to hide who you really are."

Not always, I thought. I told him about Tony, the great love of my life who left me because he was scared. Allen shook his head. "I guess some people will always be afraid of happiness." Allen sighed. He took my hands in his. "Promise me that will never be you, Kevin. Promise me you'll be happy."

"Are you happy now?" I asked him.

"The happiest I've been," Allen said. "I have wonderful friends." He raised his glass to me, "I have wonderful sex, and I am involved in so many exciting things." I knew that Allen was on the board of directors of some major gay nonprofit groups, and that his dinner parties, some of which I had been invited to, were legendary. "I have finally found my place in this world, and I wake up excited to start each day. How many men in their sixties can you say that about?"

Allen loved to mentor me. He taught me about fine wines, good clothing, gourmet food, and even opera.

He also taught me about myself. One night, we were talking about how I always hated school. I told him about my restlessness, my forgetfulness, and how quickly I'd get bored with whatever the teacher was saying.

Allen told me to hold on and got a book from his shelf. I couldn't see the cover, but Allen started reading me a quiz from it. Did I have trouble reading things unless they were very interesting or very easy? Did I have difficulty planning and organizing my work? Did I sometimes speak impulsively, only to regret it later? Did my thoughts ever bounce around like a ball in a pinball machine? Did I have a chronic sense of underachievement?

I felt like he was reading the story of my life.

Allen told me that more than five "yes" answers to the fifteen questions indicated I was a likely sufferer of Adult Attention Deficit Disorder. I had fourteen.

The next day, Allen got me an appointment with a psychiatrist friend of his. Two days later, I took my first Adderall, a long-lasting form of Ritalin. Adderall helps people with AADD function better. It helps us organize our thoughts and focus more acutely.

Immediately, I felt as if a fog in my mind had lifted. I started getting more organized, accomplishing more. I sent away for information on some master's programs and was seriously thinking of returning to school.

That's just one of the many ways Allen changed my life. Now, I was on my way to return his copy of Gore Vidal's *The City and the Pillar,* a classic book I couldn't have gotten through before meeting Allen.

But first, I had to figure out how to get there. Although Allen's apartment was only a few subway stops from where I was, I made it a general rule not to take the trains. Three years ago, I was the victim of a pretty horrific mugging/gay bashing on the IRT.

As a result, I took a course in self defense using Krav Maga, the Israeli fighting technique, at The Gay and Lesbian Community Center. But the best defense was not to put yourself into a compromising position.

While being little and cute is a valuable asset for a hustler, it isn't helpful on public transit.

So, the question was, do I walk in the stifling heat, or do I grab a cab?

Hey, I just got a hundred dollar tip.

"Taxi!"

Pulling up to Allen's apartment building, I saw right away that something was wrong. A crowd was gathered on the street, and strobe lights from police cruisers and an ambulance made everything stop-motion.

"You can let me off here," I said to the driver, half a block from where everyone was gathered. As curious as the next guy, I walked over to see what the fuss was about. In New York, people stop and watch any street drama for as long as they can. Accidents, murders, messy public break-ups, people slipping on ice: they're all part of the city's free entertainment.

Which was good because who could afford Broadway anymore?

As I approached the cluster of onlookers, I overheard their remarks. "Oh, how terrible," an elderly man who lived in Allen's building said to his wife. I wasn't sure if he was talking about the emergency or the sight of his miserable-looking spouse in her nightgown.

"He was such a nice man," a middle-aged woman in shorts and a tank top said to a young girl who looked like her daughter. "I mean, I never met him or anything, but he seemed so nice."

"That dude is, like, pancake city," a teenager with four rings in his right eyebrow, and, strangely, no other visible piercings said to his friend.

"What happened," I asked him.

"Some old guy did a Spiderman off his balcony," the teenager said. "Only, I guess he ran out of web fluid."

His friend snorted.

Suddenly, I got an uneasy feeling. Pushing my way to the front of the crowd, I saw something that broke my heart. A body lay on the ground covered by a dark green blanket with NYPD stamped across it. Only the top of the head was visible, but it was enough for me to recognize familiar gray hair with a kidney-shaped bald spot.

"Allen!" I cried, not even aware that I said it out loud.

I don't know what I was thinking, but I ran over to the body to embrace it. I heard the crowd give a collective gasp and I knew I just added considerably to their evening's entertainment.

"Whoa there, son," said a middle-aged African-American police officer who ran over to grab me. "Now, calm down. You know this guy?"

"Yes, I think he's a friend of mine," I told the officer, whose badge read "Blake." "His name is Allen Harrington. He lives, lived, in apartment 10K."

"That's right," Officer Blake said. "I'm sorry to say there's been an accident. Your friend fell from the balcony."

Tears welled up in my eyes. I blinked them back. Lights from a police car flickered over the officer's face as I looked at him in disbelief. "What do you mean 'fell?' What happened?"

"Well, do you know if he's been upset about anything lately? Or depressed?"

"No, I, God, what are you saying? You think he killed himself." Despite the heat, I felt myself shaking.

"We don't know anything yet, sir. I'm just asking, is all."

"No, he was like the happiest guy in the world. He had nothing to, I mean, he would never . . ." I wanted to tell the officer how strong Allen was, how happy. But thinking of those things made the sadness of his death hit me like, well, like a body hitting the ground.

That thought was enough to do it. I started crying uncontrollably. Giant hiccupping sobs that made me sound like a seal.

"Awww, Jeez," Officer Blake said, embarrassed. A plump, fiftyish woman standing at the periphery of the crowd ran over with a tissue. She put her arms around me and pulled me close to her fleshy bosom.

"Poor baby," she cooed. "Was that your daddy, honey?"

That's the great thing about street theater. The audience can join the cast at anytime.

"No, he was my friend," I cried as she hugged me. It was actually kind of comforting to be held like that, but then I looked down and saw that she wasn't wearing any shoes and that her toes were black with dirt. She didn't smell too good, either.

I disentangled myself from the probably homeless woman's embrace. "Um, thanks for the tissues. I'm fine now."

I turned back to Officer Blake. "Listen, you have to find his killer. There's no way this guy would hurt himself."

"Tell you what," he said, anxious to avoid another scene. "How about you give my partner a statement, and we get this all on the record, OK?"

"OK," I said, still feeling shaky. I kind of wanted to go over to Allen and touch him one last time, but I didn't want to know what lay beneath that police blanket.

I could feel the crowd's attention divided between watching the body and watching me. I knew that my red-eyed, red-cheeked snotty face was probably quite the sight.

"Hey, Tony," Office Blake shouted. "Can you come here?"

"Just wait here and he'll be right over," Officer Blake said. "You can tell everything you know to Officer Rinaldi."

Then, the past walked towards me.

Tony Rinaldi.

The only man I ever loved.

The only man who ever left me.

Until tonight, when Allen left me, too.

Seeing Tony again was like seeing the dead brought back to life.

He looked at me like he'd seen a ghost, too.

I had just enough time to make out his still-familiar features before I fainted.

CHAPTER 2

Do Old Flames Still Burn?

OK, I THOUGHT, back at my apartment, that could have gone worse.

I could, for example, have thrown up on him. That would have been worse. Or my head could have exploded. That would have been worse *and* messier.

Oh, who was I kidding? We don't see each other for seven years, and I greet him by passing out.

It *couldn't* have gone worse.

But I had an excuse, right? I mean, first Allen dies, and then Tony appears. There are only so many shocks a system can stand.

As a computer geek, I know all about systems crashing. Too much input and the whole network comes crashing down.

I was definitely suffering from data overload. The attention deficit doesn't help, either. According to the books, it's at moments like this that I'm likely to be distracted by a million small details and forget to focus on the big picture.

Focus, Kevin, focus.

Tony couldn't have been nicer about the whole thing, but in a detached, professional way. In front of the other cops, he kept calling me "sir," offering to get me water or a chair. Finally, when everyone else drifted away, he whispered to me, "Listen, I know we have to talk. How about I get your address and take your statement at your place? You OK to get home? I could have someone take you."

I told him I was fine. I gave him my address and he said he'd be over as soon as he finished up at "the scene." He figured it would be another hour, hour and a half, tops.

That was an hour ago. Plenty of time for me to replay our conversation in my head a million times. What did he mean by "we have to talk?" Did he mean about Allen or about us? And why come to my place to do it? Couldn't we have spoken just as well there? Does he always interview witnesses at their homes? I didn't see him inviting himself over to Homeless Lady's house, although I guess she didn't have one, being homeless and all.

I thought for a moment about whether homeless shelters counted as "homes" before I realized I was getting distracted again.

Focus.

I ran around the apartment, putting the dirty dishes under the sink (no time to wash them), making the bed, and taking the porn off the nightstands. I considered changing into something sexier, but I figured that would look contrived. But I did comb my hair and wash the snot off my face.

I was doing some push-ups to pump up my pecs when I stopped myself.

Why was I bothering? He probably has another boyfriend by now. Even if Tony was interested, and he did nothing to signal that he was, would I want him back? It took me a long time and a lot of tears to get over him. Did I want to put myself through that again?

Tony Rinaldi had caused me nothing but pain.

Which is why I couldn't understand the feelings I had the whole time we were talking in front of Allen's building.

The lightheadedness. The pounding heart. Even under the terrible circumstances that had brought us together, the sheer joy I felt seeing his face again.

That squishy feeling in the pit of my stomach. I wondered if an antacid would help.

Shit.

Tony knocked ten minutes later. "Hi," he said, immediately extending his arm for a handshake. Making it clear that he didn't want a hug.

In front of Allen's building, I couldn't get a good look at Tony. But standing in the light of my hallway, I saw him clearly. He looked incredible. His boyish features had matured, maybe hardened a little. His cheekbones were more defined, his lips even fuller.

His body was still prime. Wide shoulders tapered to narrow hips. I could see the bulge of his biceps and the flatness of his stomach underneath his white dress shirt.

I knew the view would only improve from the back.

There was also something a little haunted about him, a little tired. Maybe it was just the years, or the lateness of the day, or the stress of the job. Maybe it was all the work that having to deal with Allen's death would bring. Maybe it was the heat.

Maybe it was seeing me again.

I shook his hand.

"Come in," I said. "It's good to see you. I think." I gave a little shrug.

"Yeah," he said, a slight chuckle in his voice. "It's good to see you, too."

"But weird."

"Yeah, weird," he agreed.

We stood at opposite ends of the room like boxers waiting for the bell to ring. I knew why I didn't want to get any closer. I didn't trust my hands to behave themselves.

"How about something cold?" I offered.

"That would be great."

I got us both beers. When I returned, Tony was sitting in a chair across from the sofa. I handed him his drink and took a sip of mine. I licked my lips. As Alicia Silverstone so memorably said in *Clueless*, anything that draws attention to your mouth is good.

"I'm breaking a couple of rules by having this now," Tony observed as he opened his bottle. "I'm here on official business, you know."

He was joking, but he was also making sure I knew why he was here: Sorry guy, nothing personal. I felt something inside me sink, but I willed myself not to react.

"Too bad about your friend," he said. "How did you know him?"

I'm not ashamed of what I do for a living, but it never even occurred to me to tell Tony how I really met Allen Harrington. I figured I'd get the false origin of our relationship out of the way as soon as possible, so I could stick to the later, more relevant, truths. "We met at a party. We'd get together once a month or so for dinner, a show, whatever. He was a great guy."

Tony fidgeted. "Some of his neighbors said that he was, uh, gay."

"Yeah, so?"

"Well, I was just wondering, if you two were, um, boyfriends."

"No. He was just a friend. I told you"

"Just checking." Tony took a long swig from his bottle. "You're probably not even into that stuff anymore, right?"

"Friends?" I asked stupidly.

"No, you know, gay stuff."

Maybe it was just all the shocks of the day, but I really couldn't follow him. "What do you mean?"

Tony's face was starting to get red and his voice louder. "What do you mean what do I mean?"

Was he trying to confuse me? "Uh, say what now?"

Tony sighed exaggeratedly. "I mean, you know, fooling around with guys."

Was he insane? "Of course I still fool around with guys. I'm gay, Tony. Just like you."

"Whoa!" Tony stood up. "Wait a minute!" He held out his left hand. "I'm married." A gold band around his ring finger confirmed it.

OK, I hadn't noticed the ring. Call it denial. But, give me a break.

If I had a dollar for every man with a wedding ring I've done, well, I'd have a lot of dollars.

"Being married doesn't make someone straight, Tony."

"It makes *me* straight, damn it." He took a breath and seemed to will himself to calm down. "That's not what I meant. I mean, I've always been straight."

I made a vow that I'd grab his gun and shoot myself in the foot before I cried in front of him again. Instead, I decided to play it steely, like Faye Dunaway in *Mommy Dearest* when she faces down the Pepsi board of directors, hissing, "*Don't fuck with me fellas, this ain't my first time at the rodeo.*"

"Don't pull that shit with me, Rinaldi. You fucked me, remember? I sure do."

"That was teenage experimentation, Kevin."

"And I fucked you."

"Yeah, well you'd have to call that part a failed experiment, wouldn't you?"

I had to grant him that one.

"You told me you loved me."

"That was my dick talking."

Now, Tony was the one who was lying.

"Well," I said, "dumb me, huh? Cause I sure loved you."

"I know," Tony said. He came over to the couch, sat next to me. Looked me in the eyes. "And I'm sorry. I knew that you had feelings, and I used you. And I . . . cared about you, too. Very much.

"But, I didn't want to be . . . that way," Tony continued. "And, I blame myself. I was older than you. I shouldn't have let it happen."

I felt tears in my eyes again, bit my tongue hard. Tony waited for me to say something, but what could I say?

"I shouldn't have come here," Tony said. His eyes looked even darker than when he arrived. When did he get so sad?

He stood up. "But I just wanted you to know I was sorry for hurting you. I also wanted to let you know I was sorry about your friend killing himself. And I thought that maybe we could be friends. But we can't be more than that, not again. I'm not gay."

Tony walked to the door.

He looked at me one more time, waiting for me to do something. But what? Was I supposed to run after him? Beg him to stay? Throw myself at him? Forgive him? Say good-bye?

I kind of wanted to do at least four of those things. But I knew I'd be making a mistake. So I did nothing.

He opened the door.

"Tony."

He turned around.

I walked towards him. Damn he smelled good.

I ran my hand through my hair and licked my lower lip. "You're wrong."

An expression that could have been anything from desire to annoyance flashed across Tony's face. "Kevin, I told you, I'm *married*."

"No," I said flatly. "Not about that. About Allen. He didn't kill himself. Come back in, and I'll tell you about the man whose murder you should be investigating."

So, for the next thirty minutes, I told Tony about Allen. I told him how happy Allen was and how optimistic he had been about the future. I told him of Allen's many important roles in the community, his involvement with nonprofit groups, and of his deep and abiding friendships. I told him of Allen's estrangement from his family, but his hope that his kids would eventually come around. I told him I couldn't think of anyone less likely to leap off a balcony than Allen Harrington.

Tony listened intently, leaning forward, occasionally asking relevant questions and taking notes. I could see what a good cop he must be.

I was only occasionally sidetracked by the sensual arc of his neck, his sexy way-past 5:00 shadow, his silky hair.

After I shared everything I knew, Tony sat back in his chair.

"He sounds like a great guy."

"He is," I said. "Was."

"I wanted to hear everything you had to say so that you would know that I'm taking you seriously. But now, you need to listen."

Tony leaned forward again. Close enough so that I could smell the beer on his breath. I tried not to be distracted by the way his lips moved.

"There were no signs of forced entry, and no signs of a struggle. The doorman said he didn't see anyone suspicious entering or leaving. Everything points to a suicide."

"Was there a note?"

"No, but those are a lot less common than the movies would have you think."

"I just don't believe he could have killed himself."

"It's what I know for now," Tony said. "But come by my office in a day or two and we can talk again." He stood up and handed me his card.

"Listen," he asked, "was Allen expecting you tonight?"

"No, I was just dropping something off."

"Well, he was expecting someone. He had an open bottle of wine out, and two glasses. Untouched."

Tony walked to the door.

"Kevin, I'm sorry if I upset you. Thanks for letting me come by. It was, um, good to see you."

I joined Tony at the door to let him out. But first, an experiment. I stood close to him. Too close. The top of my head was at his chin.

He didn't step away. I could feel the heat coming off his chest, his breath on my face.

His breath was coming faster now.

Was he remembering how our bodies fit so well together? How hot it had been?

I looked up at him.

"Kevin," he said, a little hoarsely. "I can't do this."

I make my living by knowing men's desires. I could read the hundred subtle little signs that said he wanted me.

Plus, he had a hard-on.

"Do what?" I leaned in a little closer and stood up on my toes. "This?" I brought my lips closer to his.

"Please . . ." he said, a starving man refusing a meal. "I told you, I can't."

I got closer, my lips a millimeter away from his. He didn't back away.

But I did.

"OK, then," I said, extending my hand. I gave him my butchest handshake. "Thanks for coming by."

Tony stepped backward and I slammed the door. Fuck you, Tony Rinaldi. If I never see you again, it will be too soon. I hope your dick falls off.

After Tony left, the waterworks started again. This time, the feelings were mixed: sadness, anger, frustration, fear.

It had been a long time since I cried. Now, twice in one night. This was not good. This was not *me*.

I looked at my watch. Midnight. Still enough time to meet Freddy at the club. I traded my T-shirt for a tank that said "Twinkie" on the front and "Filled with creamy goodness" on the back.

No time for subtlety. I was going out to get laid.

I hooked my earbuds into my iPhone, put on my favorite podcast, the funny and fabulous *Feast of Fools,* and walked the ten blocks to Blow, the latest club to open in my neighborhood of Chelsea. It has a large bar area, a smaller dance floor, and an even smaller back room.

I found Freddy exactly where I expected to, dancing alone, eyes closed. I also found the usual gaggle of guys watching him, some surreptitiously, some goggle-eyed.

Freddy was quite the sight. Five foot ten inches of hip-shaking goodness. Thickly muscled but not over built, with a classically handsome face. Broad nose, wide lips, and a supermodel smile. Freddy's ass was the stuff of legends. And he could move it like nobody's business: Watching Freddy dance could bring a dead man to erection.

Freddy is the twenty-six-year-old African-American adopted son of a nice Jewish couple from Cleveland, OH. Raised rich, liberal, and white, he's a strange mix of contradictions and common sense. Butch and campy, Semitic and street, well-read and foul-mouthed, Freddy never ceases to surprise me. He's also endearingly sweet, terrifically loyal, and blessedly nonjudgmental.

Tonight, he was wearing black jeans that could have been painted on, and a white T-shirt tight enough to show the nipple rings underneath.

When I was a freshman at New York University, Freddy was student president of the school's Gay/Straight Alliance. We had a brief fling, but, as it turned out, Freddy had a brief fling with pretty much everyone. Freddy was the guy everyone wanted, and, if they were passably attractive, could get.

I, on the other hand, haven't slept around that much. Well, not if you didn't count the guys who paid for it. Freddy couldn't understand my choice of profession, but I couldn't understand his uncompensated promiscuity. So we made a perfect mismatch. All wrong as lovers, but perfect as best friends.

I watched the guys watching Freddy for a few minutes before I joined him on the dance floor. "Hey, baby," I said, grabbing his backside. "You got a license to drive that thing?"

"Sugar!" Freddy shouted. He gave me a big, strong hug. "So, are we on full slut alert tonight?" he asked, eyeing my shirt.

"Mothers, hide your sons," I warned.

But I wasn't feeling it anymore. Now that I was at the club, my bravado was gone. I wished I were home in bed. Alone.

"Honey, when you go out cruising for some strange, it usually means you've had a shitty day," Freddy said. "Come buy my black ass a drink and tell me all about it, bubela."

"So, Twinkie boy," he said as we sat in a booth in the quietest corner of the noisy bar, "what's gotten in your cream?" I told him about losing Allen and finding Tony.

"Oy vey," Freddy said, after hearing my tale of woe. "Talk about drama. You write that up as a screenplay with you as a woman, and Angelina Jolie and Ashley Judd will be scratching each other's eyes out to play that shit."

"Like Ashley could last a minute against Angelina," I said, trying to join in the joke. But my heart wasn't in it. I put my head down on the table and moaned. "What am I going to do?"

Freddy tousled my hair. "Fuck Tony."

"He didn't even like it the first time."

"No, I mean fuck him for not believing you. Solve Allen's murder yourself!"

"Good plan," I answered with sarcastic enthusiasm. "Let me get the Hardy Boys out of the backroom and you call Nancy Drew!"

"Like that bitch would be any help," Freddy answered. "If it weren't for that dyke friend she hangs out with, she never would have cracked *The Case of the Missing Dildo.* Although," Freddy continued, "I wouldn't mind doing the *Hardy Boys.* That Shaun Cassidy had some back for a white boy."

We sat in silence for a moment. Well, as much silence as you can find in a club where Britney was playing loud enough to burst your eardrums.

"Tell you what," Freddy said, "how about I help you?"

"If I were planning an orgy, you'd be the first person I'd call. But

I think we should leave the criminal investigations to the professionals. Tony will put it together."

"Honey, please, he can't even figure out if he likes dick," Freddy answered. "If you want Allen's murderer to come to justice, you better break out some serious Charlie's Angels action. Come to think of it, they were always going undercover as whores, so you'd be perfect!"

"A. I hate you," I said. "B. I wouldn't even know where to start."

"Well, let's see, the man had a lot of money and two estranged sons who hated the fact that their father was a faggot," Freddy observed. "Anyone else you know have reason to see him dead?"

I had to admit that Freddy had a point. Here we were five minutes into the case, and we already had two more suspects than the police.

"Not offhand," I answered.

"What about crazies," Freddy asked. "He know any?"

"Well, judging from the crowd in the street tonight, about half his neighbors seemed certifiable," I observed. "But this is New York."

"OK, we'll start with the sons, then," Freddy answered. "Homophobia and greed: two good motives right there."

Just then, a six-foot-tall, cappuccino-colored Latino man interrupted us. He was handsome, but kind of seedy, too. "Hey, cutie," he said to me, "I couldn't help but notice your shirt. Think I could sample some of that creamy filling?"

"Gee," I answered, "as subtle and attractive an offer as that is, I'll have to decline."

"No problem," he answered, smiling. "How about you, sexy?" he said to Freddy. "Wanna dance?"

Freddy looked up at the guy's eyes, and then craned his head around to read the back of the menu. "How about I just take you home and plow you like the fields of Idaho, instead?"

"Sounds good to me," said tall, dark, and easy.

"Honey, you don't mind, do you?" Freddy said, getting up from the booth. "We'll get serious about crime solving tomorrow. Kisses!"

I left too, and grabbed a cab home. Two A.M. The light was blinking on my answering machine. I checked the caller ID: my mother. I'd get it tomorrow.

Tomorrow was a busy day. I had to be at my volunteer job by 11:00, which meant I should be at the gym by 9:00. For me, working out is not an indulgence. It's a job requirement. I have to maintain the merchandise.

I stripped down to my boxer briefs and washed up. I felt like shit. A quick glance in the mirror showed I looked like it, too.

I got into bed and said a little prayer for Allen.

I was asleep before reaching amen.

CHAPTER 3

Meeting Mrs. Cherry and the World's Nicest Sadist

THE NEXT MORNING, I had a protein shake and my attention-deficit medication and hit the gym.

I was between sets on the leg press machine, lying on my back with my knees drawn up to my face. Leg presses are supposed to infuse you with testosterone, but this position always felt gynecological to me.

Why did Allen have to be the one to die, and Tony the one to resurface? Why couldn't it have been the other way around?

OK, that was cold. And I didn't mean it.

Well, not really.

If I really meant it, that would indicate that I still gave a shit about whether Tony lived or died, and I didn't want that to be the case.

No, the only case I wanted to deal with was Allen's.

I finished up my workout, showered, and headed off to my volunteer job. Time to make the donuts.

"OK, everyone," I called. "You guys at the front of line are going to open a bag and put a sandwich and a container of soup in it. You pass it down to the next person, who puts in a yogurt and an apple. The last person rolls the bag closed and affixes an address label. Questions? Comments? Concerns?"

I was talking to a group of local high school students, who were volunteering with me at The Stuff of Life, a charity that brings meals to homebound people with AIDS. I run the lunch shift a few times a week. The students were there for the day. We have different organizations that staff our lunch shifts: churches, businesses, schools, and even dating services have all brought in volunteers.

The fifteen students were lined up at tables in The Stuff of Life's vast, stainless steel kitchen. They seemed like a nice group, a little bit restless, but polite and well-behaved. Normally, I would have enjoyed their company, but today I couldn't help but feel preoccupied.

A skinny girl who still thought Goth was hip, raised a hennaed hand. "Do these sandwiches have, like, ham in them? Because I can't touch them if they do. I, like, don't eat meat."

"Actually," a pretty blond girl next to her said, "she can't touch them if they have any *food* in them, because she's like, anorexic."

"I am *not* anorexic," Goth girl replied. "I'm just not like you. I don't eat everything I see. Or *everyone*."

The other kids issued a collective "oooh."

I was afraid things would turn into a catfight, when Blondie said "You know the only one I eat is you, honey" and kissed Goth Girl on the lips.

"God," said another girl, "do you two have to be such total lesbians all the time?"

Goth Girl looked at her watch. "Umm, yes, we do" and gave her girlfriend another kiss.

This time, the crowd gave an "awwwww."

"OK, everyone," I said, "assuming no one else wants to start making out, let's get started."

An obviously fey boy raised his hand and jumped up and down. "Oooh, sir! Sir! I'd like to start making out!" Everyone laughed.

"Nice try, kid, but how about you make some lunches instead?"

"And, ladies," I said to the happy lesbian couple, "you'll be happy to know the sandwiches are tuna."

After the lunches were made and the students left to make the deliveries, I went to visit The Stuff of Life's director of volunteer services, my friend Vicki. Vicki is a sleek power dyke, who wears her jet black hair in a pompadour that makes her resemble a young, prettier Elvis Presley. Her black jeans and black western shirt tucked into a wide black leather belt with an oversized silver buckle only increased the resemblance.

"Hey, boy," she greeted me. "How's tricks? And I do mean 'tricks.'" She winked broadly. Vicki thought the fact that I hustled was the biggest hoot this side of non-vibrating strap-ons.

"That's so funny." I frowned. "I'm laughing on the inside."

"Whatever," she said. "So, how were the kids today?"

I told her about the two little lesbians.

"That's so cute," she said. "I wish I could have been that open in high school. I didn't have the nerve to hold my girlfriend's hand till I was a senior in college. God forbid someone thought I liked girls or something."

It was hard to imagine that Vicki had ever been mistaken for a heterosexual, but I decided to hold my tongue.

"So, how are things, really?" she asked. "You look down."

I told her about Allen.

Vicki was sympathetic. "Oh, Kevin, I'm so sorry for you. I knew Allen, too. He was on our board of directors. He was a great guy, a big contributor, too. He worked a lot with Roger Folds, our development director."

Freddy had suggested I talk to people Allen knew. Roger seemed like a good place to start. I asked Vicki where he sat.

"At his home, as far as I know. He's been out for week.

"It's weird," she continued. "Roger's on a kind of sabbatical or something. He broke up with his partner a few months ago—walked in on the guy sucking off the UPS man or something. Anyway, he got really depressed, and said he needed some time off to 'find himself,' or some shit like that."

"You don't sound too sympathetic," I said.

"Roger's a big old drama queen. It's cute at first, but when you're responsible for raising millions of dollars for an organization that feeds sick people, you should really pull your shit together.

"You know, now that I'm thinking of it," Vicki continued, "I think he and Allen had some kind of falling out. I seem to remember him saying something nasty about Allen, but I don't remember what.

"But he's been talking all kinds of crazy shit lately."

I asked Vicki how I could get in touch with Roger. She gave me his home number.

I left The Stuff of Life at around five. I had a working date at six, so I decided to go see Mrs. Cherry before heading home to shower and change. On the way, I called Roger Folds, but he didn't pick up. I left a message.

Mrs. Cherry lives in Hell's Kitchen, a neighborhood in Manhattan which is always halfway between ghetto and gentrification. For awhile, they called it "Clinton," but it didn't stick.

In today's heat, Hell's Kitchen seemed appropriate.

Mrs. Cherry buzzed me into the building and I took five flights of stairs to the top floor, where she had bought and combined three apartments into one. She opened the door and I was greeted by the combined smells of Chanel Number 5 and stale marijuana.

"My darling, darling boy," she enthused. "Look at you. Look at you! Turn around." She squeezed my ass. "Yes! Look at you! No wonder you're one of my top boys." She took my T-shirt and pulled it up to my chest. "Look at that flat belly, those rosy nipples. Absolutely delicious, perfect." She pinched the skin around my waist. "You see this, though? I shouldn't be able to squeeze even this much. I want you to have the body fat percentage of a fifteen-year-old bulimic virgin, darling. Can you do that for Mama?"

Mrs. Cherry might have been appraising me like the prize horse in her stable, but she did it so blatantly and affectionately that I wasn't offended.

At 5 foot nothing and about 200 pounds, Mrs. Cherry was no great beauty. Her heavy makeup, large beehive wig, and outrageous jewelry made it impossible to ascertain her true features. God knows what she looked like when not in drag. Wearing a large flowered caftan with a string of gardenias woven into her hair, she resembled a large, mobile botanic garden.

Mrs. Cherry guided me into her vast living room and sat me in a dark purple velvet couch piped with gold brocade, under a gold chandelier, and next to a marble fountain. Mrs. Cherry's place is huge and as ornately decorated as a New Orleans brothel. She once told me she took the set design of Brooke Shield's *Pretty Baby* as her inspiration.

"Darling," she said, in her usual breathy whisper "I heard about Allen. Such a terrible, terrible loss. Such a nice man. And such a good customer! Tell me *everything* you know."

It was ninety-seven degrees outside, but you could have kept veal fresh in Mrs. Cherry's apartment. I could barely hear her over the five air conditioners she had running.

I told her what I knew about Allen's death and about running into Tony.

"A mystery," Mrs. Cherry enthused. "I love a mystery." Mrs. Cherry plucked a small fan from her artificial bosom and waved arctic air into her face.

"Well, I don't love this mystery," I answered. "I hope they find out who killed Allen."

"Oh, I wasn't talking about *that* mystery, darling. I meant the mystery of your ex-lover's sexuality. Does he want to suck your dick, or not? Of course, he'd be insane if he didn't. Even *I* want to suck your dick, and everyone knows I'm a big fat dyke."

I couldn't always tell when Mrs. Cherry was kidding. I'm pretty sure she didn't know, either. But that was part of her charm.

"But you're right; Allen's death is curious, too. Hmmm . . . you know what we need, darling?" she asked. I shook my head. "Cocktails!"

Mrs. Cherry disappeared behind a beaded curtain and returned moments later with two perfect martinis.

"I'd offer you something stronger," she said, handing me my glass, "but I know what a boy scout you are. Besides, you have a date tonight, remember?"

I assured her I did, and we talked some more. When I was ready to leave, she gave me a peck on the cheek. "Now, go make yourself beautiful, darling," she said. "And make Momma some money."

I got home at seven and had a protein shake. I checked my answering machine. Caller ID showed I had another message from my mother. That was two in two days.

To say that my mother is high maintenance would be like saying that Lindsay Lohan enjoys an occasional drink. Or, used to enjoy. Let's give Lindsay a break, OK?

My mother's messages often ran for several minutes, during which she'd either lecture me on how I should be living my life, or detail the minutiae of how she was living hers.

I couldn't deal with her just now, but I promised myself I'd listen to her messages tomorrow.

The next call came from a law office. "This is Susan Oliver calling from Messner, Baker, and Stern. This message is for Kevin Connor. Mr. Connor, please call me to discuss an urgent personal matter. Thank you so much." She left her number.

I didn't think I owed anyone enough money that they would have gone legal on my ass, so I figured it was safe to call her back. I got her machine and left her a message with my cell phone number.

My e-mail was mostly spam, except for a message from Freddy. "I can describe that boy from last night in three words: Dee Lish Ous. Have you solved Allen's murder yet? Call me!"

I took a shower, shaved my face, chest, and balls, and put on a pair of tan khakis and a light blue Izod polo shirt. My client tonight was a regular, and he liked me to look preppy.

In the cab to his apartment, I thought about something Mrs. Cherry had said about Allen. "He was such a good customer." Freddy had asked me if I knew anyone else who knew Allen, and I had forgotten about Randy Bostinick, the hustler I recommended to him.

Unfortunately, I hadn't known Randy as well back then as I did now. If I had, I wouldn't have made the recommendation. Because as hot as Randy is, he's also a little bit nuts. I've heard a few stories of Randy going off on guys in clubs when he thought they were being rude to him.

I also knew more than one of his old boyfriends who was seen trying to hide a black eye or swollen cheek. They learned the hard way that steroids and crystal meth may make a boy beautiful, but they don't do much to improve his anger management skills.

I had my own story, too.

Once, when Randy and I were at a bar together, a guy approached me. The guy was cute, but he had an intense stare that made me a little uncomfortable. He leaned over to say something, but I couldn't hear him over the crowd. I asked him to repeat himself, but it sounded like he was mumbling.

I didn't want to be rude, but I couldn't understand what he was saying. I shook my head, but the guy just tried again.

"Hey," Randy bellowed from behind me, "can't you see my friend's not interested? Buzz off."

But the guy just leaned closer and tried to talk right into my ear. Randy, thinking the guy was moving in for a kiss, had enough.

He put down his beer—some horrible American brew that only he would have the nerve to drink in a trendy gay bar—grabbed the guy by the shoulders, and threw him against the wall. All eyes in the bar turned our way.

"Hey, punk," Randy shouted. "What the fuck is your problem! I told you, he's not interested. What are you, fucking deaf or something?"

Well, imagine our embarrassment when it turned out that he was. That's why his speech wasn't very clear, and that's why he was staring. He was trying to read my lips. That's also why he didn't hear Randy telling him to back off.

Once the misunderstanding was made clear, Randy went from sixty to zero as fast as he had previously accelerated. He was especially gratified to learn that the guy was trying to ask me if Randy and I were together, because he was interested in Randy.

"I owe you a drink," Randy said to the still-shaking deaf guy. "And if you want, I'll take you home afterwards and touch you up nice all over."

The deaf guy was reading Randy's lips and he looked like he couldn't believe what he was hearing. Seeing. Whatever.

You could see how tempted he was by the prospect of spending time with Randy, but he was also wondering if he shouldn't just leave now rather than risk his life with this beautiful nut.

But after a Cosmo and twenty minutes of watching how Randy's impossibly strong shoulders tapered down to slim hips and an unbeatable ass, he decided that even if Randy killed him, it wouldn't be a bad way to go. They left together, and Randy later told me "deaf guys are hot! He had a mouth like a Hoover, great fingers, and, after sex, I didn't have to make any conversation or anything."

Still, despite a happy ending, Randy's run-in with the deaf guy gave me firsthand knowledge of how out of control Randy could get.

Tony told me that Allen was expecting someone the night he was killed.

Could it have been a handsome hustler with a bad temper?

Randy was strong enough to throw a man off a balcony.

But why would he want to?

Under other circumstances, I would have called Tony with my suspicions. But I couldn't tell him how I knew Randy without revealing too much about myself.

I might be determined not to want Tony anymore, but I certainly wasn't about to let him know about my hustling. That might make him not want *me*. I couldn't have that!

No, I'd have to follow up with Randy on my own.

Two hours later, I found myself in an apartment on the Upper East Side, a high-priced neighborhood filled with wealthy dowagers and young investment bankers. If only they knew what their neighbors were up to.

I heard a telephone ring, but I was all tied up. Literally. Seated in a chair, my hands bound behind my back, my ankles lashed to each other. I was also nude, gagged and blindfolded.

I could hear my tormentor answer the phone. Muffled voices conspired. Then he came back to where he had imprisoned me.

"I'm so sorry," said my client, Melvin Cuttlebeck. His thin, high voice was hushed. "That's my boss on the phone, and I really have to take this call. It will be about ten minutes. Shall I untie you?"

"No, I don't mind," I said through the gag, which, to be honest, wasn't on tight enough to be effective anyway.

"Fabulous," Melvin whispered. "I wouldn't want you to be uncomfortable. I'll be back in a jiff."

I wouldn't ordinarily do this kind of scene, but Melvin Cuttlebeck must be the world's most solicitous sadist. Although he enjoys the fantasy of binding and dominating me, he's terrified of actually causing any pain. Or even discomfort.

As a result, he always ties me loosely enough so that it doesn't chafe. In fact, I could probably just slip out of tonight's ropes.

In our first session, Melvin spent over an hour showing me different knots and how to open them. "I wouldn't want you to feel the least bit trapped," he told me. "This way, you know that you can always get yourself free. After all, what would happen if I had a heart attack or something? Why, you could be stuck here for days!"

In the background, I could hear Melvin saying "yes sir," and "right away, sir," while whoever was on the other end of the phone did most of the talking. I felt sympathy for poor Melvin. Of course someone so obsequious on the job wanted to be the boss in the bedroom. It wasn't his fault that he was too sweet to actually hurt someone.

I've been seeing Melvin every month for almost a year now. Sometimes, we even do phone sessions. Melvin's about five feet, seven inches tall and thin as a rail. I think he likes me because I'm one of the few guys he's bigger than.

A few minutes later, Melvin returned. He cautiously took off my blindfold and gag, and stood before me in a black leather harness and chaps with no pants underneath. His smallish penis quivered.

"I'm back, boy. You better beg me not to hurt you."

"Oh, please, sir, please don't punish me," I said. "I know I've been a bad boy, but I'm sorry, sir. I promise I'll be better." I tried to act frightened, but probably just sounded whiny.

"Sorry, boy, but it looks like a spanking for you."

Melvin untied me and laid me over his lap. He brought a hand down on my ass so softly that I barely felt it. "That's not too hard, is it?" Melvin whispered, breaking character for a moment.

I fought hard not to giggle. Giggling was definitely a mood killer. "That's just right," I whispered back.

"Good, then here's another one!" he shouted.

This one was even gentler. "Ow!" I cried.

"That'll teach you," Melvin said.

"Please, sir, no more, no more!"

After a few more faked pleas and ten more soft slaps, I felt a sticky wetness on my belly as Melvin ejaculated.

"You're such a good boy," Melvin beamed as he stuffed a generous tip into my palm. "I have a lot of meetings with my boss this week. Maybe I could call you in the next few days?"

"Anytime," I told him.

Outside, the air was a humid fog that covered everything like a wet blanket. Thanks to Melvin's quickness on the draw, it wasn't even 7:00. I still had the whole evening to . . . well, I'd figure that out after I got home.

There were no cabs, so I walked over to a nearby hotel, where taxis always waited.

I turned on my phone and hooked up my Bluetooth headset. It always makes it look like I'm talking to myself, but in New York, that's not uncommon. Even the crazies avoided me.

The first message, from my mother, I skipped. That made three. I would call her as soon as I got through the others.

The second was from the woman in the law office. She told me she would be in her office late and that I should call anytime.

I hit the callback button.

"Susan Oliver here."

"Yes, Ms. Oliver, this is Kevin Connor returning your call."

"Mr. Connor!" Ms. Oliver sounded very happy to hear from me. "Thank goodness. You were last on my list, and the reading is tomorrow."

"The reading?"

"Of the will."

"What will?"

"Allen Harrington's will," she said as if explaining herself to a three-year-old. "He died, you know. Quite tragic." Then, "Oh dear, I hope I wasn't the one to break it to you."

"Oh no, I was there the night he was murdered."

"Murdered?" she sounded confused.

"It's a long story."

"In any case, there is a bequest to you in the will, and you are required to be there."

"Required?" I asked.

"Mr. Harrington left specific instructions as to whom he wanted in attendance."

"Who?"

"I'm afraid I can't release that information. May I count on your coming?"

Ms. Oliver gave me the time and place. I told her I'd be there.

I called Freddy and told him about my problem: I wanted to honor Allen's wishes, but I didn't want to meet his homophobic sons, whom I was sure would be there. What if the crazy ex-wife showed? It sounded like a real freak show.

"Darling, you know I'm always there in your hour of need," Freddy assured me.

"Yes, well, it's nice to have your support."

"No, darling, literally. I'm there. I'll be your bodyguard. Besides, it's on my lunch hour."

"It's at ten o'clock in the morning."

"I'll take an early lunch."

"You don't have to do that," I said, hoping he would.

"Darling, it's no trouble at all. You know I love a good soap opera. Besides, there could be a sizable inheritance at stake."

"I doubt it," I said. But it would be nice.

"Did you solve his murder yet?"

I told Freddy what I remembered about Randy Bostinick, and about Roger Folds, the development director at The Stuff of Life.

"See, that's two more leads than you had yesterday," Freddy encouraged. "Now, you're in luck with Randy because he works out at my gym. If that boy injects one more dose of steroids, I think he's going to grow hair on his elbows. Although, I have to say, he does look fabulous. I'd do him."

"Him and what army?" I ask. "Oh yeah, any army."

"Ha-ha, very funny. In any case, he's there every morning at around eight, so he won't be hard to find.

"Plus," Freddy continued, "we'll get a look at the family tomorrow. Maybe we can force a confession at the reading of the will. You know, when they're all emotional and everything."

"What did you have in mind?"

"I'll start with an easy question to break the ice. Something like: 'which one of you bitches killed your father?' "

"Subtle."

"Well you know me, darling. The soul of discretion."

"On second thought, maybe you should just stay at work. I'll fill you in later."

"Don't be silly, lamb. I'll behave, I promise. Now, I have to pick out something appropriately funereal to wear. Do you think black sequins would work, or is that too Liza?"

I hung up on Freddy and was climbing into a cab when my cell rang again. "Hello," I answered.

"It's Tony."

I resented the surge of excitement I felt when I heard his voice. "Hi."

"I need to show you something," he said.

"OK," I said. "What?"

"Show, not tell. Where are you? Can you meet me?"

I told him I was in a cab inching its way downtown.

"Fine," Tony said. "Meet me in the lobby of Allen Harrington's apartment building."

I gave the taxi driver a new destination.

CHAPTER 4

An Unexpected Guest Ruins Everything

EVEN THOUGH OUR last meeting had ended pretty tragically, I'd be lying if I didn't say I was kind of excited about seeing Tony again. And kind of hating myself for feeling that way, too.

Why did he want to see me? At Allen's building no, less.

What did Tony want?

I'd find out soon enough.

All the doormen at Allen's place knew me by now. "Kevin!" the cute young one who admitted me when I got there exclaimed, "how ya doing, buddy?" He smiled broadly, revealing perfectly white teeth against his dark Latino skin. Like many of the really handsome young men working jobs like these in New York City, Ricky was an aspiring actor/model.

"I'm OK," I said, not smiling back. "You heard about Allen."

"Right, right." Ricky's expression turned to one of concern. "Aw, man, that's too bad about your friend. I'm sorry."

"Yeah."

"So, I guess you're not going to be coming around much anymore, huh?"

"Probably not."

"Hey, I'm not supposed to be doing this but," Ricky reached into his pocket for a notepad and pen, "why don't you take my number. Maybe we can get together or something," he said writing.

He handed me the paper.

I liked Ricky, but I wouldn't be calling him. I had enough on my plate. Still, I thought, looking at his striking features, maybe I could pass his number along to Freddy as an early Christmas present.

"Thanks," I said, pocketing the note. "You take care."

Tony was standing a few feet away with a glare on his face. "What was that all about?" he asked as I approached.

"He was expressing his condolences."

"By giving you his number?"

"You could see what he wrote from here?"

"I'm a cop. I see everything. Besides, what else would he be giving you? A prayer card?"

Tony looked genuinely annoyed. He also looked extra-yummy in his navy suit, starched white shirt, and red-and-gold striped tie. The only concession to the day's heat was the undone top button of his shirt. Just that little suggestion of impending nudity was enough to fixate my attention on his bobbing Adam's apple, which distractingly screamed "lick me, lick me!" Was Tony's irritation at Ricky giving me his number a sign of jealousy? God, I hoped so.

"Why am I here?" I asked him.

"I want you to see something." He showed me a key in his hand. "In Allen's apartment."

Walking into Allen's apartment was an eerie experience. Although I had been there before when he wasn't home, this felt entirely different. It was as if the walls and floors and tables and chairs all knew their owner wasn't coming back. His absence was a vacuum sucking out all the air. I felt lightheaded and took a deep breath.

"You OK?" Tony asked.

"Fine." But I really wasn't.

"Look around," Tony said. "What do you see?

I did as instructed. Allen's place was, as always, immaculate. Even an alien, landing on Earth for the very first time, would have known that a man of wealth and good taste lived here.

On a small table by two wingback chairs was the open bottle of wine Tony had told me about, along with two glasses.

On his small antique desk, Allen's reading glasses sat next to a pen and a scattered pile of papers. Some kind of financial forms. An uncapped fountain pen lay on top of a printed out Excel spreadsheet dense with numbers on which Allen had apparently jotted his last written words. "Call T. S." The pen was an expensive Mont Blanc.

Allen had a thing for nice writing instruments. A row of similar pens stood like soldiers in a mahogany holder at the back of his desk. Any one of them could have paid half my monthly rent.

His last written words, I thought to myself. I ran my finger over them. Just a few days ago, Allen's gentle hand had rested there. I sighed.

"Something interesting?" Tony asked.

"No, just . . ." what could I say? "Nothing."

I continued to look around. Everything seemed normal. Horribly wrong without Allen there, but normal nonetheless.

"I don't get it," I said. "What did you want to show me?"

"What do you see?"

"Nothing," I said. "Well, nothing weird or anything. What's the point?"

"Sit down," Tony said to me. I settled on the couch. Tony sat in a chair across from me.

"So, everything looks normal?"

I nodded.

"Nothing broken? Nothing missing? No blood?"

I could see where he was going.

"No signs of a struggle? Or a robbery?" Tony continued.

"I get it," I said.

"I wanted you to see," Tony said, "because I know how you are. You're not going to let this go unless you see for yourself. So I showed you."

This was Tony's way of looking out for me. It was actually pretty sweet. But he was wrong.

Something about the note.

"Come here." I took him over to Allen's desk. "He had just written this." I pointed out the note. "Call T. S."

"Who's T. S.?" Tony asked.

"I don't know," I said curtly. "That's not the point. This is: Why would he make a note to call someone if he was going to kill himself? Wouldn't he have known that he wasn't going to be around to make that call?"

"He could have written that days ago," Tony answered.

"No," I said. "That's a good fountain pen.You can't leave it uncapped like that, it'll dry out. Allen was very careful with his pens."

"Kevin, look around. This place is untouched. There was plenty of cash in a drawer in his dresser, and a lot of expensive . . ." he gestured at the paintings and furnishings, "stuff here that nobody bothered to take. There's no reason to think that this man was murdered. I don't think an uncapped pen is evidence of a crime."

He looked at me with serious eyes. "Nothing here is evidence of a crime."

Suddenly, I noticed how warm it was in there. Had someone turned off the air conditioning? I felt a little woozy again.

I thought a hug from Tony might be the perfect antidote, but that didn't look likely.

"I need a drink," I told him. "Can I grab a bottle of water from the frig?"

"Go ahead," Tony said. I went into the small kitchen and opened the refrigerator. A rush of warm air whooshed out. I looked around the side and saw that it was unplugged. Apparently, the air conditioning isn't the only thing turned off when someone dies.

All the fresh food had been removed. There was still bottled water, but it was warm and unappealing. Also left behind were a few other non-perishables, including a six pack of Budweiser beer, which I knew Allen would never drink. He must have gotten it for a guest.

Allen was always considerate like that.

Now, I felt like I was going to cry again. Which I was determined not to do in front of Tony.

"There's nothing cold," I said, coming back into the living room. Again, Allen's absence weighed on me like an anchor. "Can we get out of here?"

"Sure," Tony said. "There's a bar right down the street. Why don't we get something to drink?"

We walked without speaking and were there in five minutes. About twenty men and women stood by the bar, laughing and flirting. Framed pictures of famous athletes lined the dark wood walls. Cigarette smoke and the wails of Aerosmith filled the air. If this place were any straighter, I'd melt like a vampire in daylight. We took a quiet table in the back.

Tony went to the bathroom. When the overly made-up waitress came over I ordered bottled water for myself and beer for him. It was waiting when he got back to the table.

"Hey," he said, after taking a huge gulp of his beer, "didn't I tell you not to tempt me with alcohol on the job?"

I couldn't talk about Allen anymore. I didn't want to think about death and suicide and murder. I just wanted to flirt with this man I've pined for since before I had pubic hair. I wanted to see where it would take me.

I bit my lower lip. "Funny," I said, "I remember something about temptation, but that wasn't it."

Tony rolled his eyes.

"Anyway," I added, "you can only tempt the willing."

Tony leaned closer to me. "You know what I did after I left your place last night?" he asked. "I went home and fucked my wife's brains out."

"Hmmm, what do you suppose had you all worked up?"

"Actually," Tony picked up his beer again, "I fuck her brains out every night. That's my point, Kevin. I'm straight." He drained his glass and signaled the waitress for another.

I wondered if he wasn't trying to get drunk enough to fuck *my* brains out tonight. Not that I'd mind.

"Listen," I said. "If you called me here to reject me again, mission accomplished."

"No, I didn't. I'm sorry. I called you because I wanted you to understand what happened to Allen. I didn't want you making yourself crazy that he was murdered. But as far as the stuff between us," his voice dropped a couple of decibels, "I don't want to lead you on. It's just . . . you know how you get me all worked up. I mean, defensive. Even when we were kids, you were always looking at me, always wanting something."

"Yeah, well, we're not kids anymore. And now you know what I want." I gave him the full works: Took off my glasses, flipped my hair back and ran my tongue over my lips.

"I know." He loosened his tie a little more.

"And you are tempted, right?"

"Maybe a little."

"Just a little?"

"You know I really cared about you, right?"

"Enough to break my heart?"

"You weren't the only one with a heart," he answered.

"Could have fooled me."

"But now there's someone else's heart I have to think about."

If I had to hear about his wife one more time, I was going to scream.

Just then the waitress brought Tony's beer over, giving him a long stare. "Anything else I can get you?" she asked.

"No, thanks," he said, not even looking up.

She stood a moment longer. "*Anything*?" She thrust her hips out. This bitch was about as subtle as a hysterectomy.

"I'm fine," he said to her. Then to me, "So, what were you up to tonight when I called you?"

Well, I thought, I was just headed home after being bound and lightly spanked by a harness-wearing accountant who wouldn't hurt a whore. "I was kind of tied up."

"Do you have somewhere else you need to be?"

An occasion to say a line I rarely use. "I'm free."

"Good, because I wanted to tell you something else about Allen."

Ugh. I really wanted to be done with that topic by now. I knew I wasn't going to convince Tony I was right until I could come up with some kind of evidence. And I was tired of hearing him always telling me I was wrong.

"Go ahead," I said.

"I'm going to share something with you, but it's off the record, OK?"

I mimed pulling a zipper across my lips.

"When I got to the station this morning, the captain wanted to talk to me. Turns out that Allen's death is not an entirely random thing."

That got my attention. "What do you mean?"

"There's been a rash of suicides in the gay community lately. Six in the past three months. Almost all of them were guys with no history of depression, no illnesses, none of the usual warning signs."

"How do you know they weren't murders?"

"In most of the cases, the evidence was pretty clear. There were a few notes, too."

"I thought you said those weren't that common."

"They're not. But they're not unknown, either."

"I don't understand what this has to do with Allen," I said. "Suicide isn't contagious."

"No, but it can spread. We see it all the time in colleges, high schools, social groups."

"Yes, but that can only happen if people know about the suicides," I said. "I haven't heard anything about these."

"We're trying to keep it quiet," Tony answered. "And the families generally don't want the death listed as a suicide, either, so that helps keep it out of the papers. But that doesn't mean that these guys didn't travel in the same circles, or know of each other." Tony handed me a list of names. "Any of these familiar?"

I looked at six lives lost to despair. "No." I went to hand it back to him but he waved it away.

"Keep it. Maybe something will come to you," he said.

I put the list in my wallet.

"But, you couldn't say that Allen didn't know any of these guys, right?" Tony asked.

"No."

Tony finished his second beer. "I'm just saying I want you to be careful."

"Careful of what?"

"Careful that nothing happens to you."

"Careful that I don't catch suicide? Don't worry, I've had my shots."

"That's not funny."

Unbidden, the waitress came over to replace Tony's beer. "There you go, honey," she told him. If she stuck her breasts out any further, she'd poke his eyes out. Meanwhile, my long-finished soda sat unnoticed in front of me.

"Uh, hi," I said to her. "Two people sitting here."

She ignored me. "You sure I can't get you something to eat, honey?" she asked Tony. I could swear I saw smoke rising from her pelvis.

Tony shook his head and gave her a steely cop's glance that sent her scurrying away. I felt like applauding.

"Kevin," he said, "there's no evidence that anything other than a suicide took place in that apartment. I spent my entire day talking to his neighbors. Nothing."

"Fine," I told him. "I'll figure it out."

"What do you mean?"

"I mean, if the police won't do their jobs, then I will."

Tony took another long swallow of beer. His glass was almost empty. That made three beers in ten minutes. "I'm not hearing this."

I noticed a little slurring in Tony's words. That son of a bitch—he *was* trying to get plastered enough to sleep with me!

It was the oldest line in the world: "Boy, was I drunk last night. I can't remember a thing! Hope my tossing and turning didn't bother you too much."

How rude!

How pathetic!

How wonderful!

I extended my leg under the table so that my calf pressed against his. He didn't move away.

"Listen, I said, "I could really use your guidance on this. Why don't you come over to my place so we can talk?" I gave him my puppy dog stare.

Tony looked at his empty glass. "Jesus, was that my third? Guess I was thirstier than I thought. But I should be getting home."

He stood up, staggered a little, and then sat back down again with a thud. "Guess I shouldn't have had all those beers on an empty stomach, huh? Can't drive now."

We went outside, grabbed a cab, and rode cross town. We didn't say anything on the way, but I sat real close to him and could see his body responding. Despite the air conditioning, the taxi felt hot.

I wanted to sleep with Tony again. I didn't care about the circumstances. Lust be not proud, and all that.

If he needed the cover of booze to let him do it, fine. I just wanted to prove that he really did still want me.

Once we had that established, we could go on from there.

As we boarded the elevator to my building, Tony looked at me seriously. "You know what I was saying about being totally straight?" he asked.

"Uh-huh."

"Well, maybe, for you at least, I'm a little bi."

The elevator doors closed and Tony closed in on me. I've worn cologne that didn't cling to me as tightly as Tony did. His kisses were deep and passionate.

Meanwhile, his hands traveled down to my ass, stroking, kneading. I felt him hard against me. I answered in kind. His lips traveled to my neck, chewing. He licked his way back to my mouth.

My hands traced the scalloped muscles of his back, ran over his expansive biceps. Small moans escaped my mouth, quiet echoes of his deeper groans.

"God, you feel so good," he panted.

"Mmmmm," I said. I didn't trust myself to say anything. My heart was pounding a nostalgic rhythm of happiness, desire, and fear.

I didn't know where this was going, but getting there sure felt great.

The elevator door opened and it took us a moment to disengage. Then, a mad dash to my door.

I fumbled for the key.

"Hurry," Tony said. He pressed himself against my back.

God, I wanted him. I wanted him badly.

I put the key to my door, but the doorknob turned before I could insert it.

My door was unlocked.

I live in New York City. I *never* leave my door unlocked.

Someone was in my apartment. Someone uninvited.

First Allen, and now this.

Did someone know I was looking into Allen's death? Someone with something to hide?

Was I next on the killer's list?

I turned to Tony, who picked up my concern.

"Let me check it out," he whispered.

He rested his hand on his pistol and flung open the door.

A shock of horror ran through me. The sight that greeted me was more frightening than seeing Allen's body in the street.

My mother, sitting on the couch. Two suitcases, a cosmetics bag, and a hat box by her side.

"Darling!" she said. "Momma's home!"

I didn't faint again, but the room did spin.

My mother embraced me in her ample bosom. "You look wonderful, honey." She pushed me away. "And what about me? How do I look?"

My mother is 5 feet, 8 inches of Long Island chic. She carries maybe thirty extra pounds, mostly in her chest. She was wearing a blood-red sweater with the words "Sexy Bitch" stamped in rhinestones. Her black stretch pants were tucked into knee high red vinyl boots. Her hair was teased into a high confection that could have hidden a family of squirrels.

"You look great," I told her.

"I've always loved your honesty, honey."

"How did you get in?"

"I explained to the super that I was your mother, and that you hadn't returned my messages for days."

"He let you in because I didn't return your calls?"

"I might have said something about your being insulin dependent and that you were prone to diabetic comas."

"Mom!"

"Well," she waived her hand at me, "you should have called."

She turned to Tony. "Now, who's this fine specimen? Wait a minute—Tony Rinaldi?"

Tony sobered up real quick. "Hi, Mrs. Connor," he mumbled.

"Tony, honey," she yelled, pulling him towards her in a hug that would have killed a lesser man. "Are you two crazy kids finally back together?"

"Not exactly," I told her.

"Umm, I'm married," Tony said.

"You're married?"

"To a woman."

"To a woman?"

"I'm straight."

"You're straight? You're not straight."

Tony threw him arms up and turned to me. "What is it with you people?"

"What is he talking about?" my mother asked me.

"Tony is saying that he's heterosexual and that he's married to a woman," I said to my mother. I turned to Tony. "My mother is expressing disbelief because she knows about our history and because we were just making out in the hallway."

"You were making out in the hallway?" my mother asked.

"Sorry, I thought you heard us," I said.

"Why were you making out with a married man?" my mother asked me. Then to Tony: "Does your wife know about this?"

"No!" Tony shouted.

"Well, I'm sure she'll be thrilled to know you're fooling around," my mother said. "God knows I was when I found out what my Henry was up to."

"What was Dad up to?" I asked.

"Why do you think I'm here?" my mother asked.

"Why *are* you here?"

"Haven't you been at least *listening* to my messages?"

The answer, of course, was no. Now I was paying the price. I grimaced.

"You're father's been slipping it to Dottie Kubacki; that's why I'm here." She gestured to her bags. "With these."

"You're giving me his luggage?"

"I'm moving in."

Seeing me on the hot seat made Tony happy. Grinning, he put his hand on my shoulder. "I hate to leave when this is getting good, but I better be going home."

"To your wife?" my mother asked, pointedly.

"Yes," Tony growled.

"I'll walk you downstairs," I said to Tony.

Tony took my mother's hand. "It's been a pleasure seeing you again, Mrs. Connor. Kevin was right, you look wonderful. You haven't aged a day since I last saw you."

Whatever negative impression my mother had of Tony evaporated like water on a hot stove.

"You've always been such a dear," my mother said, kissing him on the cheek. "Now, you two just run along. I'll wait up here." As if I were worried she'd leave.

"OK, Mom, I'll be right back. And whatever you do, don't unpack."

I rode down the elevator with Tony. "Is it even possible that she could have worse timing?" I asked him.

Tony looked down at his crotch. "Not that I can see," he answered. "You want me to shoot her? We can say we walked in and mistook her for a burglar."

"No," I said. "I'm too mad at my father to let him off the hook that easily. Dottie Kubacki?"

Dottie was a widow who lived two houses down from mine, five away from Tony's old house. Almost as wide as she was tall, Dottie was not exactly the husband-stealing type.

"Maybe there's been some kind of mistake," Tony said. The elevator door opened and I escorted Tony to the door of my building. Even this late, the air still felt as if it had been baked in a kiln.

"I'm going to walk to my car," Tony said. "That'll burn off the beers. You go back upstairs and enjoy your mom."

"I was hoping to enjoy *you*."

We stood awkwardly by the door. Here we were in another doorway. Half in, half out. Going in opposite directions.

I didn't think it appropriate to give him a kiss goodnight, but I couldn't imagine parting with a handshake. I decided to go for a compromise and hugged him. He hugged me back.

"Are you gonna be OK?" he asked.

I nodded into his chest.

Tony put his lips to the top of my head. "You know you have me all confused, right?"

I nodded again. I didn't want to let go, but I did.

"You'll be fine," Tony said. "I'll call you tomorrow."

"Would you really do it?" I asked

"Call you?"

"Shoot her."

Tony grinned again. "So far," he said, "you have a pretty good record of making me do things I shouldn't."

Yeah, I thought, but we hadn't actually *done* anything yet.

I watched him walk until he was gone. Then I went upstairs to face the fresh horrors that awaited me.

CHAPTER 5

The Storm Settles In

I OPENED MY apartment door and found my mother unpacking her bags. "I thought I asked you not to do that."

"Don't be silly," my mother said, shaking out a garment bag. "Do you know how hard it is to get wrinkles out of silk?"

"As a matter of fact, yes. But Mom, what are you doing here?"

"I told you. I found out a few days ago that your dad was . . . involved with that bitch Dottie Kubacki. There was no way I could stay in the house after that. I would have kicked him out, but where would he have gone? Dottie's? I'd cut his legs off, first. I tried to call and tell you that I was coming, but you never answered my messages."

"What about Kara?" Kara was my married sister who lived in a big house in New Rochelle. A house with at least two guest bedrooms.

"You know she wouldn't want me there. Besides, those kids would drive me crazy before too long."

"'Too long?' How long do you plan on staying?"

My mother started opening closets. Well, closet. There was only one. "Where's your ironing board?"

"I don't have one. And stop going through my things." I was glad I hid my porn the other night when Tony was coming over, but it wasn't *that* well hidden.

"How can you not have an ironing board?"

"Kara has an ironing board."

"And five-year-old triplets who should have their vocal cords cut," my mother answered.

"I only have one bed," I whined.

"I don't mind if you sleep on the couch."

There was no use arguing with my mother. She's like a force of nature when she gets like this: determined, inevitable, implacable. I've found that people are either appalled or amused by her. I was usually both.

So I helped her unpack. Tomorrow, I would call my father and have him get her back. It was inconceivable to me that he was actually having an affair with anyone, let alone with a woman who needed to have her dresses made at Omar the Tentmaker's. I was more likely to sleep with Dottie Kubacki than my father. I was sure it was all a big misunderstanding.

After an hour spent turning on the couch, I realized I'd never get to sleep. The heavy snoring from my bedroom assured me that my mother wasn't having the same problem. But then again, there happens to be a very comfortable bed in there.

Maybe I'd get to use it again someday.

I got out of bed and sat at my computer. I decided to see if I could find out a little more about Allen's sons before I met them at the reading of the will tomorrow.

First, the younger one. A Google of his name led to a few relevant links. The first was to the financial firm Ingerson Investing. Paul managed two of their largest mutual funds.

His picture was in the annual report. A handsome man, he was posed standing in front of his desk, arms crossed across his chest. His grim, serious-guy expression was meant to convey gravity and strength. But the slimness of his build, his thin lips, the two-hundred-dollar haircut, and the perfect tailoring of his suit spoke to a certain effeteness. He seemed more likely to study himself in the mirror than to study financial reports.

I followed a few links to his funds, and sure enough, they had underperformed the market. I looked at the stocks he had recently bought for the funds, and some of them were real dogs, companies whose malfeasance or misfortunes had made the front pages. Unlike his father, who had a Midas touch with investing, Paul seemed to have the instincts of a born loser.

Another search led me to an article from the *New York Times.* Paul and his wife were pictured at a cancer fundraiser at the Ritz Carlton. "Investment fund manager Paul Harrington and wife Alana," the caption read.

Paul looked even spiffier here. Gucci shoes, a suit that fit him like it was custom made, and a white linen shirt buckled to the collar, no tie. His wife, Alana, was attractive, but severe looking. Almost as tall as he, with sharp, birdlike features that made her smile look predatory. In a strapless white evening gown, her bony shoulders and prominent collarbone gave her the chic appeal of a bulimic. Lara Flynn Boyle would have to diet to get this skinny. Whoever said you can't be too rich or too thin never saw this picture.

Next, I searched the name of the older brother, Michael. The first link took me to the Center for Creative Empowerment Therapy. There on the homepage was a picture of Michael, with a caption reading "Founder and Leader."

Although the picture was just a head and shoulder shot, you could see Michael Harrington was a powerfully built and stunningly good-looking man. Square jawed, heavily muscled, with sharp cheekbones and electric blue eyes. Although there was some resemblance between Paul and him, Michael seemed to have gotten both brothers' allotment of testosterone.

Like his brother's official portrait, Michael's also showed him unsmiling. With his stern expression and piercing eyes, Michael gave you the feeling that if his "creative empowerment therapy" (whatever that was) didn't work, he could just beat the neuroses out of you.

Hunky as he was, he could have made a fortune with Mrs. Cherry doing just that.

A click on his picture took you to his bio. I was just about to read more about him when an instant message popped up on my screen.

"Angel, what r u doing up?" Freddy typed.

I wrote him an abbreviated synopsis of my evening, making out with Tony, and my mother's moving in.

"Just when I thought ur life couldn't get any more dramatic," Freddy wrote back. "What tragedy will befall you next? A plague of locusts? Boils? A new Celine Dion album?

"Speaking of crazy divas," he continued, "would u say hello to ur mother for me?

I assured him I would.

"Good. Now go to bed. We have to be beautiful for the reading of the will tomorrow."

I looked at the time in the Windows taskbar. 2:45 A.M. Ugh.

I signed off and lay on the couch for another hour until sleep came.

CHAPTER 6

Things Go Worse Than Expected

THREE HOURS LATER I was awakened by the sound of grenades exploding in my kitchen. "What the hell?" I shouted.

"Honey," my mother said cheerily. "I was just looking for where you keep the food."

Welcome, Hurricane Momma. For one blissful moment, I had forgotten about my new roommate.

"I don't keep any food," I groaned.

"Toast?"

"Toast is food."

"Coffee?"

"Nope."

"How about some tea?"

"I have protein powder, milk, and bananas."

"Maybe some eggs?"

"Am I going to have to get out of bed?"

"You're not in bed," my mother reminded me. "You're on the couch. And yes, you have to get up. Momma's going to take you out to breakfast at that greasy spoon on the corner. You know, breakfast is a very important meal. The most important of the day, I always say. I don't know how you can be productive if you don't start out with a good breakfast . . . "

Maybe I should have taken Tony up on that offer to shoot her.

After our breakfast, my mother and I went our separate ways: She to the beauty parlor she runs in Hauppauge, Long Island, I to my apartment to change. I told her that the super would let her in if she got home before I did, but she assured me that he had already given her an extra key. Great.

I put on a pair of tan khakis, a white dress shirt, tan boat shoes, and carried a blue linen blazer, the outfit I wear when a client requests "a nice, clean boy." I considered wearing a tie, but the blistering heat made me decide otherwise. I don't know how people who have real jobs survive in this city.

I took a cab to the law office where Allen's will was to be read. Standing outside was Freddy, looking spectacular in a black suit with a white silk T-shirt underneath. The outfit was just this side of *Miami Vice,* but Freddy could pull it off.

"What happened to the sequins?" I asked, getting out of the cab.

"I thought, 'why detract from my natural beauty?'" Freddy answered. "You look very *Lands End,* darling."

"Thanks for coming." I kissed him on the cheek. "These people scare me."

"Well, Auntie Freddy will protect you," he said, ushering me inside. "You know there isn't a white person in the world who scares me."

We rode the elevator to the forty-fifth floor, where we entered the offices of Allen's law firm. I could see why rich people would trust them with their finances. Everything about the place screamed old money and new tax loopholes. Even the mail clerks were better dressed than me.

Two receptionists sat behind a long mahogany desk. One looked as if she was in her mid-sixties, with silver hair sprayed into a stiff wave seen only in fifties horror movies and *Town and Country* magazine. Her facelift was pulled so tight that every time she blinked her hairline moved down an inch. From the way she was looking at Freddy and me, it was impossible not to imagine she had one hand on the police call button.

The other woman looked to be in her mid-thirties. She was attractive, but in a less artificial and frightening way. I told her we were there for the reading of Allen Harrington's will.

After checking my name against a printed list, she ushered us to a plush waiting area, where we sank into brown leather armchairs that cost more than I made in a month. And I make a lot in a month. An older man sitting across from us snorted. A passing attorney looked at Freddy and me questioningly.

"May I bring you something?" the nicer, younger receptionist inquired. "Coffee, tea?"

"Valium?" I asked.

"Five or ten milligrams?" She winked.

"Fifty," I answered.

The receptionist whispered. "Don't be intimidated. Most of them take the train back to Brooklyn just like the rest of us."

"You're a doll," Freddy said to her. Then, to me: "See? I told you there was nothing to be afraid of. I'm sure everything's going to go fine. How bad can it be?"

Ten minutes later, the receptionist took Freddy and me to a swank, windowed corner office, where the other invitees were seated at a small oval conference table.

I recognized the Harrington sons, Michael, the oldest, and Paul. Michael was as handsome and well-built as he appeared in his picture. His forehead was high and distinguished. Strong cheekbones pointed the way to a perfectly sculpted nose and thick lips.

He had a football player's body. Bulky and dense, with well-rounded shoulders and biceps that peaked even under his suit jacket. You could have posted a billboard on his expansive chest.

Paul was even more effete than he looked in his picture. He was dressed in true metrosexual style, in a Hugo Boss suit and two-tone Prada shoes that were new for this season.

In person, he was better looking, though. Thinner and less muscular than his brother, he was nonetheless trim and fit. He shared his brother's handsome features, and although not quite as striking as Michael, his blue eyes and lighter hair made him look less imposing and more approachable.

His wife, Alana, perched at his side. She, too, was perfectly turned out in a charcoal gray Chanel-like suit and an impenetrable mask of Clinique. Even seated, you could see she was taller than Paul.

She was wearing a sweet perfume that I could smell from across the table. It did little to soften her attractive but harsh features.

There were two other women in the room I didn't recognize. One was long and skinny, with small dark eyes and a short-cropped haircut. The other was short and stocky, with an attractive face that looked nervous. Her eyes were red and teary.

Their clothing was sensible and modest. I guessed Banana Republic for the skinny one and Lane Bryant for the other.

No one was speaking.

Alana regarded me and Freddy with narrowed eyes. She whispered something to her husband, who chuckled.

Michael refused to look at us at all.

So far, it was going fabulously.

Freddy and I sat, too.

Freddy looked at Michael and kicked me under the table. "Who's the hunky one?" he whispered.

I kicked him back harder. "Shhhh!"

Freddy stuck his chin out at Alana and Paul. "They're whispering!" he whined.

"I thought you were going to behave yourself," I hissed.

A door opened at the far end of the office. A tall black woman with strong features and a bald head walked through it. She was impeccably dressed in a man-tailored black suit with a white silk blouse underneath. Two-inch heels provided a percussive accompaniment to her confident stride and increased her already impressive stature.

"Thank you all for coming," she began, sitting down at the end of the table nearest the Harrington family. "I'm Tamela Steel, Mr. Harrington's attorney."

Freddy elbowed me. "*Get Christie Love,*" he stage whispered.

Ms. Steel looked at him and raised an eyebrow.

Freddy straightened up in his chair.

"The purpose of our meeting today is to go over the bequests of Mr. Harrington's will. Mr. Harrington left specific instructions . . ."

Paul Harrington interrupted her. "Excuse me, Miss, um, Beals, but is this really necessary?" He spoke in an irritated, above-it-all sigh. "I'm sure you could handle the disposition of my father's estate in a more appropriate manner. I don't know why we have to hear about it in front of" he waved his hand at the four of us who weren't part of his family "these people."

The look the lawyer gave him could have melted a brick. "It's *Ms. Steel.* And as I was saying, Mr. Harrington left specific instructions as to how he wanted his wishes conveyed. Everyone in this room is here at his request."

She leaned forward, getting in Paul's face. "His *last* request. I trust you have no problem honoring your father's last request, Mr. Harrington?"

I never heard anyone harrumph before, but I suppose that was the noise that escaped from Paul's lips.

"Hey," Freddy whispered, "did that guy just fart out of his mouth?"

"If there are no more interruptions, then," Ms. Steel continued, "some time ago, Mr. Harrington taped a video to be played for you all in the event of his death."

She pressed a button under the table, and a thin, fifty-inch plasma screen descended from the ceiling. The lights automatically dimmed and a quiet popping sound signaled the presence of hidden speakers in the wall.

"Cool," Freddy said aloud. Ms. Steel tried to give him a dirty look, but she couldn't help smiling. Like I said, Freddy has that way with people.

Although not, I couldn't help but notice, with the Harringtons. Paul harrumphed again, and Alana looked like she wanted to strangle Freddy with the strap of her Louis Vuitton bag.

The screen came on and there, suddenly, bigger than life, was the understandably serious face of Allen Harrington.

"Thank you for coming," the familiar voice said. I felt a chill down the back of my neck. "Trust me, I have never been more honest than when I say I only wish I could be there with you today."

The skinny woman I didn't know laughed aloud and then, embarrassed, covered her mouth. Her companion, though, took a sharp breath and started to quietly sob. The skinny one put her arm around her. Opposites attract, I thought.

I saw Paul Harrington staring at me, but I wouldn't return his gaze. Although I did wonder why he was looking at me when his father's last appearance was playing on a screen a few feet away.

"I'm sure this videotape may seem a bit dramatic to you, but every time I tried to write this down, I found myself uncharacteristically at a loss for words. So, I thought, why not just tape the damn thing and be done with it?

"First, I'd like to address my sons. Michael, Paul. What can I say? I can still remember the day each of you was born; they were among the happiest of my life. For so many years, watching you grow up was what gave shape and meaning to my existence. As hard as I worked, I always believed it was for you, my boys, the lights of my life.

"But you can't let anyone, even your children, become your life. And for a long time that's what I did, ignoring parts of myself that I was afraid would take me away from you. Denying the things my soul craved, denying my heart.

"But the heart can only be denied for so long.

"By the time I was ready to face the truth, I was almost dead inside. But I wanted to wait until I thought you boys could deal with my being gay. I wanted to believe that we could still be a family."

Allen's expression turned sad.

"But I was wrong.

"While you were children, I could forgive you. But now you are men, and still your minds are closed. As are your hearts. I've reached out to you both over the years, but each time I've been rebuffed.

"What you are doing, Michael, makes me especially sad."

I made a mental note—what was Michael doing?

"Still, I have provided for each of you in my will."

I looked at the Harrington boys. Paul's sudden smile made me think of a vulture finding a particularly tasty corpse on the road. Alana clenched her fist and nodded as if to say "yes!"

Michael stayed stoic.

"Oh, not as much as I could have. And not as much as I know you're hoping for. But enough for me to go to my grave knowing I did the right thing.

"Even if my boys didn't.

"Now, to my dear friend Kevin."

I could feel all the eyes in the room fall on me.

"Kevin, you have refused the gifts I've offered you over the years. But what you didn't know is that I've been taking the money I wanted to give you and investing it on your behalf.

"And, if you don't mind my saying so, if there's one thing I'm good at, it's investing."

Allen smiled.

"You've always told me that you wanted to earn enough money to put yourself through school. Well, now you'll find that you have more than enough to follow that dream. And maybe even take a nice vacation before you enroll.

"Maybe you can take that friend Freddy you're always going on about. I've got a feeling you two are going to be spending a lot of time together."

Freddy looked at me in surprise. I tried not to notice. Had I led Allen to think that my feelings for Freddy extended beyond friendship?

Did they?

And what was Allen's inheritance going to mean in my life? Had my world just changed? Again?

Allen continued. "Kevin, I thank you for your companionship. Although my own boys wouldn't let me be a part of their lives, you were like a son to me. Now, go and make me proud."

Alana turned to Paul. "Oh, please." He harrumphed in response.

"You really should see a doctor about that noise you keep making," Freddy said with mock sincerity.

"Shhh," Ms. Steel said, barely suppressing a grin.

"The bulk of my estate," Allen said "I leave to the Association for the Acceptance of Lesbian and Gay Youth." The two women I didn't know gasped and clutched each other. The heavier one blushed furiously.

"Lori, May, I believe you have the opportunity to do something wonderful with your work. I only hope that through your contributions you can help ensure that other young people don't have to face the repression and isolation I felt for so much of my life. I'm so glad I can help you begin your journey."

"Lastly, a message to my sons. Well, my biological ones, that is.

"You've wasted a lot of your lives on negative emotions. But it's not too late for you to change. Anger is the only poison in the world that kills both the giver and the receiver.

"Get over it."

The screen went black. Ms. Steel pressed a button, and it disappeared back into the ceiling as the lights came back on.

"Well," said Alana, tapping the table with her perfectly manicured nails, "I guess he put the homosexual agenda ahead of his own family right until the end, didn't he?"

Even her husband looked shocked by the bluntness of Alana's comment.

The thinner woman (Lori? May?) from the gay youth group wrinkled her nose in disgust and rose from her chair. "Ms. Steel, thank you for arranging for us to come in today. Unfortunately," she said, looking at Alana Harrington, "I'm afraid the air in here has gotten quite fetid."

Her companion stood, too. She looked genuinely grief-stricken. "I'm s-s-s-sorry about your father," she said shyly to the Harrington boys. "Your father-in-law, too," she added to Alana. "I . . . " she began, and then dissolved into heavy sobs. Her companion led her from the room.

Alana watched the two women leave.

"Well," she said, "at least we don't have to deal with any more dykes."

Tamela Steel's glare was withering. "Not. Quite."

"Oh," Alana said.

"What does 'fetid' mean?" Freddy asked.

I gave Ms. Steel credit—she managed to conclude the meeting without throwing Alana Harrington out the window. She explained that we would all be receiving notices through registered mail that explained how much we each stood to inherit, and that we would be issued checks when the estate passed through probate.

In as professional a manner as possible, she ushered us out of the office, only breaking character to slap Freddy on the ass once the Harringtons cleared the hallway. "You stick with that boy," she said, motioning towards me. "Allen Harrington was a great man. Any companion of his is bound to be a good catch."

"We're just friends," Freddy said.

Ms. Steel looked at us. "Oh, is that the story? Well, I like a good story, too."

I wasn't quite sure I knew what she meant, but she was heading back into her office and I never got the chance to ask.

Freddy and I were anxious to talk, but when we reached the elevator, Paul and Alana Harrington were waiting there. Michael was nowhere to be seen.

"Well, well, well," Alana trilled. "If it isn't the boy toy and his dusky boyfriend."

"'Dusky?'" Freddy asked me. "What is this, *Mandingo?*"

Paul put a limp arm around his wife. "Just ignore them, darling. I would never have brought you if I had known you'd have to associate with whores."

"Hey," Freddy said, "*I'm* not a whore!"

I looked at Paul, then at Alana. He might be good looking, but there was no way he was man enough for a shark like her. Unless he had a twelve-inch dick, there was no way she married him for anything but his money. "Speaking of whores," I said to her, "what was it that brought you two crazy kids together?"

Alana's eyes narrowed and her already thin lips curled under. The veins in her neck stretched taught as guitar strings. "You *trash,*" she hissed at me. "How dare you talk to me that way? Do you have any idea what I do to boys like you?"

I could tell that Alana was used to her imperial manner intimidating folk, but I'm a little gay guy who's faced bullies since junior high. This bitch had no idea who she was dealing with.

"You seemed real broken up about Allen's death," I said to her. "You, too, Paul. So let me ask you a question: Who do you think killed him?"

Alana blinked twice and Paul opened and closed his mouth like a guppy.

"My father's *suicide* was tragic," an impossibly deep voice came from behind us. Michael Harrington had returned. He walked over as tall and imposing as a god; his words booming like a pronouncement from the heavens.

"But it was the unavoidable result of a 'lifestyle' that he chose for himself. A lifestyle that can lead to nothing but despair and an early grave. A lifestyle that, perhaps, is more accurately called a 'deathstyle.'"

Freddy looked at him with a mixture of desire and disgust. If there was anything that made him angry, it was a good-looking man who was too horrible a person to be worth fucking. That was nature at its cruelest, and it was not to be borne. "You're kidding with this shit, right?"

"I don't know what your relationship with my father was," Michael said to me, ignoring Freddy as a statue might ignore the pigeon that crapped on it. "But I'm sure it was tawdry."

He reached inside his jacket and, for a quick moment, I thought *he's going for his gun!* But instead, he pulled out a small black leather envelope and handed me an expensively printed ivory card with raised lettering: Michael Harrington, founder, *The Center for Creative Empowerment Therapy.* "Perhaps we can talk about it someday." He looked at me as if he wanted to eat me up, but not in a good way, if you know what I mean. I was reminded of the Big Bad Wolf.

I slipped his card into my pocket and instinctively took a step backwards. "Maybe you can tell me what exactly you were doing that made him 'especially sad.'"

"I can assure you," Michael said, "my father made me infinitely sadder than I ever made him."

"He must be turning over in his grave to see you still so bitter," I said.

Michael's mouth turned up a little. "There will be no grave. He's scheduled for cremation as soon as the coroner releases his body. There will be no funeral, either. Ashes to ashes . . ."

"Dusk to dusky," Freddy finished.

This time it was Alana who harrumphed and Paul chuckled at her discomfort. This did not look like a happy marriage.

Michael looked confused, the first time I saw him shaken. Good going, Freddy.

We all stood and stared for a moment before we were interrupted by a perky looking young woman. "Oh, look!" she said excitedly, "you all forgot to push the elevator button. No wonder you've been waiting so long!" She quickly corrected our oversight.

A moment later the elevator door opened and the Harringtons stepped inside. I started to follow, but Freddy held me back.

"We'll wait for the next one," he said. "The air in there is too fetid."

"Fuck you," Alana snapped as the door slowly closed.

"You got yourself a real class act," Freddy shouted to Paul. But by then, they were gone.

"I *hated* those people," Freddy said once we got outside. We both took off our jackets in the oppressive summer heat. "I mean, I expected not to like them, but I *hated* them."

"Yeah, well, they were pretty easy to hate," I answered.

"They all did it, you know. The creepy, fruity one, the sexy but crazy older brother, the hag from Hell, they all did it. It's like *Murder on the Orient Express.* But the old movie, not the shitty television remake with, God help me, Meredith Baxter Birney. The guys probably knocked Allen out, and that bitch threw him over the balcony."

Freddy was being ridiculous, but something he said caught my interest. "You thought Paul was fruity?"

"Oh, please," Freddy said. "Sister was a step away from wearing hot pants at Gay Pride. Definitely a closet case. I mean, Prada shoes? Hello!"

"I'm sure some straight boys wear designer footwear," I answered.

"Yeah, but he also couldn't take his eyes off you, or didn't you notice?"

"Well, I caught him looking once, but I thought he was just giving me a dirty look."

"Oh, they were 'dirty' all right."

I'd have to think about that. "So what about Michael?"

"I don't know. What was with all that crazy shit anyway? 'Deathstyle?' I thought you told me he was running some kind of psychiatric treatment center. He sounded more like a preacher than a doctor."

"I thought so, too," I answered. "But, you know, when people start mixing religion with therapy, they get pretty nutty."

"I think we better visit that place of his, don't you?"

I put my arm around him. "Why? Do you want his 'help'?"

Freddy pulled me closer. "He did say there was still hope for us."

"Amen," I laughed.

"Speaking of 'us,'" Freddy said, "what was Allen talking about when he said he thought we'd be spending a lot of time together?"

"I don't know," I answered.

"You didn't tell him we were a couple, did you?"

"No, why would I?"

"Because, that's not what you want, right?"

I was suddenly aware of the size and strength of Freddy's arm around me. Of his slightly sweaty, musky smell. Of the heat coming off his body on this already hot day.

"Of course not," I said a little too quickly. "I mean, that's not what either of us wants, right?"

"Of course not," Freddy answered hastily. "I mean, why fuck up a good friendship, right?"

"Right," I said.

“Right,” Freddy said.

We were both quiet for a minute.

“Although,” Freddy continued, “now that Allen’s left you a fortune, maybe I *should* marry your ass.”

“I don’t think I’m rich,” I said. “But maybe I can go to graduate school earlier than I thought.”

“And maybe,” Freddy said, “you can stop being such a big whore.”

“Hey,” I said, “it worked for Alana Harrington!”

CHAPTER 7

A Client a Boy Could Fall For

I WALKED FREDDY to his office and took a cab back to my apartment. I put the air conditioner on high and checked my messages. Just one. "Tony. Call me."

One crisis at a time, I thought. When Tony visited the other night, I did a casual sweep of my porn. With my mother, Snoopy McSnoopy staying over, I had to really hide it.

I also had to call the only man who could save me.

I put on my headset and dialed. He answered on the first ring.

"Dad," I began, "what the hell is going on?"

"Kevin, I have some rough news for you," he said. "Are you sitting down?"

"No." I was, in fact, pulling dirty magazines out of my dresser.

"Sit down."

"Dad!"

"All right, it's your funeral. So. Your mother. I have to tell you: She's nuts."

"That's your news?"

"She's really lost it this time, Kevin. She has it in her mind that I'm making the whoopee with Dottie Kubacki."

"So I've heard." As I listened to my dad, I piled four *Honchos,* an *Advocate Men,* and my Kristen Bjorn DVD collection on the floor.

"I mean, Dottie Kubacki? How? Have you seen how large that woman is? Could a person even find her, excuse my French, vagina? Do I look like Jacques Cousteau to you?"

"Well, why is she upset?" I was under the bed trying to reach an old issue of *Freshmen.*

"Why? Who knows where that woman gets her ideas from? Call those people from that *CSI* show, they can solve a murder based on some toilet paper and a toenail. Maybe they can figure her out."

"All right, well, you have to work this out with Mom. She can't stay here."

"Why not?"

"Dad!"

"Listen, you know how she gets. Give her a week, she'll find something else to be nutty about."

"A week!" I found an old *Playgirl* in the back of my nightstand.

"Maybe two."

It takes a lot of drama to be heard in my family. "I'm going to wind up in the loony bin if she stays here one more night. Do you know what it is to lose a son?"

"Please," my father asked. "Don't rush me. I'm just beginning to enjoy losing my wife."

Before I hung up, I got my dad to promise to call my mom at work before the day was over. I filled a backpack with my lubes and condoms and stuck it as far back as it would go in the cabinet under the kitchen sink.

The phone rang. Caller ID told me it was Tony. Did I want to pick up? Yes.

"Hey."

"You didn't return my call," Tony said.

"I just got in."

"Where were you?"

"What are you, my keeper?"

"Just concerned."

"Oh." That sounded nice coming from him. "I'm fine. You should have tried my cell." I told him about the reading of Allen's will.

"Huh," Tony said, "they sound like the family from hell."

"It was pretty grisly."

"If you go to the funeral, you'll have to see them again," Tony said.

I told him that there wasn't even going to be a funeral.

"That's pretty cold," Tony said. "I guess they really did hate him."

"See?" I asked

"Denying him a funeral isn't the same as killing him, Kevin."

"I got the feeling they couldn't wait to cremate him. Guess he wasn't dead enough, huh?"

"Yeah, well, you can't kill the past."

"You sound like you're talking from experience," I said.

"You ought to know," Tony answered.

Yeah, I did.

"There were about a million reasons why I wasn't happy to find my mother in my apartment last night," I told him. "Want to guess the biggest one?"

"Hey, watch that mouth. I'm at work."

"Come on over. You can watch my mouth."

"Enough," he said in the cop voice I suspected he used in the interrogation room. "Listen, about what you said before . . . "

"About last night?"

"About trying to solve Allen's 'murder.' Just walk away, Kevin."

"I'll think about it."

"Don't think, do. And stay away from the Harringtons. They sound nuts, and nuts can be dangerous."

"Then I better stay away from my mother, too."

"That goes without saying. So, I have a question for you: How much do you think Allen left you?"

"Oh, I don't know. A couple of thousand?"

"Huh. An inheritance. Know what that makes you?"

"Grateful?"

"A suspect." Tony, sounding glad for once to have the last word, hung up.

I lay down on my couch with a groan. Now I was a murder suspect. Great.

I was tired, stressed, and hungry. I started to think about the day's events, but that hurt my brain. So, I opted for my own personal form of meditation: Replaying *The Way We Were,* scene by scene, in my head. Fade in: A young, unconventionally attractive Jewish girl hands out flyers at a protest rally . . .

Two hours later, I was awakened by the sound of my front door rattling. Someone was trying to get in. There was enough weirdness and violence in my life lately that I felt even more than my usual New York paranoia. I sat up quickly, becoming aware of both a stiff back and an attractive crust of dried drool on my cheek.

I ran to the door and looked through the peephole. I could see the top of someone's head, but he or she was standing too close for me to see who it was. I leaned in closer just as the door swung open and knocked me on my ass.

"Ow!"

"Damn key keeps getting stuck," my mother greeted me. "You really should have the super look at it. Never mind, I'll tell him. I want to talk to him about getting another rod installed in the closet, anyway. And maybe a nice shower head. One of those that rain on you, you know? What are you doing on the floor?"

I stood up to give her a hug. I didn't want her living with me, but she was still my mother. "Hi."

"Hi, yourself." She took my face in her hands. "Sweet boy. What's that on your face." She licked her thumb and reached out to swab my cheek.

"Drool," I said, jumping back. "And keep that thumb to yourself."

"You always did drool a lot," she said, coming in and taking off her shoes. "And not just when you were a baby, either. I remember you were in the first grade, and your teacher asked me what we were giving you to drink at home because your chin was always wet and covered in . . ."

"Enough!" I shouted. "As charming as this trip down memory lane is, can we skip any more stories about my bodily functions?" I followed her as she walked into my kitchen.

"Oh, please, don't even get me started on your poopies! I remember one day, oh, you must have been three years old, I had you dressed in the cutest white outfit and . . ."

I picked a knife off the counter and pointed it at my chest. "That's it. I'm cutting my heart out right now."

My mother opened up the refrigerator. "Don't be such a drama queen."

"'Drama queen?'"

"I run a beauty shop, darling. I can talk *gay*. And there's still nothing to eat in this thing."

"I go out a lot."

"Tell you what," my mother said. "How about we hop in my car, drive out to somewhere where there are real supermarkets, Queens or Brooklyn or something, and go shopping. Let's pretend real people live in this apartment."

"I don't cook."

"I'll cook." She walked over to the stove. "Does this thing actually work, or is it just for show?" She turned the dial and the pilot light caught. "Hallelujah! We have fire! Now I know how the cavemen felt."

The truth was, my mom's cooking didn't sound half bad. Neither did a fully-stocked kitchen. I didn't have a client tonight, or any other plans, either. I was thinking of staring at the phone all night hoping Tony might call, but I could always do that tomorrow.

Besides, she'd be a captive audience on the car ride, and I could use the time to plead my father's innocence.

Four hours later, I was fat and happy sitting at my computer. My mother was in the bedroom watching *Matlock* or something.

It had been a fun evening. Although I didn't get anywhere on the

Dottie Kubacki front, ("I know what I know and don't ask me what I know, all right?") we did tear up the supermarket and filled my cupboards with more food than I knew they could hold. The apartment still smelled of her signature liver with cabbage and onions, which sounds disgusting but is really delicious. And there was still about ten pounds left over for tomorrow.

The evening made me remember that when I wasn't embarrassed or overwhelmed by my mother, she was pretty good company.

A stocked kitchen. Home cooking. A shower that rained on me. Maybe having her here for awhile wasn't going to be so bad.

"Hey," my mother's voice came from the bedroom. "Where's that magazine I was reading last night?"

"What magazine?" I asked her.

"The one in your nightstand. With all the naked men."

Oh. My. God.

She had to go.

I was typing the phrase "how to kill your mother" into Google when I got an instant message: "R u free?"

It was from Marc Wilgus, one of my favorite clients. I typed back "I'm available, but never 'free.'"

"LOL," Marc replied. "Seriously. I'm bored & horny. Wanna cum over?"

Marc was a great guy, and sex with him was always fun. I'd do him for free, although I wasn't about to tell him that.

"C u in 20," I answered. I didn't want to interrupt my mother's show, so I left her a note saying that I was meeting some friends.

Marc opened his door and immediately pulled me inside, pinning me against the wall and kissing me hard and deep.

It was probably the movie *Pretty Woman* that popularized the myth that prostitutes don't kiss. Think about it: Does it really make sense that a hooker would suck Richard Gere's dick but not make out with him?

In fact, it's our clients who usually avoid the lip lock. If a guy wants to kiss me, and if he's clean and doesn't have bad breath, I'm not adverse to some tonsil hockey.

Least of all with Marc. He was as good a kisser as he was everything else.

All around us, computers buzzed and whirred. Marc worked out of his apartment as a reverse-hacker. Security companies hired him to try and break into their client's computer networks. If Marc found an opening—and he always did—the security company knew to develop appropriate countermeasures.

In other words, Marc made his living doing things most people would go to jail for. But then again, so did I.

In addition to being good at sex, Marc was handsome as hell. He was just a little taller than me which made him kind of short. His body had obviously never seen the inside of a gym. Sometimes he'd call himself "fat" but he wasn't. He wasn't in great shape like a cover boy, but he was warm and strong and his skin was the smoothest I've ever felt. He must have been in his mid-thirties, but he could pass for younger. He had luxuriously black curly hair that I could spend hours running my hands through.

Had I met him under other circumstances, I might have been tempted to go out with him, except for one small thing: I wasn't entirely sure he ever went out.

Marc lived his life almost entirely on the Web. He ordered groceries and meals on the Internet. His movies, music, and pornography arrived over his FIOS line. He even hooked up with me through Mrs. Cherry's Web site.

"Mmmm," I said, pulling away from his embrace. "It's been kind of a long day. Do you want me to grab a shower?"

Marc licked me from my neck to my ear, whispering, "only if I can join you."

I put my arms back around him, hooking my thumbs into the back of his jeans. I started pushing down. "Wanna get wet?"

Marc pressed his impressive bulge against me. "I'm already getting wet."

"Sweet talker."

Marc took my T-shirt off and put his lips to my right nipple. He sucked hard and I gasped with pleasure.

"Fuck the shower," Marc said, putting his hands under my ass. He lifted me off the ground and I wrapped my legs around his back. He carried me towards the bedroom. "Let's fuck."

An hour later, I needed the shower even more. Marc lay on top of me, the drying evidence of my orgasm threatening to permanently glue us together. Marc tossed his condom on the floor, where it landed with a wet plop.

"Damn, that was good. How much," Marc asked playfully, "would it cost to have you move in?"

"More than you could afford." I ran my hands down his back.

"Hey, careful what you say," Marc smiled. "You're talking to a man who can hack into the bank accounts of seven of the world's ten richest men."

"Only seven?"

"The other three haven't hired me yet to try," Marc answered. He rolled off me, finding out too late how sticky dried cum can be. "Ouch!"

"Love hurts," I said.

"You're telling me," Marc answered. "And I haven't even paid yet."

"Listen," I said, thinking of the uncomfortable couch and my mother's snoring awaiting me at home, "if you want I can stay the night."

"I'd like that," Marc said, "but I'm kind of in the middle of breaking into the satellite systems of a small Central American nation. I better get back to work."

"No problem," I said, disappointed.

I couldn't help but think that Richard Gere never kicked Julia Roberts out.

Maybe I should have held back on the kissing.

After I got dressed, Marc slipped two hundred dollar bills into my hand. "I'll settle the rest up with Mrs. Cherry online," he told me.

"You're great," I said, giving him a hug.

"You too," he said. "What's your schedule like next week?" I told him the nights I was free, and he said he'd get back to me. It was a silly dance we did, because we both knew he'd never schedule a date in advance. In Marc's virtual reality, everything came to him when he wanted it, and he never knew what he'd want from one moment to the next. If he saw me online when he was horny, he'd get in touch and we'd get together. If I wasn't available, another rentboy would enjoy his generosity.

Although he always told me I was his favorite.

Which I didn't doubt, because he was my favorite client.

"Maybe next time," he said, "you could do it."

"Do what?"

"You know," he said, shyly. "Spend the night. If you want to, I mean."

Marc looked sweet and vulnerable, even younger than he usually did.

Maybe Marc's earlier rejection of my offer to stay had less to do with his work than with his fear of getting too close to someone. It wasn't an accident, I thought, that he's locked himself in this computer wonderland.

Maybe he wasn't locking himself in as much as he was locking everyone else out.

Maybe he needed someone to knock down the door.

He was sweet, he was handsome, he was sexy, and he was rich. Maybe that someone should be me.

Maybe this kind of thinking gets a hustler in trouble.

"Give 'em your mouth, your dick, and your ass," Mrs. Cherry once told me, "but do me a favor: keep your heart to yourself."

"Maybe I can," I told Marc.

But I knew I probably shouldn't.

I sneaked into my apartment somewhere around one. My mother's snoring combined with the lumpy couch to defeat any chance of sleep. I tossed and turned for awhile, but eventually gave in to pharmaceutical assistance and popped an Ambien.

What do you get when you cross someone with hyperactivity with a sleeping pill? Someone who *can't wait* to fall asleep. *Get it?*

So, after ten restless minutes, I popped another pill. That did the trick. Sleep hit me like a hammer.

CHAPTER 8

In Which Our Hero Goes to the Gynecologist

"GOOD MORNING, GORGEOUS!" someone shouted into my face. I groggily opened my unwilling eyes. Features slowly came into focus: blood-red lipstick, long, false eyelashes, heavily teased wig. Oh my God, I thought, a demented drag queen has broken into my apartment!

Then I remembered.

"Mom. What time is it?" I croaked

"Wake up time," she said. She leaned over to kiss me on the cheek. "Smell."

I covered my mouth. "I haven't brushed yet," I explained.

"No, you don't smell," she said. "Well, maybe a little. I mean: smell." She took a deep breath.

I did too. Oh my god. Bacon. French toast. Hazelnut coffee. If I hadn't woken up with a morning erection (thank you Lord for the blanket that covered my lap), I'd have sprung one there and then.

"See what you can do with food?" my mother said. "It's called 'cooking.'"

After breakfast with my mother, I went to the gym. I was doing pull-ups, my least favorite exercise, and thinking about what Tony told me.

"Just walk away."

He was right, of course. I had about as much business solving a murder as Sherlock Holmes did turning tricks.

Still, several things nagged at me.

Not the least of which was that I couldn't believe Allen would have killed himself.

I don't care what Tony told me about a recent rash of gay suicides. Allen was a happy, vital man, and he never would have taken his own life.

Someone must have killed him.

But who?

His children were obvious suspects.

Both Michael, the tall, handsome one, and Paul, the fey dandy, hated their father. Perhaps they had other motives, too. Maybe they didn't believe he had cut them from his will. Were they expecting a windfall from Allen's fall from a window?

There were other suspects, too.

I still had questions about Randy Bostinick, the hustler I had hooked Allen up with. Randy had a killer temper. But did he have a *killer's* temper? I couldn't say.

Then there was Roger Folds, the development director at The Stuff of Life. While I didn't have any reason to think he was capable of murder, it was pretty strange that he stopped coming to work right around the time of Allen's death. And his co-worker Vicki had told me something else . . . what was it?

Focus, Kevin, focus.

Ah yes, she thought Roger and Allen had been fighting about something.

And I still didn't know enough about Paul and Michael Harrington. What was Paul doing with that shrew Alana? And what was up with Michael's group, The Center for Creative Empowerment Therapy? It sounded like a quack factory to me.

All these thoughts swirling around in my head—it was time to get organized. My psychiatrist often told me that people with AADD should make lists. I was lazy about following his advice, but I felt overwhelmed enough to admit I needed all the help I could get. I took my iPhone out of my shorts. Along with a very small canister of Mace I kept on my keychain (we little blond boys need all the help we can get), it was something I carried with me all the time. I opened up a note and started typing.

1. Follow up with Roger Folds—fight?
2. Talk to Randy Bostinick
3. Research Paul and Michael Harrington.
4. Look into those gay suicides—was that true?

Then, just for the heck of it, I added

5. Fuck Tony

I wasn't sure how I meant that last item, but what the hell. Either way would be immensely satisfying.

I looked over the list. Items one and two looked pretty doable. With the help of the Internet, I could at least get started on three and four.

Item five I had waited seven years for. I could afford to wait a while longer.

My first to-do, talking to Roger Folds, I might be able to make short order of. Feeling pumped from the gym, I walked to The Stuff of Life for my morning shift. By the time I got there, the summer heat had deflated my pump, soaked through my shirt, and left me a sweaty mess. Yuck.

I got to The Stuff of Life early and headed straight to Roger's office. The door was closed. I knocked, once quietly, once with a little more oomph. No answer.

Next I went to see Vicki. She was sitting with her feet up on her desk, back to the door, phone held to her ear. Black cowboy shirt, black jeans, black boots. Black hair slicked back like Elvis. She was talking on the phone. "So I said to her, 'listen honey, I wouldn't eat her pussy with *your* mouth,' and she said . . ."

I tapped on the door to let her know I was there.

Vicki held up a finger.

"Hey, listen, someone's at the door. I'll call you back later. Yeah, love you too, Mom." She hung up the phone.

"Jesus," I said, "you talk to your mother like that?"

"Please," Vicki rolled her eyes, "once my mother found out I was a dyke, she got more interested in lesbianism than I am. She read every book she could find on the subject, rented *Desert Hearts*, and begged me to take her to a gay bar."

"Did you?"

"Of course! She had a great time. Haven't you ever taken your mother out?"

"We went to the supermarket last night."

"That's not what I meant."

"Listen, there's not a gay bar in New York big enough to hold me *and* my mother."

"You should try it. Maybe you guys could come out with me and my mom sometime. Who knows, maybe our moms will hook up."

I put my fingers in my ears. "La, la, la, la . . ."

"OK," Vicki said, laughing, "I take it back. So, if you didn't come here looking to hook your mother up with some hot lesbo action, what does bring you my way?"

I explained that I was looking for Roger Folds.

"Well, don't look here," Vick answered. "He quit."

"When?"

"Yesterday. He said he never wants to come back, either. Just asked if someone could bring his personal stuff to his apartment." Vicki pointed to a cardboard box sitting on her floor. "That's it over there. He doesn't live too far from me, so I figured I'd do it. Give me a chance to tell him what an asshole I think he is."

"Listen," I said, "think you could tell him in a letter? Cause I'd *really* like to see him."

"Can't imagine why. But if you wanna deliver his shit, be my guest. Just be sure to send my disregards."

"Thanks. I'll pick it up when I'm done." I kissed Vicki on the cheek. "Tell your Mom I said 'hi.'"

"Hey, tell her yourself when your mother brings her home for Christmas. As her date."

"Ewwwww."

My talk with Vicki had taken longer than I expected. I had to hurry to the kitchen to get today's volunteers started on the meal preparation. I was racing down the hallway, not really looking where I was going, when I ran smack into a wall. "Oomph!"

"Sorry," the wall mumbled.

"It's OK," I said, realizing that the wall, in fact, was a woman. Not a heavy woman, but large and solidly built, with the muscles of a high-school football player.

Our eyes met with a flash of recognition. The Wall blushed and looked down at her feet.

"Lori," a voice called from down the hallway, catching up to us, "I got the papers we need and . . ."

The taller, thinner woman recognized me immediately. "Oh!" she said. "Hello. Connor, right?"

"Kevin," I corrected her. "I met you two . . ."

"At the reading of Allen's will," she finished my sentence. "I'm May. And this," she said gesturing towards to her companion, "is Lori. My partner at the Association for the Acceptance of Lesbian and Gay Youth, as well as in life."

They were the women from the group Allen funded in his will.

Lori shifted uncomfortably. "Huh," she said by way of greeting.

May put her hand on my shoulder. "I'm so sorry for your loss. I could tell you and Allen were close. The way he spoke about you in that video—it was obvious he cared. You must have been very special to him."

Had anyone talked to me with compassion about Allen's death, I wondered? I found myself tearing up.

"Thanks," I said. "He was a very good man."

"He was obviously a big fan of yours," I said. "Of your work."

"Yes," May said. "I think the plight of queer youth really touched him. After all he had been through. And his son of course."

This was new. "His son?"

"Well, you know he didn't have much contact with either of his children, right?"

"None," I said.

"Right. Still, he kept track of them. Tried to be involved. He told me that he thought one of them might be gay, but that he had gotten married anyway. It made him so sad to think that his son might be making the same mistake he had."

The only one of the sons who was married was Paul. "Did he say what made him think that?"

Lori, or as I would always think of her, The Wall, cleared her throat. "We r-r-really have to go, May." For such a big girl, her voice was soft and breathless. You could see how shy she was, too, as she continued to regard her shoes as if they were the most interesting things on Earth. I always wondered what quiet people like her did with all their feelings.

"One minute," May responded. She gave Lori a reassuring pat on the back. I wondered if Lori wasn't a bit impaired. May turned back to me.

"No, he never said."

Freddy thought Paul seemed a little light in the loafers, too. Although I wasn't sure what difference it made.

We stood awkwardly for a moment. "So, do you work here?" May asked me.

I explained that I was a volunteer.

"That's wonderful," May enthused. "Good for you."

"Hey," I said, "maybe I could do some work with you guys," I offered. "Kind of a way to honor Allen's memory."

Lori and May looked at each other. "We're not really set up for that," May said.

"Well, let me know if I can help. Do you have a card or something?"

"Not yet," May smiled. "That's what Allen was helping us with. Infrastructure costs. We're kind of a start-up. Allen had been looking to build an organization that catered specifically to the needs of sexual minority youth, and he was very impressed by some of the work Lori and I had been doing with homeless teens. But maybe I could take one of yours?"

Not surprisingly, I didn't have any business cards. What would they say: "Kevin Connor, Male Prostitute?" I wrote my number on the back of a safer-sex flyer hanging in the hallway.

I wanted to talk to them some more, just in case they might have known something about Allen that would have helped me understand what had happened to him, but I really didn't know what to ask. I also had to go run my lunch shift. But there was one last thing I wanted to ask them.

"Listen, everyone tells me I'm crazy," I said, "but I just don't believe Allen would have killed himself. Do you?"

May shook her head. "I've been saying the same thing to Lori since it happened. He was very involved with us in the formation of the Association. We spoke every day. He went over our books, he helped us develop grant applications, he even introduced us to other potential major donors. Allen lived passionately. I think it must have been some terrible kind of accident. I just can't believe he'd take his own life."

For the first time since I'd bumped into her, Lori looked up. I was struck by just how pretty her features were. "You d-d-don't know," she said quietly. I recalled that she stuttered at the reading of the will, too. Maybe it was embarrassment that kept her so quiet.

"Don't know what," I asked.

She turned to me with tears in her eyes. "You don't know what someone could d-d-do. What they're c-c-capable of. Until they do it." Her shoulders started to shake.

May put an arm around her. "In our line of work, we see things that are very hard to believe, Kevin. Parents who beat their own children half to death, who throw them into the streets, just because they find out that they're gay.

"If you saw these parents in the market, or at church or school, they'd probably look like any other loving parent in the world. But when they find out the truth about their kids, when the reality doesn't fit perfectly with their expectations, well, you find out just how disposable some children in this society are."

You could hear May's passion in her words and you could see Lori's empathy on her pained and tear-streaked face. I saw why Allen believed in their vision.

"Kevin!" A call came from the kitchen. "We've got to get started! We need you!"

I put out my hand. "Sorry, but it sounds like I really have to go. But I'm glad I ran into you. Give me a call."

May took my hand in both of hers and pulled me in for a kiss on the cheek. "Take care of yourself, dear."

I extended my hand to Lori, too. She shook it limply. Even though she wasn't squeezing, I could feel the strength in her fingers. She really was a gentle giant.

Which made me remember how she was crying at the reading of Allen's will.

What happens to the feelings of quiet people like her?

Maybe they come out as tears.

After finishing my shift at The Stuff of Life, I called Roger Folds and got his machine. I left a message that I was a volunteer with the agency and that I had his things. I asked him to call me with a convenient time to drop them off. I took the box home with me.

It would be wrong for me to go through Roger's things, I thought, as I went through his things. Unfortunately, there was nothing interesting. Some pens, a desk blotter, a few framed certificates, and an *American Idol Season One Greatest Hits* CD. Not exactly an admission of murder, although possession of an American Idol CD must violate some law somewhere.

I checked my answering machine. No messages.

My iPhone chimed the love theme from *A Star Is Born*, reminding me that I had a client appointment in an hour. I made a quick lunch of leftover liver and onion, brushed my teeth three times, used mouthwash, and grabbed a quick shower before running out the door.

Midday appointments usually mean a married client, and this one was no exception. Dr. Richard Applebaum was one of the Upper East Side's most prestigious gynecologists. He and his beautiful wife appeared regularly on the pages of the society columns.

On the third Thursday of every month, Richard closed his office at noon to catch up on paperwork. At two, I'd arrive to put his stirrups to a few unintended uses. I don't know how long he lasted in bed with his lovely wife, but I was usually out the door by 2:20.

"You're such a good boy," Richard said, as I laid back on his examining table, where, only moments earlier, he'd showered me with a voluminous, if typically premature, ejaculation. "Is there anything you need written?"

Dr. Dick was my contact for pharmaceutical assistance. He was always willing to write me a prescription for whatever I wanted. And although I never took recreational drugs (who knows what's in that Ecstasy you buy on the dance floor?), I wasn't above the occasional Xanax, Ambien, or Viagra.

"Nothing, thanks, Dr. Applebaum." I wiped something off my chin. Yuck. "That was quite a load you shot there."

"Sorry about that," the doctor chuckled. "Here." He reached up to my hair. "You got some there, too."

"Jesus, what are you eating?"

"Good nutrition, son, exercise, and plenty of rest. Keeps a man vital, you know?"

And quick, too, I thought. Although I had to say that for a man in his late fifties, he did look pretty good.

"Listen," he said, handing me towel. "I was sorry to hear about your friend Allen Harrington."

"You knew Allen?"

"Oh yes, we traveled in some of the same circles, you know." I wasn't sure if he meant high society or gay-older-man circles, but I nodded.

"Allen knew of my . . . extracurricular interests, and he once mentioned you."

"A recommendation?" I asked.

"Yes, although he made it clear that he hadn't, shall we say, sampled the goods."

Lovely.

"Yes, Allen's tastes ran towards the more beastly, you know. Although what he saw in all those vapid muscle boys, I can't imagine. Not when he could have had a sweet kid like you."

"Aw shucks." I shrugged.

"Imagine his surprise when I told him that I had already made your acquaintance. I remember he said 'Ah, Richard, you always did have a way of finding the better things in life, didn't you?'"

I smiled.

"He was a very good man, and I know you two remained friends. I'm sure you'll miss him."

"Listen," I said, "do you believe he would have killed himself?"

"Suicide?" Dr. Dick asked. "Of course not. Who's saying that?"

"The police."

"Why, that's absurd. Allen Harrington was one of the strongest, bravest men I knew." Dr. Dick glanced over at the wall, where a portrait of him and the woman he was married to hung in a simple gold frame.

A reminder of the double life his friend had left behind.

His face clouded over with regret.

"Yes," Dr. Dick said. "He was one of the bravest men I knew."

Sitting in a taxi on my way back to my apartment, I felt a little sad for Dr. Dick. As accomplished as he was professionally, who knows if he was happy?

I, however, was thrilled with the hundred-dollar tip in my pocket, and the confirmation that yet another person thought Allen incapable of suicide.

I wasn't sure how I felt about Allen pimping me out, but I suppose that was just his way of looking out for me. After all, if I were a plumber, I wouldn't object to a referral. So why should I mind Allen recommending my sexual services?

Meanwhile, I was kind of horny. I hadn't cum in my eleven minutes of sex with the good doctor, but the blowjob he was giving me at the moment of his sudden climax had me boned up pretty good. And although he had offered to "bring me to completion," I declined his kindness.

So now what?

I checked out my cab driver in the rear viewer, but he was too freaky looking to fantasize about.

My iPhone vibrated in my pocket. As nice as it felt, I decided to answer it.

"Hey, it's Tony. Can you drop by my precinct later?"

Best offer I had all day.

"How about now? I'm in a cab."

"Great," Tony said. "Just tell 'em you're here to see me."

CHAPTER 9

Too Many Balls

SURE ENOUGH, THE desk clerk called Tony, who came out to join me. I wasn't expecting a hug in front of his fellow officers, and I didn't get one. "Come this way," Tony said, stiffly.

Tony looked great in his usual outfit of dark blue dress slacks, white shirt, and blue striped tie. He held a manila envelope in his hand.

He led me to a small room with a rectangular table and four chairs. He nodded towards the mirror that lined the far wall. "Two way glass," he cautioned me.

Translation: Don't try any funny stuff.

"What's up?" I asked him.

"Take a look." Tony handed me the folder.

A memo to his chief summarizing Tony's findings on Allen's case. The coroner's report found the cause of death to be—no surprise—the fall from his window. He found no other bruises or injuries inconsistent with the fall, although he did note that the back of the head and several other parts of the body were crushed in a way that made a complete analysis impossible.

There was also no sign of forced entry to Allen's apartment and the doorman hadn't announced any visitors.

"Satisfied?" he smirked.

"Why are you showing me this?"

"To keep you out of trouble. Also, to let you know I was only kidding when I said that you were a suspect." He smiled.

"I assumed you were."

"Don't be so sure. After all, you were mentioned in the will. In any case, that's always the first question we ask. 'Who benefits?'"

"I didn't even know I was in the will," I told him. "Let alone for how much."

"Fifty-seven thousand, two hundred and seven dollars," Tony said. "And seven cents. At least that's what the account was worth yesterday."

My mouth dropped open.

"Surprised?" Tony asked, still grinning.

"How do you know?" I asked him.

"We're the police," Tony said. "We know these things. I also know that the amount he left each of his kids was just about double that. Not exactly chump change, but, given what his boys earn, hardly an inducement to murder."

I thought for a moment.

"They hated him," I said, half to myself.

"A lot of people hate their parents," Tony said. "But they don't kill them."

"No, they don't." So, the Harrington kids had no financial incentive to see their father dead. I had to admit that Tony was making sense.

"Kevin," Tony looked at me gently. He put his hand on the table as if he were going to take mine. Then he glanced at the mirror and pulled it back. "I think you're wasting your time. I think you're mourning Allen and you're looking for someone to blame. I think you might just have to accept that Allen killed himself."

Suddenly, I felt a lot less sure of things. "I need a minute," I said. My thoughts were coming fast and furious. Had I taken my medicine today?

I lowered my head and looked up at him. Blinked back tears.

"Kevin," Tony said. He got up from his seat and came behind me. He put his hands on my shoulders. "Kevin."

I wanted to be strong, but the possibility that Tony was right devastated me. He was the professional here. What was I even doing doubting him?

"I just . . ." I began, but there was a lump in my throat that blocked my words. I rubbed my eyes. "I'm just so sad," I admitted. "I really loved him, you know?"

Tony sank to his knees and put his arms around me. "It's OK," he comforted me.

"Two way glass," I reminded him as we embraced.

"Fuck 'em," Tony answered.

After a few minutes, I told Tony I was all right and he returned to his seat. "Can you talk a little more?" he asked me.

"Sure."

"Listen, that's a pretty big chunk of change Allen left you. Just what was going on between you two, anyway?"

"Just friends," I told him. Tony raised an eyebrow. "I swear. I think he liked having a young man he could mentor and look out for. Especially since his own kids were estranged."

Tony nodded. "OK, I buy it. But if that was your relationship, then maybe he didn't feel comfortable sharing his problems with you. After all, if he was your father figure, maybe he didn't want to seem weak in front of you."

"I don't know. Maybe."

"We may never know," Tony said. "All I'm saying is that you need to move on. The evidence shows that Allen killed himself. And that's not exactly rare these days."

I remembered something Tony had said at the bar.

"That's right, you told me about that—a series of gay suicides."

"Yeah, but that's off the record."

"Did you ever find out if Allen knew any of the other victims?"

"There's no evidence either way."

I tried to think of another question, but I was at a dead end.

Dead. End.

I shuddered.

My phone rang.

"Do you need to get that?" Tony asked.

"Not now," I told him. We just looked at each other. How beautiful he was at that moment, his face showing nothing but concern for me. I felt teary again.

"Are you going to be all right?" he asked me.

I nodded. I brushed my hair out of my eyes and looked at him sadly.

"I wish I could kiss you right now," Tony said.

But you always have a reason not to kiss me, I thought, *don't you, and there's a two way mirror, and my dear friend is dead, and we can't go to your place because your wife might be home, and we can't go to my place because my mother might be home, and someone just left me over fifty thousand dollars and that kind of kills my last excuse not to go back to school, and if you knew what I really did for a living you'd probably kill me and I think I'm falling in love with you again and you hurt me so much the last time and oh, this is all so complicated!*

Too many balls in the air.

Time to let one drop.

With Tony no longer investigating Allen's death, there was one less reason for us to keep seeing each other.

Especially since he was married. To a woman, yet.

I had to tell him that this was it for us.

Another dead end.

At least I'd be the one to end it this time.

I was just about to tell him so when he said, "Listen, Kevin, with me closing the case and all, I guess that means we have to decide if we're going to keep seeing each other. And I think, maybe, we should talk about it."

"What?" I said louder than I intended to.

"Well, I just think that you're looking for something more than I am, and while I can't deny that I'm attracted to you, I just don't want to . . ."

"No way," I interrupted him. "No way are you dumping me again."

"I'm not dumping you," Tony said. "I'm just saying I don't want to hurt you down the line . . ."

"So you're hurting me now?"

"No, what I'm saying is . . ."

"What you're saying is bullshit," I told him. "And you can't break up with me, damn it, because I was just about to break up with you."

Tony raised his eyebrows. "You were?"

"Yes."

"Well, I wasn't breaking up with you," Tony said. "I was just saying we need to talk about it."

"Oh, yeah?" I said. "Oh, yeah?" I couldn't believe how angry I was with him, but at the same time, I wasn't sure what I was angry about. After all, I had been thinking the same thing.

Then I realized I was angry because I was afraid. I had built a great wall around my heart, and I didn't want to get hurt again.

Even my hustling was all about separating sex from my feelings.

Feelings, I thought, were overrated.

I sat stumped as to where to go from here.

"Anyway," Tony said, "how can we 'break up'? We aren't exactly going out. I'm not sure there's a word for what we're doing . . . ."

Silence. We sat and looked at each other for a minute that felt like ten.

"OK, maybe you're right," I said. "Maybe we shouldn't see each other anymore."

"I didn't say that," Tony said. "I just said I didn't want to hurt you again." He reached out and put his hand on top of mine. "Is that really so wrong of me? Not to want to hurt you?"

"No," I answered softly. "Not so wrong."

"If I didn't care for you so much," Tony said, "I wouldn't be so torn up about this."

"So, you could see me if you liked me less?"

"You know what I mean."

I sighed. "Yeah."

"So, what do you want to do?"

I want you to leave your wife, I thought. I want you to marry me and I want to bear your children and I want you to love me forever. Like I've loved you, Tony. Ever since we were kids growing up down the block from each other. Forever. Is that too much to ask?

"I don't know," I answered.

"Neither do I."

We sat quietly for a moment.

I drew my hand away.

I realized I had a very important question for him.

"Tony, just tell me this: are you really happy? With your wife, I mean."

"Yes," Tony said with the quickness of a practiced liar. Then he bit his lip, frowned. "No. It's complicated."

"Happy is complicated?" I asked.

"I don't want to give you false hope."

"How about real hope, then?"

Tony smiled, but it was a sad smile.

"Things would have been a lot simpler if we hadn't run into each other," Tony said.

But we did. At the scene of Allen's death. Allen, who was always trying to arrange things for me, who was always trying to lead me to what's best for me.

Had he led me to this?

Suddenly, I didn't need Tony's hope anymore. I had my own.

"Tell you what," I said. "How about we just take some time? Figure this out. Give ourselves some space."

"'Space.' Is that what you really want?" Tony asked.

"No, not really," I said. "But it's what I get."

Walking out of the police station, I felt strangely buoyant. I should have been sad, but I just felt relieved.

If things with Tony were meant to be, they'd be.

If not, I'd go on.

Either way, it was nice not to have to think about it for a while.

My phone vibrated in my pocket to tell me I had a message.

It was Roger Folds, the fund-raiser from The Stuff of Life. He was letting me know that he was home for the evening. He would appreciate if I could drop off his stuff.

Now that Tony had me convinced Allen's death really was a suicide, I was tempted to skip it.

Still, I told Vicki I would take care of it, so I would.

CHAPTER 10

If One More Person Calls Me a Whore . . .

"YOU'RE WEARING THAT?" my mother asked, appalled, as I got ready to leave my apartment.

I was dressed in flip flops, short denim shorts, and a tight white T-shirt that rode high on my belly.

"What happened?" she continued. "Did you buy Jessica Simpson's used wardrobe off eBay? You look like a hooker."

I was dying to say, "Yes, Mom, I am a hooker," but it sounded too much like a *Lifetime* movie starring Tori Spelling, so I just shrugged.

"It's hot out," I said.

"Please, it's hot in Long Island, too, but you don't see me parading around like the Whore of Babylon."

"Speaking of Long Island, have you spoken to Daddy today? Have you two worked things out yet?"

"Please, I'll let you know when I speak to your father. Don't be so excited to get rid of me."

"I don't want to get rid of you," I said. "I just want to get you out of my apartment."

"Very nice," she told me. "You weighed nine and a half pounds at birth, you know. It was like pushing a piano out of my . . . "

"Stop!" I screamed. "Stay as long as you like." I picked up the box of Roger Folds's stuff off the floor where I'd left it.

"I have to drop this off for a coworker. I'll be back later."

"I'm making a brisket for dinner. I'll save you some."

Can I just tell you something? I love my mother's brisket.

On the cab ride to Roger Folds's apartment, I had to admit my mother was right: I did look like a whore. But tonight, it was for a good reason.

Roger Folds had a reputation as a big old letch. More than once I heard complaints from staff members and other volunteers that he had made an inappropriate comment or untoward advance.

He liked them young and pretty.

Vicki had said she overheard Roger arguing with Allen before Allen's death.

Knowing what they were fighting about might give me insight as to what was on Allen's mind before he committed . . . before his death.

My experience as a hustler has taught me that a horny man has loose lips.

It was worth a try. In any case, it would keep my mind off Tony. Which was, I decided, my new rule in life: Anything that kept my mind off of Tony was A Good Thing.

Roger lived in an old building on the Upper West Side. An expensive neighborhood, but if Roger had a rent-controlled apartment, he could live there cheaply.

I rang the bell and he buzzed me up. An elevator that smelled slightly of urine brought me to the seventh floor. I knocked at his door.

Roger opened it to reveal a tubby man of about five foot five. His head was mostly bald, except for thin strips that rested like twin caterpillars above each ear. He wore black sweatpants and a black T-shirt with the logo from *Miss Saigon* on it.

"Thanks," he said, reaching out for the box. He took it and put it on a table by the door. He looked at me for a half a minute, hungrily.

If there's one thing I know, it's when a man wants me. I hooked my thumb inside the waistband of my shorts and waited for him to invite me inside.

"OK, bye," he said, and closed the door in my face.

What the fuck?

I knocked on the door again.

Roger opened it a crack.

"What do you want?" he snapped.

"Nothing," I said, "it's just . . ."

"Fine, then," he said. "I already thanked you. Are you waiting for a tip?" Roger opened the door and reached over to the same table where he put the box. He picked up his wallet. "I must have a buck or two here somewhere . . ."

"No, listen," I said. It was apparent that, despite my youthful yumminess, Roger didn't want me around. But I had to talk to him. "I, uh, I need to use your bathroom."

"Oh, *that*." Roger opened the door. "OK, fine. Just be quick about it."

Roger's apartment was decorated in 1980's theater fag. The art deco furniture looked as if it came from the road show of *Anything Goes*. Posters from Broadway musicals lined his walls.

He showed me into the bathroom, where a signed 8x10 picture of Stephen Sondheim hung over the toilet.

I really did have to go, so I peed, flushed, and washed my hands.

Just for good measure, I "accidentally" left the snap of my shorts open.

I came out to find Roger standing by the door.

I ignored him and walked into the living room. "Listen," I said, "it's hot as Mars out there. Think I could get something cold to drink?"

"There's a bar down the street," Roger said not looking at me.

I laced my fingers together and stretched my arms over my head, letting my T-shirt ride up even more and thrusting out my basket.

"Come on, man. I'm hot and sore from carrying that heavy box. Just some water would be great."

This time, Roger did look at me. If this were a cartoon, his eyes would have fallen out of his head and bounced off the floor. Oh, he wanted it all right. But he was fighting it. I wondered why.

He cleared his throat and looked away.

"*Fine,*" he snapped, walking into the kitchen. "I'll be right back."

I sat down on a sleek black leather couch. Roger returned and handed me what had to be the smallest glass in his kitchen.

"*Here,*" he said.

"Nice place you got here," I said, although it wasn't.

Roger just looked at the wall behind me, willing me to finish my water and leave.

"While we're talking," I said, even though we weren't, "why'd you leave The Stuff of Life, anyway?"

Roger looked at his coffee table.

"I'm sure it's none of your business."

"I'm just saying, everyone liked you so much, and you did such a good job," I lied again.

Roger looked at me. "What did you say your name was?"

I told him.

"You're the kid who left a message on my machine the other day, aren't you?"

I wasn't sure if he'd placed me. I smiled, winningly I hoped. "Guilty as charged."

"What did you want?"

This guy is all charm.

"I just wanted to make sure you heard about Allen Harrington's death," I told him. "Seeing as you two were friends and all."

Roger sniffed. "Yes. Well. We were. Poor man. What a loss. Although I can't say I was surprised."

"What do you mean?"

"Suicide. It's just so cliché isn't it?"

I leaned forward. "How's that?"

"Oh, please." Roger stood up, began pacing. "It's the oldest story in the world: Old queen can't stand the fact that she's getting older. She looks in the mirror and sees herself turning into the kind of old man she made fun of when she was younger. Fat where she should be thin, soft where she should be hard." His voice took on a weird sing-song. "So sad, too bad."

I hated what Roger was saying, but I needed to see where this was leading.

"You think that's why Allen killed himself?"

"It's the lifestyle, darling," Roger said. He became increasingly agitated and started waving his arms around. "Don't you see? It's *wrong*. It's immoral and wasteful and against God's will. It leads *nowhere*. Don't you see?

"I tried to tell Allen that, but would he listen? Of course not! Just a few days before he died, he was on the phone with me; we got into a terrible stew."

"What were you fighting about?"

"About me. About how I was growing and changing, and about how much that scared a man like Allen."

"Allen was scared?"

"Allen was scared of the *truth*." Roger sat next to me. "But the truth shall set you free!" he shrieked hysterically, reaching his hands to heaven.

This guy was nuts.

"What truth?" I asked.

Roger sat next to me and took my hands. "The truth, my darling. The truth about homosexuality."

I thought he was coming onto me, and then realized it was worse. He was trying to *save* me.

"*You don't have to be gay*," Roger crowed. "You *can* change. But did anyone at The Stuff of Life want to hear that? Of course not! They were so stuck in their old ways of thinking—I didn't dare bring it up! Look what happened when I tried to share it with Allen—he turned on me!

"That's why I had to get out of there. Don't you see? Away from all that cognitive dissonance and deathstyle."

That word. Where had I just heard it?

Focus, Kevin, focus.

And what was this odd mix of religion and psychobabble?

Roger squeezed my hands tighter. It was starting to hurt, but I didn't want to say anything and break his stride.

"You had to get out," I repeated his words, a trick I learned in my psychology classes to keep a person talking.

"I did." He squeezed even tighter. Ouch.

"It must have been hard for you," I said.

"Yes! Yes! To see them all, wasting their lives, wasting away in sin. I tried to tell Allen, I did, but I was too late. If only I had reached him sooner."

Roger surprised me by breaking into tears. He buried his face in his hands. At least he let go of mine.

When the feeling returned to my fingers, I patted his back. "It's not your fault," I told him. "You did your best."

"I know, I know," Roger sobbed. "What hope did I have of changing him? Not even his own family could help him."

What did *that* mean?

I was about to ask when Roger grabbed my hands again. This time, I could have sworn he was *trying* to break my fingers.

"But it's not too late for you, my boy. Look at you, you think I don't know what you are? Dressed like a whore?"

I swear, if one more person calls me a whore tonight . . .

"It's all about sex, isn't it? Getting it up and getting it off. *Disgusting,*" Roger hissed. Beads of sweat dotted his forehead.

"Of course, you're young, you're beautiful. Look at you. Those sexy legs in those tight shorts. The way they show off your ass, so fucking tight. That bulge in your shorts. Your T-shirt so snug with those little nipples jutting so proudly, so proudly out at me."

The way Roger was talking, even though I didn't want to, I had to look down. Yep, there it was—his erection tenting out his sweatpants.

No doubt about it, he was one sick puppy.

Roger shook his head as if tossing a bad thought out of his mind.

"Of course I want to fuck you right now, and I know you want me to. But I don't have to give into it, and neither do you. You can reprogram yourself, son." Roger got up and ran over to the desk. Grabbed a business card and thrust it into my hand. "They can help."

I looked at the card, and handed it back to him.

I didn't need it.

I already had it.

The Center for Creative Empowerment Therapy.

The group run by Allen Harrington's son, Michael.

"Deathstyle." Now I remembered hearing Michael say it at the reading of his father's will.

Roger Folds was Michael's—what? Patient? Student? Disciple?

Here it was: The first link I had between people who might have wanted to see Allen dead.

I didn't need to connect the dots. They were connecting themselves.

I got out of Roger Folds's apartment as soon as I could, skipping the elevator and running down the stairs.

That guy was a *freak*, I thought, as I hit the street. *Jesus.*

The evening was just starting to turn to night, although you wouldn't know it from the ever-present heat and humidity. Still, even the stale summer air felt good after being trapped with that born-again lunatic.

The Center for Creative Empowerment Therapy. Shit. Allen Harrington's son was running a group that promised to convert gays to heterosexuality.

I knew a little about scams like that from various new reports.

They usually are based on religion, but Michael's group sounded like it threw in some pop psychology, too.

Shit!

How twisted was *that*?

Did Allen know?

Of course he knew.

I remembered something Allen had said in his video. "What you are doing, Michael, makes me especially sad."

And Roger's words: *not even his own family could help him.*

But Allen never said anything about his son to me.

Maybe Tony was right—Allen wanted to be strong for me. He didn't share his burdens. I had to admit I didn't know Allen as well as I thought I did.

And if Tony was right about that, maybe he was right about Allen's death being a suicide, too.

How did Allen feel when he found out what his son was up to?

He must have been devastated.

He must have wanted to *die*.

The realization hit me like a blow to the stomach. I felt dizzy and leaned against a street lamp.

Shit!

Did Allen really kill himself? Was this why?

"Excuse me," someone shouted. It took a moment to realize he was shouting at me.

I looked up. A middle-aged man with a Donald Trumpian combover sat at the curb in an expensive Lexus.

"Yeah?" I asked him.

"You working?" he whispered loudly.

"What?" I went closer to his window.

"I said, 'are you *working*?'" he asked nervously.

I looked down at myself. The skimpy T-shirt, the Daisy Duke shorts still unbuttoned at the waist.

"Sorry, I don't work the streets," I said.

"Oh, please," the man said. "Look at you. Let's not play hard to get. I got fifty bucks for your time. We could do it right in the car."

"Sorry," I said, leaning in. The guy might have been an asshole, but the air conditioning coming from his expensive car felt great. "First of all, I am *not* working. Second of all, if I *were* working, it would cost you a hell of a lot more than fifty bucks."

"Sixty?"

"No!" Now I was getting offended. "Do I look like the kind of guy you could have for sixty bucks?"

"Well, how much, then?"

"Listen," I said, deciding to give him some advice, "if you're going to haggle over price, don't drive a Lexus."

"It's a lease," he clarified.

I had enough of this nonsense. "Sorry, buddy, but . . . " I began.

Then I heard my name called out.

"Kevin?"

I turned around and saw Freddy, with a Versace shopping bag in each hand and a horrified expression on his face.

He looked me up and down.

"Are you *streetwalking?*" he asked, appalled.

"Excuse me," the man inside the car called out. "But I saw him first. We were in the middle of a negotiation here and . . ."

"No we weren't," I shouted back at him. Freddy frowned. I shouted at him. "I *swear.* Stop looking at me like that."

Freddy leaned over into the car and dropped his voice an octave. "Listen, man. You want to deal with my boy, here, you gots to deal with me. I'm his pimp, and unless you show me five hundred large real quick, we're gonna have us some problems."

The man showed his appreciation for Freddy's words by demonstrating just how quickly a really nice car can accelerate.

"Asshole," I yelled after him. Then, to Freddy: "That guy was trying to get me to go with him for sixty bucks!"

"How much were you charging?" Freddy asked.

"Nothing! I'm telling you, I was just walking, well, leaning, and the guy pulled over and propositioned me."

"You were standing out here dressed like that and you're shocked that someone thought you were hustling?"

I had to laugh. I twirled around for him, showing off my trampy style. "You like?"

Freddy looked at me hungrily. He dropped his bags and pulled me towards him. He ground his crotch into mine.

"I like," he said hotly into my ear.

Damn, he was built.

An old woman stepping into her building yelled at us, "Get a room!"

I laughed and pushed Freddy away.

"No, seriously," Freddy said, picking up his bags. "Why are you dressed, well, half-dressed, like that?"

"It's a long story," I said. "Come on, I'll tell you about it over a snack."

Freddy and I went to a nearby Starbucks. Freddy's heavy flirting with the boy at the counter doubled the amount of time it took to get our coffees.

I told Freddy about my meeting with Roger Folds. He listened carefully, only looking at Starbucks Boy half the time I was talking. When I told him about Roger Folds's connection to Michael Harrington, he jumped in.

"Oh, yeah," he said. "I wanted to tell you I asked some people at work if they ever heard of The Center for Creative Empowerment Therapy."

Freddy was the director of administration at a local AIDS services center.

"And?"

"Some of the counselors have clients who went there. They said it was a pretty fucked-up place. They put all this pressure on you to 'change.' A lot of guilt and lecturing and nagging. You know, kind of like your mother."

"'Kind of?'" I asked.

"Yeah, well, when I say 'kind of' I mean 'exactly.' But even worse, if you can imagine it. It sounds like they try to brainwash you. I guess it takes a lot to repress someone's basic instincts, huh," Freddy said. "Speaking of which, I wonder what Sharon Stone's up to these days. I always did think she was underrated as an actress."

"That reminds me, I have to tell you something about Paul Harrington."

"He knows Sharon Stone?" Freddy asked excitedly.

"No, what you said about repression." I told him about May's comment that Allen thought his son might be gay.

"Well, duh," Freddy responded, bored. "I already told you that. I don't understand how you can be such a big street streetwalking whore when you have the world's worst gaydar."

"I'm not a streetwalking whore," I said a little too loudly.

Starbucks Boy, whose name tag read Colin, started cleaning the table next to us. Which, by the way, was already clean. I had the feeling he didn't often walk out from behind the counter, but somehow, with Freddy around, he had a sudden urge to straighten up.

"Hey, I'm not putting you down. I love dick, too," Freddy also said loudly, and not for my benefit.

"Maybe we could start a club," Colin chimed in, taking the bait.

"You know, you'd be charming if you could just get over your shyness," I said to Freddy.

Freddy grinned, not taking his eyes off Colin's butt as the coffee slinger bent over to pick a napkin off the floor.

"Don't be petty," Freddy cautioned.

Colin came over. "So, are you two together?" he asked Freddy.

"Only for the coffee," Freddy said.

"Good." Colin handed Freddy a card from his wallet. "Here's my number."

"Oh, I think I got your number," Freddy said, taking the card from him.

Colin gave me and my outfit a long look. "Your friend is cute, too," he said to Freddy, "but I don't think I could afford him. You're not a call boy, too, are you?"

My mouth dropped open. "Excuse me," I said. "Sitting right here."

They ignored me. "I know," Freddy mock-whispered. "He's a little obvious. But when you're working the streets, you can't afford to be discreet."

"Hey!" I said.

"Doesn't it scare you?" Colin asked me. "Just going with anyone?"

"I don't just 'go with anyone,'" I hissed. "I'm not a whore."

"Well, not that *kind* of whore," Freddy clarified, smirking.

"I hate you," I told him. Then, to Colin, "I'm glad to see you're not afraid of catching my friend's scabies."

"Scabies?" Colin asked.

"Little mites that live under the skin. Extremely itchy and unpleasant. Very contagious, too."

"Mites?" Colin wasn't the brightest light on the tree.

"Bugs."

Colin looked terrified.

"You have bugs under your skin?" he asked Freddy.

"My friend's just funning you," Freddy said. He stood and pulled up his T-shirt. "See," he said. "Does that look like scabies to you?"

One look at Freddy's flawless abdominals was enough to convince Colin that he'd suffer far worse than a skin infection to run his tongue down those furrowed ridges.

He put his hand on Freddy's belly. "Call me."

Then he turned to me. "Maybe you're the one with the scabies. Given your line of work and all." He walked away triumphantly.

Freddy snorted coffee through his nose.

"Very attractive," I told him. "Now can we get back to work?"

Freddy and I talked some more about my conversation with Roger. Freddy asked to see my to-do list. He knows I'm lost without it.

I handed him my iPhone.

1. Follow up with Roger Folds—fight?
2. Talk to Randy Bostinick
3. Research Paul and Michael Harrington.
4. Look into those gay suicides—was that true?
5. Fuck Tony

"Hmm," Freddy said, "let's start with number five."

"Magic Eight Ball says 'future looks dim' on that one."

"Oh, sorry to hear that," Freddy said. "You really need to get laid."

"I get laid almost every day."

"I mean by someone who's not paying for it."

"Details, details," I sighed.

Freddy gave the list another look. "OK, you took care of number one. Why not just work your way down?"

I took the list back. "Talk to Randy, huh?"

"He should be at the gym tomorrow."

"You know, even before I talked to Roger, Tony had me halfway convinced that Allen really did kill himself."

"And now?" Freddy asked.

"Now, I guess I have more reason to think it might be true, but I still can't believe it."

"Just talk to Randy. I've watched enough episodes of *JAG* to know that you follow up on every lead."

"You watch *JAG?*" I asked. I couldn't think of a straighter show. Well, maybe *Everybody Loves Raymond.*

"Did you ever see that guy who plays the lead?"

"Jag?"

"I'm not sure if that's his name, or just the name of the show. I don't actually have the sound on. But who cares about that. I have something to add to your list."

"What's that?"

"We should go to Michael's Harrington's place. *The Center for Creative Cunnilingus,* or whatever it is. Check it out."

"Talk with Michael?"

"Naw, that lovely little chat we had with him at the reading of his father's will was more than enough for me, darling. But let's see what his organization is like. I think they have open houses where they tell you about their programs."

"Do you really think we should?"

"Honey, what would Farrah Fawcett Majors do?"

"Are we *JAG* or *Charlie's Angels* here? You're mixing your metaphors."

"We watch *JAG,* but we *are Charlies Angels,* OK? I'm the glamorous Farrah and you can be the serious one, what's-her-name? The one from that movie with that cutie from the *Rookies.* What was it called? *My Husband's a Fag?*"

"Kate Jackson. And it was Michael Onkean and the movie was *Making Love.* For its time, it was actually a pretty daring film about a closeted married man who . . . "

Freddy rolled his eyes. "Tangent, darling, tangent."

"Whatever," I said. "Like all that talk about *JAG* and *Charlie's Angels* was so on topic. Speaking of which, how come you get to be Farrah?"

Freddy pulled his T-shirt down, stretching it across his chiseled pecs. "Honey, check out the boobage. It's all about the nipples."

CHAPTER 11

Is That a Foot in My Lap or Are You Happy to See Me?

THE NEXT MORNING I woke up at six, groaned, turned to go back to sleep, and remembered that I had to meet Randy at the gym. Shit. I dragged my ass out of bed and was about to make a protein shake when I realized something amazing. I heard no crashing pans, no loud snoring, and no invitations to "wake and embrace the day." Just silence.

My mother was still sleeping.

Finally, a little peace. I had my drink, took my meds, grabbed a quick shower, shaved the usual places, and began the important task of choosing my outfit for the gym. I needed something tasteful, yet erotic, simple, but seductive, revealing but not too . . . aw fuck, let's face it: I needed to dress like a whore again. Randy wasn't the type to be interested in my sparkling conversation.

I threw on a pair of skimpy, almost translucent white running shorts with side slits. Truthfully, they looked more like underwear than pants. I squeezed into a tight little white T-shirt that has a picture of a baseball player and the word "Catcher" on it. I put on sneakers with no socks, a combination I found unsanitary but sexy. I took a look at myself in the mirror and realized there was just one thing missing: Nipple action. Freddy was right: It's all about the boobage.

There's an old stripper trick I learned from the movie *Showgirls*. If you apply ice cubes to your nipples, they'll harden and stick out.

Knowing how much Randy liked juicy tits, I figured I better meet him with my headlights on high.

I grabbed two ice cubes from the freezer and held them to my chest. But they melted too quickly and started dripping onto my shorts. Shit, I looked like I wet myself. I wanted to look excited to see Randy, but not that excited. I stripped off the shorts, put the ice cubes back on my chest, and leaned over so that the drips would fall harmlessly into the kitchen sink.

"What, I shudder to ask, are you doing?"

My mother was standing behind me.

I dropped the ice cubes.

"Mom!" I screamed. "Hello! Naked here! Could you give me a minute?"

"Oh, please, like I haven't seen that little tushy a million times." She swatted my ass.

"Mom!"

"Could you please stop screaming like that, darling? Maybe we can save the outraged 'Moms' until after I've had my coffee." She reached around me to fill the pot.

I grabbed some paper towels off the roll by the sink and wrapped them around my waist.

"What were you doing, anyway?" my mother asked. She looked in the sink, then at me.

"My lord, were you icing your nipples?"

If I turned any redder, I would have exploded. "Mom!"

"Again with the 'Mom!'" she got herself a cup.

"I was not," I said through gritted teeth, "icing my nipples."

"Liar. Look at those things. You could take someone's eye out."

"Listen," I told her. "I really am going to die if you say one more word."

"I used to do the same thing before my dates with your father, may the Lord rest his soul."

"Dad's not dead," I reminded her, pulling on my skimpy shorts.

"Well, not yet," she said a little wistfully.

I threw on my shirt and hurried to the door. "I gotta run. "

"Wait!" my mother cried after me. "You forgot your pants!"

Randy worked out at Pexx, a hot new gym in Tribeca. His magnificent body had made Randy a bit of a legend in NYC gyms and he usually belonged to the best and newest ones. This was partly because A. new gyms often hired him to create some buzz, and B. he had already slept with all the really hot guys at his last gym, so why not move on?

I took a cab to Pexx and arrived there sweaty and aggravated. Like most taxi drivers, this one didn't believe in using air conditioning. I growled as I handed him the fare.

Pexx was a high tech gym, all stainless steel and industrial carpeting. The air was chilled to a polar degree—I could have skipped the ice. Electronic dance music pounded from invisible speakers. I went to the front desk and told them I was thinking of joining. They gave me a day pass and I was in.

I walked into the weight room and spotted Randy right away. All I had to do was follow the stares of half the guys in the room.

Randy was lying on an exercise bench doing chest presses. He was wearing baggy green basketball shorts. The curve of his red underwear, and the throbbing menace within, was clearly visible. His muscles bulged obscenely beneath his tight tank top. His arms looked as hard and smooth as marble straining beneath the heavy weight.

I remembered my own workout straining beneath Randy's heavy weight and felt a tingling in my groin. Stop that, you're here on a mission.

Randy finished his set and sat up, bumping his head on the weight bar. He rubbed his head, cursed, and looked up. His eyes rolled in their sockets. If this were a cartoon, he'd have stars and little bluebirds circling around his head.

Then he saw me. "Kevin," he shouted.

He jumped off the bench and picked me up, effortlessly spinning me around. "You look tasty as ice cream," he said, hugging me close.

"Thanks, you too."

His hugging started to turn into grinding. "No, I mean really, really great," he said huskily. "You know I always was kind of sweet on you. Such a hot little-brother piece of trim you are." He grabbed my ass. "I missed these cupcakes."

Randy spoke his own language of primal needs: everything was either sex or food. I pushed myself away. "What a surprise to see you here," I lied.

Randy looked me up and down. I don't know if eyes can smolder, but his seemed about to burst into flames. All this sexual attention was starting to get to me.

"Come on, work in with me," Randy offered. I looked at the three forty-five-pound weights on each side of the bar. "What," Randy smirked, "want me to throw some more crackers on that?"

"Ha-ha," I said, "very funny." I walked around to the back of the bench. "How about I spot you?"

Randy lay back down. "How about you just stand there and inspire me." In this position, he was looking right up my shorts. "I see London, I see France . . ." he began.

"Just lift," I said. And he did, impressively, his body a perfect symphony of strength and symmetry.

And he was right—he didn't need the spot at all.

I stood there for two more sets, and we made some small talk. Randy continued to flirt outrageously, and I continued to remind myself that I didn't come here to get laid. I needed to know what he knew about Allen's death.

I was trying to figure out how to bring up Topic A when Randy sat up.

"Your turn." He took two plates off each side. This I could handle.

I lay on the bench and grabbed the bar. Randy's crotch loomed like heaven above me. His cotton-enclosed cock coiled menacingly.

It seemed to be growing.

I felt myself hardening in sympathetic response.

"Look at you down there," Randy whispered huskily. "So fucking sweet and creamy. Such a smooth milkshake of a boy. I could slurp you right up."

I put my hands on the bar to lift, but my blood seemed to be rushing elsewhere.

"I could rip those shorts right off with my teeth," Randy purred.

My eyes were riveted to his growing crotch, which seemed to be lowering.

Growing and lowering.

Then all of a sudden his half-hard cock slipped out of his underwear and flopped on my forehead.

"Hey!" I sat up suddenly.

This is when I learned A Very Important Lesson that should be part of every SAT study course: In an accident where a rapidly ascending big head impacts a slowly descending little head, the little head is going to get hurt.

Or, in simpler turns, when you head butt someone in the crotch, it's gonna hurt.

"Shit!" Randy screamed. He grabbed his balls and doubled over. "Holy fuck!"

I jumped off the bench and put my hand on his back. "Sorry, sorry, I got kind of startled."

"Ow!" Randy hopped up and down a little before crouching again. "Fuck me, that hurts!"

"OK, OK," I said, "I'm sorry." I waited a few minutes until he seemed to be breathing normally again.

"I feel terrible," I said, flinging back my bangs and biting my lower lip. It's one of my most seductive moves. "Let me buy you a protein shake and make it up to you."

Randy nodded. "You got it, little man. And then we can talk about why you really came here."

"What do you mean?" I asked him.

"You didn't come here just to work out, did you? You think I aced Allen Harrington."

Holy shit. "I do?"

"Well, I figured as much when you saw me there that night," Randy said.

"I did?"

"In front of his building."

"Oh, that. Yeah, well, sure, I saw you and all," I lied again, "but, you know, I didn't think, well, did you?"

"Come on," Randy said, extending his hand. "Let's get that drink."

Following Randy to the gym's café, I tried not to be distracted by two things: 1. his admission that he had been to Allen's apartment on the night of his death, and 2. his perfect, muscular ass. Focus, Kevin, focus.

We ordered protein shakes (I hadn't actually done any working out, so I got the best-tasting and least healthy one), and sat in a booth.

Randy started. "So, do you really think I killed Allen?"

I didn't know what to say, so I took a long sip of my shake. Stalled. But Randy just waited.

"Well," I said, "no, of course not."

"But you've seen me pretty angered up, right?" He was referring to the night he almost beat a deaf guy to death on my behalf.

"Were you angry at Allen?"

"Maybe I should be charging you for this information." Randy grinned. "You know my time is costly, right?"

I took a dollar out of my pocket and slid it to him.

"Nice, try, creampuff. I was thinking more along a trade." Randy's foot, which he managed to slip out of his sneaker, landed in my lap. "Maybe take it out on your ass. You look real sexy in that little pair of underwear you're wearing." He slipped the dollar into his bag.

Once a hustler, always a hustler, I thought. Not that I was throwing any stones.

"It's not underwear," I said, trying to ignore his toes scraping up and down my crotch. "They're gym shorts."

"Look like underwear to me."

"My mother said the same thing."

Randy's foot began tapping against my balls. I felt myself start to swell.

"Your mother?"

"It's a long story. She's kind of living with me now."

This revelation was so startling that Randy stopped moving his foot.

"You're kidding, right?"

"I wish."

"Poor little dude." Randy looked genuinely sympathetic. "You got yourself a whole world of troubles, don't you?"

I nodded.

"Well, then, I guess I'll stop torturing you." He smiled, evilly. "Unless you like to be tortured, little dude." He started with the foot-tapping again. "A little teasing. You like that? You like to be teased, little dude? It feels like you do." His voice was getting a little husky.

I was fully hard now. I knew he knew it, too. Damn, he was good at this.

"You know how much I like you, Randy." I decided a little flattery might help me get the subject back where I wanted it. "Damn, you're like the hottest guy I've even been with. I know Allen thought so, too. He never stopped thanking me for referring you."

That stopped the foot again. "Allen," Randy said. "That is some fucked up shit."

When in doubt, plunge right in. "So, what were you doing there that night?" I asked.

"Allen and I had a date," Randy said.

I remembered the Budweiser I'd seen in Allen's refrigerator. It was for Randy! But he also had two wine glasses set out. So he must have been expecting someone else.

"How was it?" I asked.

"How was what?" Randy looked puzzled. Well, he looked more puzzled. He always looked a little puzzled.

"The date."

Randy started the whole foot-rubbing thing again. "What are you, the cops?" He pressed against me. "Is this your nightstick?"

I let out a small moan.

Randy grinned.

"Come on, man," I said.

"You want more, baby?" Randy purred. "I could eat you up real good. Let me take you home and lay you out like lunch."

Randy was distracting me with his food fetishes again, but also with that damn foot and the sexy huskiness of his voice. What were we talking about again?

"Or I could just do you right here," Randy continued. "Slip right under this table and pull down those little white briefs you're wearing. Take you in my mouth. Would you like that, baby? Think anyone would notice? Think they'd watch? Bet that would make it even hotter."

I was about to lose all conscious thought when I realized what Randy was doing.

I sat back, pulling away from him.

"You're hustling me," I told him.

"Huh?" Randy looked

I looked at him angrily. "You're playing me. Dirty talk and that sexy whisper and that tricky little foot of yours. I'm not one of your customers, Randy."

Randy's face crumpled like a little boy's. "I'm just doing what guys like me do, Kevin. Don't you like it?"

"Of course I like it. But I'm not here for a goddamn foot job. I came here as a friend."

"Why?"

"Because Allen was my friend, too, Randy. Something terrible happened to him and I just want to know what it was."

"You really cared about him," Randy said.

I nodded.

Randy looked even sadder. "I did, too, Kevin. He wasn't like the other guys. He would talk to me, you know. He always wanted to know how I was, if I was taking care of myself. He used to try to teach me stuff, about investing, shit like that. Told me I had to think about my future. He always wanted to help me, you know?"

I nodded again.

"But of course, I never took him up on it, right? Big stupid Randy. All muscles and cock and no fucking brain. That's what everyone thinks, right? Well, you know what? They're right. That's me, always thinking about the next workout, the next trick, the next hit."

"I don't think you're stupid, Randy." I wasn't exactly lying, either. Randy had people smarts. He knew how to play them. And it's not easy to be one of the hottest hustlers in a big city. Randy knew how to work it.

"I don't think Allen did, either," Randy said. He let out a big sigh. "So, what do you want to know?"

"How was your date with Allen that night?"

"We didn't have it."

Now it was my turn to look confused. "But you told me you did."

"I did. Have it, I mean. But I didn't *have* it. I mean, I had just gotten to his building when he called me on my cell to cancel."

"That wasn't like him."

"No. But he said something came up and he couldn't see me. He said if it didn't go well, it might only take a minute, but he was hoping it would take a lot longer. He didn't want me to wait."

"It must have been important for him to cancel you at the last minute like that."

"Yeah, that's what I figured. So, I went down the street and had a coffee for awhile and then decided maybe I'd go by his building and give him a call—see if his meeting was over. You know Allen—he said he'd pay me for my time. I'd'a taken the money, but I thought maybe if he was available I'd go earn it, too."

"And when you got back to his building . . . "

"That's when I saw him. All laid out like that. All broken." Randy's face crumbled again. "And I saw you, too. I almost went over to you, but I didn't want to have to explain to the cops what I was doing there, you know?"

"Yeah, that might have been awkward."

"Plus, you were talking to that super-hot cop, and I didn't want to crash your party."

He was talking about Tony. "Yeah, well, that party was over a long time ago. But I understand why you stayed back."

"I really am sorry for you," Randy said. "I mean, Allen was my best customer, but I know he was your best friend. I think it's great that you're doing this for him. Trying to figure out what happened. I'm sorry I was such an asshole before."

"You weren't an asshole, Randy. You were just doing what you do. And it's not like I hated it," I couldn't help adding.

"Oh yeah." Randy grinned. "Well, the offer for a little under-the-table action is still out there, baby."

"Maybe some other time." I smiled back. I was about to say goodbye when I suddenly thought of something.

"Listen, you said that Allen cancelled because something came up, right?"

Randy nodded.

"And then you said you came back because you thought his

meeting might be brief—he did say he was meeting someone, right?"

"Yeah, he said someone had just called and said it was really important that they talk. 'In person.' I remember he used that phrase. He said he didn't know how it was going to go, though. That's why he didn't know how long he'd be."

"He didn't say who it was, did he?"

"Yeah, he did." Randy said. "It was his son."

"His son!" I shouted. The guys at the next booth turned to look at us. I repeated myself more quietly. "His son. Did he say which one?"

"Did he have more than one?"

"Why didn't you tell the cops?"

"How would I have explained what I was doing there?"

I knew the feeling. "Got ya."

"You're not gonna tell them, are you?"

I ran my fingers over my chest. "Cross my heart."

Randy's foot found its way back into my lap.

"So, what do you say?" he asked. "Do I still get to sink my hot dog into your toasty buns?"

I stood. As much fun as Randy would be, his revelations inspired me to a different kind of action. "Not this time, Randy. Can I take a rain check?"

"A check? Naw. You know I only take cash, Kevin."

"I knew it!" Freddy screamed when I told him about Randy's revelation. "I knew it was one of those freaky kids of his. It had to be the big one, the religious nut. Michael. That other one couldn't throw a basketball off a balcony, let alone a grown man."

We were sitting in Freddy's office, where I headed immediately after my conversation with Randy. I couldn't wait to tell Freddy my news in person.

"And I'm so proud of you," Freddy said, ruffling my head. "Charlie's littlest Angel. Although in the future, I'd prefer if you didn't come to my office in your underwear. People talk, you know."

"It's not underwear," I protested. "Oh, never mind about that. Allen hadn't spoken to either of his sons in years. Why would one of them been going over there?"

"Maybe he just wanted to get in there so he could give his dad an impromptu flying lesson."

I grimaced.

"Sorry about that," Freddy continued. "But really, maybe it was all just a setup."

"Maybe," I said. "So, what next?"

"Now, I think you call Tony and tell him what you learned."

"I'm not speaking to him."

"Honey, this isn't a lover's spat. You have 'material information in a homicide'. Well, a possible homicide. I think that's how they'd describe it on *CSI.*"

"And how would I explain how I'd come across this 'material information,' huh? Without compromising me or Randy, that is?"

"You haven't told Tony what you do for a living?"

"Hell, no!"

"Oy," Freddy sighed. "Then I guess it's back to Square One: We're just going to have to solve this case ourselves."

I sighed. Freddy was enjoying this.

"We need to get a better read on Michael." Freddy typed something into his computer. "OK, here's the schedule for the Center for Creative Empowerment Therapy. And look—tomorrow they're having a free seminar." He read on. "Oh, this is too perfect."

"What is?"

"The seminar. 'Flight from Homosexuality.'"

"You shitting me?"

"No, and listen to this: 'Flight from Homosexuality is about breaking the dysfunctional patterns that bind you from leaping boldly into a brand new life. This seminar is the perfect jump-start for those of you brave enough to boldly spring out of the death-style of homosexuality and into the promise of a healthier life-style.'"

"'*Flight* from homosexuality,'" I repeated. "*Leaping* boldly?"

"Don't forget '*jump*-start,'" said Freddy.

"Kind of heavy on the whole flying metaphor, isn't it?"

"And kind of coincidental for a guy whose dad supposedly threw himself off a building."

Shit. This was all getting very complicated again.

"Oh, and look," Freddy enthused. "Michael Harrington himself is running the workshop. Talk about a hot ticket."

"So," I said, "will you go with me tomorrow?"

"Honey," Freddy grinned, "I wouldn't miss it for the world. That hunky white boy's gonna teach this little fairy how to *fly!*"

I walked home from Freddy's office, ignoring the catcalls and come-ons that my skimpy outfit encouraged.

I had a 2:00 date with a regular. That gave me two hours to kill. I decided to go to the gym and run home for a shower. At least I'd feel clean.

Dudley Chambers was one of the top psychiatrists in the entire city—not a bad achievement in a town with almost as many shrinks as taxis. Every month, I'd sit under the handsome fifty-something-year-old doctor's desk and jerk him off while he participated in the board of director's conference call of the North American Analysts for the Advancement of Psychoanalytic Psychotherapy. That name was more than a mouthful, as was his dick, which must have topped nine inches.

With a cock like that, he really didn't need to pay for sex, but I wasn't about to tell him that.

"I swear," Dr. Chambers said, as he hung up the phone and scooted back to zip up his pants. "Your kind ministrations are the only things that get me through those excruciating calls. Imagine, seven pseudo-intellectuals who get paid all week to *listen.* By the time they get on the phone, they are so *pent up* they just can't shut up. They really should find a healthier outlet for all those repressed feelings." He patted my head. "Like I do."

I grinned.

"Come sit up here, sweetheart," he said, pointing to his lap. "Tell me what's up with you."

"Do you have a minute?" I asked.

"More than that, dear. And anything you have to say will be more interesting than the posturing of those solipsistic bores I just escaped."

I told him about how a friend had become involved with The Center for Creative Empowerment Therapy, and about their promises that they could convert gay people to be straight.

"A dreadful sham, it is." Dr. Chambers shook his head. "Yes, some small percentage of gay people want very much to change, but why is that, my dear? Because they're ill? Sick? Of course not! It's because society puts such burdens on them, because they're not strong enough to build a life for themselves. Any decent therapist, even one unfortunate enough to work at something called The Center for Creative Empowerment Therapy, would help such an individual to live a life congruent with his natural orientation.

"But some charlatans exploit these poor, tortured souls and take advantage of their desperation. They peddle false 'cures,' impossible 'conversions.' They push religion or psychiatry as tools to pervert the natural self.

"And what tools do they use? They inflict shame upon their clients, teach them to hate themselves. How else could you get someone to repress something as basic as whom they're born to love?"

Dr. Chambers scooted me off his lap and went to his bookshelf. "You should give this to your friend," he said, handing me a copy of Wayne Besen's *Anything but Straight: Unmasking the Scandals and Lies Behind the Ex-Gay Myth.* "It exposes these frauds for the sick, self-hating bastards they are."

"Self-hating?" I asked him.

"Often," said Dr. Chambers. "Many of these supposed therapists claim to be 'ex-gay' themselves. They can only justify their own cognitive dissonance by trying to convert others to their own internalized loathing. If the 'patient' buys their bullshit, they can claim that it 'works.' If the patient is healthy enough to get the hell out of there, the 'therapist' can feel morally superior. It's a win-win for these execrable exploiters of their brothers. But you know what they say." Dr. Chambers sighed.

"Um, misery loves company?"

"No, I was thinking of 'Life sucks, and so do I.'" Dr. Chambers sank to his knees. "What say we double your fee?"

If Dr. Chambers gave advice as well as he gave head, I might have to switch therapists. Feeling significantly more relaxed, and a couple of hundred richer, I hailed a cab and went home.

Should I make it to heaven, I have no doubt that the first meal they serve will be my mother's stuffed cabbage. Loading up a second plateful (note to self: double cardio at the gym tomorrow), I tried to remember why I needed her out of my apartment so bad.

Then she started to speak and it all came back to me.

"It's curtains," she said, watching with pride as I ate.

"Mmmm," I said, swallowing. "Curtains for who?"

"Not 'for who.' 'For what.' Your apartment. I was thinking curtains."

"I have blinds."

"Blinds!" my mother repeated, as if I had just uttered a heresy. "Blinds are for doctors' offices. Curtains are for a home. You need curtains. And some throw pillows. Matching. I'm thinking floral."

"OK, thanks, but I think I'll pass." I gestured around the room. "It's fine."

"My son should be doing better than 'fine.' You're always telling me that you're making good money on your consulting work. Which, by the way, I would like to know a little more about."

That was an area I really wanted to avoid.

"I'm really a blinds kind of person." I said. "I think curtains and pillows attract too much dust. I might be allergic to dust. I'll have to check that out. Besides, I like it the way it is."

"What's to like? Inmates have better rooms than this. I feel like I'm in prison here. Where's the color? Where's the drama? Where are the tchotchkes?"

"It's fine," I repeated.

"I don't know why you invite me here and ask for my opinion if you're not going to take it," she pouted.

"I love you, Mom, but I don't remember the part where I asked for your opinion. Actually, I don't remember the part where I invited you, either."

"I assume I have an open invitation to see my only son," she said.

"You do. But don't you miss your own home? Your husband? I know that Dad misses you."

"Good," she said. "Let him miss me. Now, tell me about your work."

I paused. Looked around the room pensively. Settled on the windows.

"Curtains," I said thoughtfully. "You know, now that I think about it, maybe it's not such a bad idea. What did you have in mind?"

CHAPTER 12

Visiting the Spider in His Web

THE NEXT DAY I hit the gym (double cardio), volunteered at The Stuff of Life for the lunch shift, and then polished off a quick client at an uptown church (don't ask).

At 6:45, I met Freddy in front of the building on the Upper East Side where the Center for Creative Empowerment Therapy has its offices.

Once again, I went for the preppy look: Brooks Brothers khakis and blue polo shirt. Freddy looked dashing in black Juicy Couture jeans, a white T-shirt, a silver choker, and black cowboy boots with silver tips.

"You forgot the spurs," I told him.

"I didn't want to over-excite the masses," he said, giving me a hug. "You look very Republican."

"I'm trying to look unhappy with myself," I said. "Repressed. Self-hating."

"That's what I said, darling. You look Republican."

We took the elevator to the second floor. The Center had the entire story to itself. The lobby was vast and intimidating, cold and modern in its design with lots of stainless steel and white surfaces.

"Very *2001: A Space Odyssey*," Freddy observed. "Where's HAL?"

"Straight ahead," I said, as we walked towards a handsome but blank-looking young man sitting at a long, curved reception desk. He didn't smile as we approached.

"Hi, we're here for . . ." I began.

"Straight ahead and to your left," he directed. "The big room at the end of that hallway."

Freddy rested his hands on the counter. "How, if I may be so bold as to inquire, do you know what we're here for?"

Blank Boy didn't blink. "I assume you're attending our free informational session, Flight from Homosexuality. Am I correct?"

"It's the boots, isn't it? Straight boys would never wear boots like this."

"It's the only session being held tonight," HAL answered.

Freddy leaned in closer. "What do you think?" he half-whispered. "Does this shit work?"

"It did for me," Hal said robotically. "Have a productive session."

Freddy pulled me aside as we walked towards the meeting room. "We have *got* to get out of here!"

"What are you talking about?"

"It's like a whole *Stepford* thing going on here," he hissed. "Did you see that boy? They make you straight by stealing your identity and replacing you with a pod person!"

"The pod people were *Invasion of the Body Snatchers.* In *The Stepford Wives* the women were replaced by androids. Or something like that. I don't think it was very clear. Now stop being such a baby."

"OK," Freddy said, "but if I wake up in a giant pod, I am going to be very, very angry with you. Green is *so* not my color."

The meeting room was as cold and sterile as the rest of the office. Ten rows of eight chairs apiece faced a raised white platform that served as a stage. The room was brightly lit from overhead halogens.

We sat in the back where there was a chance we'd go unrecognized.

There were about forty other men in the audience. Although the program had not yet begun, they sat silently, staring straight ahead, leaving an empty chair between them whenever possible.

"This is weird," Freddy whispered. "We just walked into a room full of gay men and no one turned around to check us out."

"They're here to eschew that kind of behavior," I reminded him.

Freddy stood up and raised his arms over his head. "Damn, I think I pulled my shoulder out at the gym this morning," he groaned. He stretched out, causing his T-shirt to ride up and reveal his flawless stomach and his biceps to bulge menacingly against the sleeves of his T-shirt. "Mmmm . . ." he moaned, "that feels better."

Every eye in the room turned to look at him. Eyes widened, jaws dropped. Lips were licked. Then, almost as one, the men, remembering why they were here, guiltily flushed red and turned away.

You could feel the defeat in the air.

Freddy grinned. "That's better."

Just then the overhead lights dimmed to total blackness. At the same time, a spotlight from behind us illuminated the stage. I could feel the floor vibrating a little before the music started to swell.

The song, incredibly, was "Sharp Dressed Man."

"ZZ top?" Freddy asked.

"I think it's like a theme song for straight guys," I answered.

Just then, from where I don't know, a tall, handsome man ran onto the stage. Michael Harrington, bursting with energy. Over the roar of the music he shouted, "You. Can. Change!" With each word, he pointed into the audience. "You. Can. Change!" he shouted louder, still turning and pointing. "You. Can. CHANGE!"

He pointed right in the direction of Freddy and me, but his expression didn't alter. Good. He couldn't see into the dark audience.

Gone was the reserved and dignified man I had met at the reading of his father's will. Michael was now in full televangelist/motivational speaker mode, and it was a sight to behold.

Suddenly the music cut off. The room seemed quieter than silent, if such a thing was possible. The loudest noise was Michael's heavy breathing. He stood still for a moment. Then, in a whisper, he slowly extended his finger and swept it around the room, pointing to all of us at once.

"You . . . can . . . change," he whispered theatrically. Another dramatic pause.

He pointed directly to a man in the front row. Still whispering, he asked him, "Can you change?"

No answer.

"This is *not* a hypothetical question," Michael's deep voice began to rise again. "This is *not* a hypothetical life. This is the real thing, man!" He got right up in the guy's face. "Can you CHANGE?"

The poor bastard in the front row wasn't getting it. "I hope so," he squeaked.

"You hope so?" Michael thundered. "You hope so? Hope is for church and for women! You are men!"

He pointed to someone else. "Can *you* change?" he bellowed.

"Yes," the man said.

"Louder!"

"Yes!"

"Make me believe it!"

"Yes!"

"If you can't make me believe you mean it, then how can you make *yourself* believe it?" Michael raged at him.

"YES!" the man screamed like a lunatic.

Michael threw his hands to the sky in a silent hallelujah. "That's it! That's the passion. You have to believe! You have the power! All of you, together now: Can You Change?"

It was hard to tell in the darkened room, but I'd say about three quarters of the audience answered with various degrees of enthusiasm, including Freddy. I turned to look at him.

"I got caught up in the moment." He shrugged. "I thought he was talking about changing my outfit."

I scowled.

But the truth was, it was easy to get caught up in Michael Harrington's moments.

Have you ever seen a TV infomercial that seemed to be too good to be true? Someone telling you that you could make ten thousand dollars a week extra income with no investment of time or money? A pitchman extolling the virtues of a vitamin that would turn back the clock and melt off the pounds? A motivational speaker promising you that his life management system can add hours to your day and years to your life?

And even though you knew—knew!—there was no way the product could meet those claims—were you ever tempted to pick up the phone and order?

Those spokespeople have their jobs for a reason. There are some people who are just natural persuaders, people whose charisma and carriage and charm strike just the right chords to be convincing on even the most spurious claims.

Michael Harrington was one of those people. Fantastically attractive, deep-voiced with authority, he strode the stage like an athlete about to set a world record.

As he spoke on, it was hard not to get excited and believe. Some of what he told us was what anyone would want to hear. We "have the power." We "are in charge." We "control our destinies."

Some of what he said were generalities that could apply to anyone, but when he looked into the audience, you felt he was looking into your soul. Your mother "loved you, but she couldn't love you enough, and not in the right ways. You worshiped your father, but you feared him, because you were always afraid you couldn't measure up. When you hit adolescence, you felt different from the other kids, apart from the other boys, frightened of the blossoming girls, awkward and alone."

Well, who didn't feel awkward when they were growing hair in new places, erupting in acne and springing inopportune boners? But if you were looking for a cure, looking for someone who understood you and could lead you to a better place, Michael Harrington would be easy to follow.

Then, he spoke specifically about homosexuality. How gay men were stuck in a developmental stage, "like a caterpillar that never emerged from the cocoon." That we needed to "break free, to spread our wings, to fly (that word again!)". That any behavior can be changed through the right kind of conditioning and support.

At the end, he threw in references to a higher power. We were not following Mother Nature's plan. We needed to get back to what the Lord had intended for us.

"I don't get it," Freddy whispered to me. "Is it God who's in charge or Mother Nature?"

"I think they're the same person," I whispered back.

"Like in drag?" Freddy asked.

Throughout the message, Michael planted seeds of self-hatred and doubt. Weren't we there because we knew we were on the incorrect path? Didn't we always sense there was something wrong with us, something deep inside? Didn't we want to live a life congruent with society's values? Didn't we want to make our parents proud of us?

"Well you can!" Michael thundered. "You have the power! And so, I ask you *one more time:* Can You Change?"

This time the crowd roared. "Yes!" they cried with one voice. They clapped and shouted and whooped it up like Oprah's audience being told they had all won brand new Buicks.

"OK," Freddy whispered, "this is a bit much."

"Ya think?"

Suddenly, the lights came on full force. We blinked in the sudden brilliance. The room became sober again. "Just by coming here today, you've all taken the first step towards reclaiming your lives and your identities as men," Michael smiled. "Any questions?"

A man in the third row raised his hand. Michael nodded at him.

"Excuse me," the man asked Michael, standing up, "I'm wondering if you'd like to go on a date?"

The audience was shocked by the audacity of the man's proposal. A few men gasped, one hissed.

Michael glowered. "Excuse me?"

"Well, since I figured that's the last time I'm ever going to ask another man out, it might as well be one who's as good looking as you!"

The audience exploded with laughter and applause. Michael grinned. The man went on.

"No, really, you can't imagine how much you've inspired me today. I came here with, well, not exactly no expectations, but pretty low ones. But a friend I know, he went through your program, and, he's really doing it, you know? He's dating a girl at work now and he says it's not too b . . . well, he says he's really getting used to it. And I just thought, well, why not; let's give it a shot, because I've been so unhappy for so long and," the man's voice caught for a moment and I really hoped he wasn't going to start crying, "well, I guess I don't really have a question." He sat back down again.

Michael smiled warmly at the man. He put out his hand. "Come up here."

The man walked to the front of the room and turned to face us. He looked to be in his early thirties. He was tall, thin, and had one of the worst cases of post-adolescent acne I've ever seen. If Michael were honest, he'd tell this guy to skip the counseling and get to a dermatologist.

Michael put his arm around him. "You're going to do it, friend. Our program combines counseling, peer support, positive reinforcement, neuro-associative conditioning, hypnosis and, where indicated, even pharmaceutical assistance that will make it impossible for you *not* to change!"

"He left out the pods," Freddy whispered.

No, I thought, but he's thrown pretty much everything else into the mix. Hypnosis? Drugs? Dr. Chambers was right—it takes a lot to suppress someone's natural orientation.

Michael pulled the guy closer and put his other hand on the guy's stomach. Right above his belt. It was almost sexual. "And the next time I put my arm around you," Michael continued, "I promise you, you won't be hoping my hand slides lower."

The room again broke into laughter and applause. Michael put both his arms around the guy and squeezed him tight. I could swear he even ground his crotch into him a little. He released him and, with a pat on his ass, sent him back to his seat. The crowd was still laughing and cheering. I looked at the guy's crotch and thought he might have gotten a little chubby from Michael's teasing.

I thought about something else Dr. Chambers said, that many of these "ex-gays" were gay themselves. Michael was totally butch and said homophobic things, but he was also single. Where, I wondered, did he fall on the Kinsey scale?

Michael looked out at the audience again. He took a few more questions and answered them with the professional aplomb of a talk show host. Every time his eyes glanced our way, we slunk low in our chairs to avoid detection.

At the end of the session, Michael marched triumphantly out a door at the front of the room to cheers and applause. Immediately, two fresh-faced young men with clipboards came in to announce that anyone interested in signing up for a discounted one-on-one introductory session should fill out one of the forms they were handing out.

"Can we leave now, or do I have to attend the individual brain washing session, too?" Freddy asked.

"Come on," I said, as we slinked toward the back door. I noticed only one other guy was leaving without signing up. A pretty-good-looking guy who was one of the youngest in the room. One of the staff members gave the three of us a dirty look.

Sorry, I thought, no sale.

Right outside the room was a restroom.

"Darling," Freddy said, "I need to powder my nose. Want to join me."

"No," I said, "I'll wait out here."

I was looking at some flyers on the wall when I felt someone come up from behind me.

I turned around. Michael Harrington was standing there.

"Leaving so soon?"

I looked up at him. And he was tall enough that I really did have to look up.

He grinned. "One might think your interest in my seminar was less than sincere. Did you really think I didn't see you there?" His words were a little harsh, but his delivery was charming, frisky. His eyes wrinkled with amusement.

It was a completely different face than the one he had shown me at the lawyer's office. Gone was the officious authority figure. Now he was playful, teasing. Provocative.

"That was quite a performance," I said.

Michael stepped closer. A challenge. "Did you like it?"

I stepped closer too. If either of us moved another inch, we'd be touching. "Very much. Very inspiring." I tossed back my hair, bit my lower lip. "You had the audience in the palm of your hand."

"How about you," he asked. "Where did I have you?"

"That depends," I husked. "Where do you want me?"

Michael's eyes burned into mine. "You're flirting with me."

"Like you were flirting with the guy you brought up?" I asked. "You know, the one you felt up in front of us?"

"That's my job," Michael said. "It's a seduction, you see? All sales are a seduction. You of all people know that."

"You seemed to enjoy it." I was trying to figure out what makes him tick.

"What I enjoy about my job," Michael said, "is the opportunity to help people."

"I bet."

"Believe it or not," Michael said, "I'd like to help you, too."

Michael wanted something, but I didn't know what. Any other man and I'd be thinking he wanted to bang me. But Michael had made a career out of hating homosexuals, and teaching them to hate themselves.

Of course, be they preachers or politicians, most of the people who are really rabid about homosexuality are just acting out on their own repression.

Or, Michael could just be playing me. But to what end? To throw me off the track of his father's murder? To convince me he really was an OK guy?

And, to be brutally honest, standing next to his rampant hotness, feeling the undeniable sexual energy he exuded, I could think of worse places I could be than *mano y mano* in his office.

I decided to play along. "Really?" I asked, doing my best to sound naïve. "You think you could help me?"

"I do. Why don't you lose your friend and come with me to my office?"

"Just the two of us?"

Michael put his hand on my shoulder. I could feel the cotton of my shirt begin to smolder. Nobody this sexy could be all bad.

"Just the two of us," he said. "It may take all night, though." He winked and gave my arm a gentle squeeze.

My knees buckled. There was something that was just very . . . compelling about this man.

"Well, maybe . . ." I began

Michael's smile widened, baring his teeth.

When you hustle for a living, there's a look you learn to watch out for. It's a look that's not just excited, not just aroused, but feral.

It's not a look that says "I want to have fun with you."

It says "I want to hurt you. And I'm going to enjoy it."

Men like that especially like to hurt cute little boys like me.

Michael Harrington had that look.

Who's afraid of the big, bad wolf? I was. I took half a step back.

"Sorry," I said, "I can't leave my friend." Speaking of which, where the fuck was Freddy? "Maybe some other time?"

Michael closed the distance between us. "You sure? Maybe you'd enjoy it?"

I took a full step back this time. "How about tomorrow?"

Michael's grip on my arm tightened. It didn't feel sexy anymore. It felt like a vise.

"Just for a minute," he said. "We'll look at my book and schedule some time for later in the week."

I hesitated.

"Come on." He put his arm around my shoulder and squeezed. He pulled me close enough that I could feel the strong bulge of his pectoral muscles.

Had I misread him? He pulled me closer, ruffled my hair.

"Don't be a knucklehead," he said. "Come on."

I was being paranoid. No one who wants to hurt you calls you "knucklehead," right? I was just about to tell him "sure" when my knight in sequined armor reappeared.

"For a man who's so fucking straight," Freddy said, "you can't seem to keep your hands off guys."

Michael looked up at him and growled. Yes, he actually growled.

Gone was the playful big brother, the charming seducer. This was the Michael I first met at Tamela Steel's office. This was the wolf.

"Ah, if it isn't the sidekick," said Michael. "Your friend and I were just going to make an appointment. How about you wait here and we'll be right back?"

Freddy moved to my side. "How about I come along?"

"That won't be necessary."

Freddy looked at me.

"We come as a set," I said, feigning casualness. "Maybe you could help my friend, too."

"I think your friend is beyond help," Michael said. He turned to me and tried to smile, but the mask was melting.

"Why, doctor," Freddy said, "that doesn't seem very Christian of you."

Michael's face twisted into a ball of rage. "You think you're clever, don't you, boy? You think I don't know what kind of filth you are?"

"I think we better go," I said to no one in particular.

"Did you just call me 'boy'?" Freddy asked.

"I'll call you worse than that," Michael said, moving toward us, his color rising.

I think he was about to take a swing at Freddy, but then the doors of the meeting room opened. Men streamed out, chatting away, making a beeline for Michael when they spotted him.

Upon hearing the crowd, Michael transformed instantly. His body relaxed and his practiced smile returned. To anyone looking, we had just had a friendly chat.

It was creepy how quickly his entire demeanor changed. As if his most intense feelings could be cycled through like premium channels on cable. In the time I had observed him tonight, I'd seen him be charming, friendly, inspiring, seductive, angry, threatening, and then charming again.

The Mirror Has Two Faces, I thought. Only a lot more than two.

"Well, gentlemen," he said to us. "It looks like you've been saved by the *Tinkerbelles.* How appropriate."

He turned away, but not before Freddy said, "Oh, yeah? Well, fuck you, too."

"Good comeback," I told him as we walked away.

"It was the best I could think of under the circumstances," Freddy admitted.

Over dinner at the new Chelsea restaurant Foodboys, I told Freddy about how I sensed that Michael had a real sadistic streak.

"Well, duh," Freddy said. "That's why I stepped in. I think if he'd gotten you into his office, you might never have come back out."

"I know. What scares me is that for a moment, maybe even a few moments, I was almost ready to go with him. He's got some crazy thing going—he's super-charming one minute, then psycho the next. He'd have made a great hustler."

"He kind of is a great hustler, no?"

"I guess so," I answered. I thought for a minute about how close I had come to stepping into the lion's den. Which reminded me: "Where were you, anyway? It seemed like you were in that bathroom forever."

"Oh, I met that guy who left the room right before we did in there. Remember him? The one with the great hair?"

"You did a guy in the bathroom at an anti-gay conversion seminar?" I asked.

"I didn't *do* him," Freddy corrected me. "I mean, OK, we made out a little, but that was it."

Knowing Freddy, "made out" could cover anything short of fisting. I decided to let it pass.

"I got his number," Freddy said. "He was really very nice. Twenty-three years old. Real religious family. When he came out in his teens, his mother stood up, went to the kitchen, and put her head in the oven."

"Really?"

"Yeah. He told me she didn't turn it on or anything, she just did it for effect. Anyway, they sent him to one of those camps they have for teenagers—you know, the ones that are supposed to make you straight?"

I nodded.

"They screwed him up pretty good. Tried to make him hate himself, but it didn't really take. When he saw the ad for the seminar tonight, he thought he'd give it one more try, but his heart wasn't in it. He told me that Michael sounded like one of the counselors at his camp, only a little more pop psychology and a little less fire and brimstone."

I figured that assessment was probably about right.

"Anyway, after a couple of minutes of fooling around, Charlie—that's his name—told me he didn't think he was going to be trying any more conversion therapies anytime soon. We have a date next week."

"You're truly a giver," I said.

"I try."

"OK," I said, "what's next?"

"Well, we know now that Michael has a real mean streak. And something about you obviously makes him nervous. To me, he looks more like a suspect than ever."

"OK, but we have to be able to prove it."

"I know," Freddy said. "Oy. That's the hard part, ain't it?"

"What's next?"

"Check your list."

I pulled out my iPhone and pulled up my to-do list.

1. Follow up with Roger Folds—fight?
2. Talk to Randy Bostinick
3. Research Paul and Michael Harrington.
4. Look into those gay suicides—was that true?
5. Fuck Tony

"OK, Freddy said, "you can cross one and two off the list. Number three—we've gotten some information about Michael Harrington—what about Paul?"

"Nothing yet," I said.

"OK, so let's leave that. What's this about 'gay suicides'?"

I shared what Tony had said about a rash of gay men taking their own lives.

"OK, so can you find out more about that?"

"Not without talking to Tony," I said.

"Well, that might get you closer to goal number five, too."

"I'll find another way." I had something in mind.

"Do that. And listen, while you have that thing out, don't forget about tomorrow night."

"Tomorrow night?" I asked.

"Sexbar?"

"Oh, right," I said. I quickly clicked over to my calendar—yep, there it was. "I got it."

"OK," Freddy said, looking over my shoulder at an Asian man with the most amazing green eyes. "What's for dessert?"

I left Freddy at Foodboys and headed home. Although it was 10:45 when I got there, my mother was sitting on the couch, purse in hand. She was wearing her black boots, a black sweatshirt, and, bizarrely, a black ski mask.

It was ninety-seven degrees out. This didn't look good.

"Don't sit down!" she called as I walked through the door. "We're going back out."

I had, as they say, a very bad feeling about this.

CHAPTER 13

A Lot More of Dottie Kubacki Than We Expected

"TELL ME AGAIN," I asked, yawning in the couch-like seat of the Lincoln Continental my mother was driving, badly, down the Long Island Expressway, "why are we doing this?"

"Your father hasn't answered the phone all evening. Why do you think that is?"

"He's sleeping?" I asked.

"He's with that bitch Dottie Kubacki," my mother hissed.

"Mom, there is no way that daddy is fu- fooling around with Dottie Kubacki." But even as I said it, I saw my mother's already death-like grip on the steering wheel tighten.

"Don't say that name to me!"

"You just said it," I reminded her.

"Well, yes, but I was careful to call her 'that bitch' Dottie Kubacki. If you say the whole thing like that, it takes the sting out."

"Fine," I said, exasperated. "There's no way daddy's seeing 'that bitch' Dottie Kubacki. For one thing, isn't she kind of heavy?"

"She's a pig!" my mother screamed, looking at me. The ear splitting horn of a tractor trailer in the lane into which she was carelessly drifting forced her to turn back to the road. "A heifer! She puts ice cream on her hamburgers!"

"Then how could you possibly be threatened by her?"

"Who knows what men like? I'd found magazines in your father's drawers—not just naked people like that pornography you have . . ."

"Mom!" I cried.

"But really dirty stuff, like two women posing together, or ladies with breasts so huge that they almost qualified for their own zip codes."

"That's hardly the equal to doing Dot . . ."

"Watch it," my mother said.

"Sorry. 'That bitch' Dottie Kubacki."

"He could be a 'chubby chaser.'" she replied. "I saw about them on *The View.*"

We exited the Expressway and drove the five local blocks to our street. But instead of pulling up to our home, my mother turned off the engine and let the car quietly drift down the street until it stopped right in front of Dottie Kubacki's house.

"I learned that from reading detective novels," she said.

"Now what?" I asked.

"Now, you go out and peek in her windows."

"What?"

"Just go up to the house and look in windows and see what they're up to." She reached into her handbag and brought out one of those cardboard disposable cameras you buy at the drugstore. "Take this. I want evidence."

"Listen, you're on your own here, Jessica Fletcher. There is no way I'm going out there to spy on my own father."

My mother looked at me coolly. "Do you know what an episiotomy is? When you were born, the doctors had to give me five stitches because you tore up my . . ."

"OK!" I said, "I'll go."

"It'll be fun," my mother said. "Haven't you ever wanted to play detective?"

If you only knew, I thought.

Just as I started to open my door, we saw a light come on in one of Dottie's second-floor windows.

"Her bedroom," my mother hissed. "Get up there."

"What?"

"There's a tree right over there. Climb up and get the picture. Do I have to think of everything?"

When my mother gets like this, you can either argue or give in. In either case, you're going to lose. I was in no mood to fight.

I got out of the car, put the camera in my back pocket, and approached the tree. I grabbed hold of the lowest branch and pulled myself up.

Years of gymnastics made the climbing part easy. I ascended from limb to limb until I got near Dottie's window. I had already decided that no matter what happened, even in the inconceivable event that my father was in there, I'd tell my mother that all I saw was Dottie, sorry, "that bitch" Dottie, getting ready for bed.

The tree got me high enough that I was looking directly into Dottie's bedroom. Which, luckily, was empty. I couldn't hear anything through the quarter-open window, either.

I looked down and saw my mother, expectant and angry, standing at the bottom of the tree. "Well?" she stage-whispered.

I put my hands together in prayer position and rested my head on them in the universal sign for sleep.

"Hmmm!" my mother observed.

I was just about to climb back down when a change in the light made me look up. There, at the window, stood Dottie Kubacki.

Nude.

I had always known that Dottie Kubacki was overweight, but to see her in the all-too-real flesh was to know the true awesomeness of nature. The Himalayas would be humbled.

She was Jabba the Hutt with pubic hair.

In fact, so impressive was the sight that I gasped. Loudly.

Dottie raised the window fully open. "Who's out there?" she asked.

Shit, I thought. The tree was thick with branches and leaves. Maybe if I stood very still, she wouldn't see me.

Dottie leaned out the window, her pendulous breasts reaching almost to the ground. Well, not really, but you get the picture. I tried to make myself invisible.

"Huh," she said, turning away.

If the front view of a naked Dottie Kubacki was indelible, you can only imagine how her backside seared itself into my consciousness. Her ass could have had its own zip code.

I looked down at my mother and motioned wildly for her to go back to the car. I was just beginning to climb down when Dottie's presence back at the window made me look up.

The only worse thing than seeing Dottie Kubacki standing naked at the window, I learned, was seeing Dottie Kubacki standing naked *with a handgun* at the window.

"I said, 'who's out there!'" she demanded, pointing the gun about a foot to my left.

"Gah!" I said. I put my foot down where I expected a branch but found nothing but air. "Shit!"

I fell about a foot down the tree until I managed to grab hold with my right hand.

"Is there someone in that tree?" Dottie demanded.

No, I thought, it's a squirrel that says "shit."

"If you're that Ferrara kid, I'm calling your parents right now," Dottie yelled. "I don't care how late it is."

She had that right—the Ferrara kids were brats.

I got halfway down the tree when the branch I was standing on cracked off.

"Shit!" I said again, as I fell, this time all the way to the ground. I landed on my ass, cracking the cheap camera my mother gave me and sending shards of plastic into my butt. "Ow!"

My impact or the noise must have set off an alarm, because all of a sudden the lights in Dottie's yard came on and a loud siren blared.

"Murderer!" Dottie screamed. "Rapist! Someone call the police!"

Lights in all the neighboring houses switched on, including ours, which pretty much ruled out the possibility that my father was at Dottie's.

My mother reached over from the driver's seat and opened the passenger door. "Would you get in here!" she yelled at me.

The thought had occurred to me.

I scampered as quickly as I could across Dottie's lawn and jumped into the car. My mother took off before my feet were all the way in.

"Gah!" I cried again. "Are you trying to kill me?"

"Kill you?" she said. "Can you imagine how embarrassed I would have been to be discovered snooping in that bitch Dottie Kubacki's yard?"

"I think your camera went into my tush," I told her, shifting uncomfortably in my seat.

"Well, that would be a new one," she observed dryly. "What made you cry out like that?"

I told her about seeing Dottie Kubacki naked.

"You poor thing," she admitted. "Well, at least you can't say she's turned you off to women."

"No, but it confirms my theory that daddy isn't sleeping with her," I said.

"How's that?" my mother asked.

"He *couldn't,*" I explained. "It wouldn't *reach.*"

CHAPTER 14

Bit by Bit, Putting it Together

THE NEXT MORNING I woke up with a long scratch along my right side and a sore ass. My mother was still asleep, snoring loudly. She was probably exhausted after a long night of almost-getting-her-son killed. I looked at the clock: 6:30.

I made a protein drink and sat down with my iPhone. My new to-do list looked like this.

1. Talk to Marc about gay suicides
2. Try to find out more about Paul Harrington
3. Fuck Tony

I debated deleting the third item, but I decided to let it stay. For now.

My plan for finding out more about the supposed "rash" of gay suicides that Tony had mentioned was to ask my client Marc Wilgus to see what he could turn up. Marc was probably one of the world's greatest Masters of the Web, and I doubted there was any information he couldn't get.

I sat at my computer and wrote him an e-mail asking if I could come by today and discuss something with him. I sent it and started surfing the Web. A few minutes later, my instant messenger beeped. Marc was online.

"Hey," he wrote, "what's up?"

"Something I need 2 talk 2 you about in person."

"U quitting the biz?"

"No, not that."

"U need 2 tell me that you have herpes or something?"

"No, nothing bad. Just need ur help."

"Come now if you want."

Of course, since Marc never left his apartment, any time was as good as any other. I had to be at The Stuff of Life at 11:00 to volunteer for the lunch shift, and then had a client at 3:00.

"Let me grab a shower," I wrote back. "C u in 30."

"Cool."

I showered, shaved all the relevant body parts, threw on frayed dungaree shorts, an Abercrombie and Fitch T-shirt, and sneakers, and headed out the door. Just as I was leaving, my mother emerged from the bedroom.

"Good boy," she said, "you're almost dressed today."

"Morning," I said, giving her a kiss on the cheek. "You recovered from last night?"

She put her hand on my cheek. "You're the one who almost broke his neck. Not to mention seeing that bitch Dottie Kubacki in such detail that not even her doctor should have to. I'm sorry you have such a crazy mother."

My mother never really admitted to being wrong, but this was close.

"Don't worry about it," I said. "At least now you know that daddy wasn't there."

"Well, he wasn't there when we *got* there. Who knows where he was before that."

I sighed.

"I'm telling you," she said. "There is something going on between your father and that woman. And I'm going to find out what it is."

"OK, well, good luck with that. I have to run and meet a friend." I turned towards the door.

"Oh, I don't need luck." She patted me right on the sorest part of my butt. "I have you."

The doorman at Marc's building gave me a look that seemed to say "Isn't it a bit early for the likes of you?" before buzzing me in. When I got to Marc's door, Marc was standing there in sweatpants and a T-shirt that said "When the robot overlords take over, I can translate." He looked cute and a little disheveled, and smelled of freshly-applied deodorant.

"Hi," he said.

"Hi."

We stood there a bit awkwardly. Usually, when he was paying for my visits, he just grabbed me and we started making out. Today, he didn't know what to do.

Was I there as a friend? A hustler? What?

I gave him a kiss on the cheek. "Thanks for seeing me."

"No problem," he said, "you want some coffee or tea?"

"That'd be great."

He walked me into his very modern kitchen, where about fifteen tall cups from Starbucks were lined up on his blindingly clean marble countertop, along with a plate of baked goods.

"I, uh, didn't know what you wanted," he said, "so I just told them to send up one of everything."

"We could have just made a pot," I said smiling.

"Um, I don't actually have a pot," Marc answered. "Or any coffee beans or real cups. Or milk. I pretty much order in whatever I need."

Like I said, Marc is the Master of the Web. But how he survives in the real world is a mystery to me.

"The only problem is," Marc continued, "I don't exactly know what is what. But feel free to take a sip of everything until you find one you like."

I eventually found a nice Chai tea that smelled deliciously of cinnamon and honey. Marc picked up a cup at random and started drinking. We both took scones and sat at the counter.

I told Marc about Allen's death. I described for him the crazy sons and my visit to The Center for Creative Empowerment Therapy. I told him about the gay suicides and how they haven't been reported in the press. That was what I needed his help to investigate.

"Wow," Marc said, after he heard the whole story. "That's what I call good customer service. Would you do all that for me if I ended up on the pavement?"

"Allen was a friend," I told him. "But the answer is 'yes.'"

Marc smiled. "I bet you would." He reached out to ruffle my hair. "You're a pretty special kid."

"Thanks. Can you help me?"

"You mean, can I illegally hack into the files at police headquarters and find out the information they're withholding from the press?"

I nodded.

"With my dominant hand tied behind my back," he grinned. "But I'll go you one better. Wait here a minute."

Marc went into his office and returned with a laptop. Flipping it open, he fussed with the mouse and keyboard.

"Give me all the information you have. I'll put it into my data mining program and we'll see what comes up."

"Data mining?" I asked him

"It's one of the information technology tools that governments use to catch terrorists. It's like a giant database that looks at millions of other databases and other information to make relevant connections.

"Like, for example, the program might notice that five people from a country with terrorist connections who all attended the same military training program have dissolved their bank accounts and booked themselves on the same flight. Each one of those pieces of data might be insignificant, but when you put them all together, well, I wouldn't want to be on that plane."

"Got it," I said.

"So download to me everything you know that's related to Allen's death and we'll see what turns up."

I rattled off all the people and places that I knew were involved, including the eight names Tony had given me of the supposed suicides, which I read off the list I still carried in my wallet. Marc typed it all in.

"OK," he said. "It will take a day or two to run that through the program. I'll call you when I find anything out."

I got up and sat on his lap. "You're wonderful." I kissed him on the lips. Now I know what he'd been drinking—he tasted of caramel.

"Mmm," he said. "You're going to get me started."

I looked at the clock. I had over an hour before I had to be at The Stuff of Life.

"And this is a bad thing why?" I asked. Then, I realized that he might think I was working.

"Listen," I said. "I'm going to tell you something I've never told another client. You know how you've been paying me over the past couple of months?"

He nodded.

"I would have done at least half those things for free."

"Really?" he said, his voice cracking like a teenager's.

"Uh-huh," I said, kissing his neck. "Maybe even three quarters." I scraped his skin with my teeth.

"Mmmm," he groaned. I felt him grow hard against me. "I don't mind paying. But it's nice to know."

"Well, today's on the house," I said. "If you have time."

Marc stood up, grabbing me behind the knees and carrying me to the bedroom. "I think I can squeeze you in."

As I pulled my shorts back on, Marc looked at me affectionately from the bed. "What you're involved in, it's got me a little worried."

"What do you mean?"

"You're dealing with a possible murderer here," Marc explained. "You said that guy Michael looked like he wanted to hurt you. I don't want to see anything bad happen to you."

I stood up and executed some Krav Maga moves and then jumped into a handstand. "I can take care of myself."

"Hey," Marc said, standing up, naked. Although we had both just cum twenty minutes ago, he looked like he was getting excited again. "Little tough man. Who knew?"

I playfully flexed my biceps. "Grrrr!"

"Where'd you learn to get all Jackie Chan like that?"

"When you're a little blond boy like me," I said, "you either learn to defend yourself or you wind up an easy target."

Marc took me in his arms. "Well, I'm impressed."

I grabbed him where it counts. "I can see."

Marc put his hand under my chin and tilted my face up to his. His eyes looked steadily into mine. "I know we've spent plenty of time together, but I guess I've never really gotten to know you. But today, well, I think I've learned a lot about you. You're smart and brave and resourceful and strong in ways that I never knew. I have to say, I like what I see."

I heard Mrs. Cherry's words in my head. "Give 'em your mouth, your dick, and your ass. But do me a favor: keep your heart to yourself."

Was she right?

I blushed.

Marc put his hands on my hot cheeks. "That's cute."

I definitely had feelings for Marc. But could I love him?

Maybe, but he was no Tony.

Tony? Shit, where had that come from? Ugh.

I threw my arms around Marc and hugged him tightly. "Thank you for helping me," I said.

Marc hugged me back. "Thank you for asking."

CHAPTER 15

A Climax, of Sorts

I ARRIVED AT The Stuff of Life about fifteen minutes before the lunch shift, planning to tell Vicki about my bizarre meeting with Roger Folds. But as I walked through the door, my cell phone rang. It was my father.

I went into an empty office to take his call.

"So," my father began, "if you don't mind my asking such a thing, what was your mother's car doing racing down our street at midnight last night?"

"Oh, you saw?" I asked.

"The whole neighborhood saw. At least no one else recognized her. For this, we should be thankful."

"It's kind of a long story," I said.

"You can start with why you were in a tree peeping into Mrs. Kubacki's window."

"She saw me?"

"She saw someone. And it doesn't take a brain surgeon to know that your mother didn't haul her fat, excuse me for saying, ass up that tree."

I told my father about my mother's suspicion that he had been visiting Dottie that night.

"Oy. That woman. She drove me to it."

"Drove you to what?"

"To Dottie, of course. What do you think?"

I was glad I was sitting down. "You mean, you really are having an affair with Dottie Kubacki? You told me nothing was going on."

"Well, what's 'nothing?'" he said to me. Then, after a moment,

"And I wouldn't call it an 'affair.' I'm not, pardon the expression, having the intercourse with her. It's not physical.

"But your mother, you may know this already, is driving me crazy. She doesn't let me live. She nags, she lectures, she doesn't let me get a word in edgewise.

"But Dottie. Dottie listens. I tell her about the war, about my parents, about my dreams, and she sits there with her chin in her hands and she looks at me like I'm the most interesting person in the world. Then, she makes me a glass of tea and homemade apple cake and it makes me feel like a man again.

"When you're as old as I am, that's a good feeling, son."

I have to admit I was moved listening to my father talk. He was right; he did deserve a moment in the sun. At the end of days, don't we all?

"So, do you want to leave Mom?" I asked.

"Leave?" my father asked. "What are you, nuts too? I love your mother. She drives me crazy, but she's still my wife. I just have a friend. A lady friend. She makes me tea and every once in a while I change a lightbulb for her. So what? The world has to come to an end because I have a friend? What is this, Nazi Germany?"

Suddenly, I understood what threatened my mother so much about "that bitch" Dottie Kubacki. She knew perfectly well that my father wasn't having sex with Dottie. But my mother also knew how difficult she could be. She was afraid that if my father had someone with whom he could compare her, that he'd realize it, too. As if he didn't know.

My mother recognized that, measured against Dottie, she might, in some ways, look bad. And if there was anything my mother couldn't stand, it was looking bad.

"OK," I said, "listen. We're gonna fix this, OK? I know you want Mom back home . . ."

"Let's not get carried away," my father said.

"Dad."

"No, you're right, she belongs here. The house, and I know you may find this hard to believe, is kind of quiet without her. Empty, too. Plus, she must be driving you coo-coo. Before you know it, she'll be putting up curtains."

"You're going to have to do something," I told him. "Something romantic. Something that shows her that she really is the most important person in the world to you. Can you do that?"

"Like maybe I should send flowers?"

"Bigger."

"Chocolates?"

"Too ordinary."

"One of those guys who come to the house dressed like a policeman and then takes his clothes off like a crazy person? She saw that once on that *View* show and loved it."

I thought I might enjoy that, too, but it didn't seem entirely appropriate. "We'll have to come up with something better than that, Dad. I'll think about it."

"You're a good boy. So, tell me: Dottie says that whoever was looking through her window saw her naked. Is this true?"

"Yes," I admitted.

"And . . ." my father asked.

"And what?"

"How was it?"

"How do you think it was?"

My father paused for a moment. "Epic."

"Yes," I said, "but not in a good way."

"No," my father said, "I wouldn't think so. The woman has a heart of gold, but it's surrounded by, and you'll excuse my French, a shitload of lard, isn't it?"

After my shift at The Stuff of Life I went to the gym, had a protein drink, and then headed off to a date with a client who paid five hundred dollars to play "salesman."

His fantasy was that he worked at The Gap, and I asked to have my inseam measured. He took a measuring tape, put one end at my shoe, extended the rest up the side of my leg until his hand was just under my balls, gave them a quick, surreptitious squeeze, and then ejaculated into his pants.

The entire thing took less than five minutes, four minutes of which was him explaining what he wanted me to do.

Sometimes, I loved my job.

I got home at 4:00 to find Tony outside my building.

"Hi," he said, looking great in his standard blue slacks and white shirt. No tie today.

"Is this a stakeout?" I asked.

"I was just in the neighborhood. Rang your bell and when no one answered, decided to wait awhile."

I took out my cell phone. "You could have called."

"I could have."

"But you didn't."

"I wanted to see you."

I extended my arms. "OK, you've seen me."

"You're going to make this hard for me, aren't you?"

"Didn't you tell me two days ago that you *didn't* want to see me?"

Tony cocked his head to the side and gave me his most charming smile. He arched one eyebrow and shrugged. "I have conflicting feelings."

I couldn't help but smile back. "There's a lot of that going around."

"Can we talk?"

Because of my attention deficit disorder, I often get lost in the details and forget the big picture. That was happening here, too, I thought. I really didn't want to talk to Tony. What else was there to say?

Just this morning, I spent time talking to Marc with whom I'd had a lot of sex, but never really spoken. It brought us a lot closer.

Now, here I was with a man who I've been talking to for days, but we haven't had sex in years.

If we did it, if we finally made love again, would it bring us closer together, too? Or would it be the end?

Wasn't it time I found out?

I thought of my to-do list. What was the last item? Oh yeah, "fuck Tony."

When I wrote it, I meant it in an angry way.

Standing here with him now, on a steaming city street with him looking cool and so handsome and smelling faintly of freshly-mowed grass, I decided it would be OK to mean it in the other way, too.

What did I want?

What was I afraid of?

Focus, Kevin, focus.

"Let me ask you a question," I said. "Are you drunk right now?"

Tony looked quizzical. "No."

"Under the influence of any drugs or other mind-altering substances?"

Tony rolled up his sleeve. "See? No track marks."

"So, whatever happens, you're ready to take responsibility for it?"

Tony saw what I was getting at. He pulled me towards him. "You mean, right now? In the middle of the afternoon? No more talking?"

I just had sex with Marc Wilgus a couple of hours earlier, but I suddenly felt as horny as I ever have. I kissed him. He kissed me back.

This time he didn't hold back, and the kiss made something inside me expand and explode into a million little pleasures.

"No more talking," I said. "But feel free to cry out in ecstasy."

CHAPTER 16

Can't Help Loving That Man

BECAUSE I HAVE sex for a living, it's easy to think I could become inured to it. Jaded.

But having sex isn't making love.

When Tony entered me, I felt like I finally had come home.

And then I came.

Just from him sliding inside me.

"Wow," Tony said. "I do that to you?"

"Now," I said, climbing on top of him, "watch what I can do to you."

Although being with Tony wasn't like being with a trick, that didn't mean I wasn't about to use everything I had learned. I rode him like he had never been rode, feeling him grow impossibly hard inside me. I stopped every time he got close and then sped up again.

"You're killing me," he cried, before finally flipping me back on my back. He made love to me slowly, and then quickly, passionately, kissing me the whole time and moaning against my lips.

My erection, which had never really gone away, rubbed against his impressive abs.

"Jesus!" he cried when he finally came. "Holy fuck!"

I shot again against his stomach.

He collapsed on top of me and buried his face in my neck. I felt wetness there.

But whether it was sweat or tears I didn't know.

I'd be lying if I said that the cuddling after sex is better than the actual act. But it does come pretty damn close.

Lying in Tony Rinaldi's arms.

I could stay here forever.

But could he?

He pulled me closer.

"That was incredible," he said.

As good as your wife? I thought. Then I chided myself: Stop it! Stop indulging your doubts and focus on enjoying the moment.

"It was OK," I said.

He rolled on top of me. "Just OK?"

"Well, it's clear you're out of practice."

Tony frowned. "Hmmm. You're right. Now, where could I get some more training, do you think?"

"Well, I do offer advanced lessons for my more promising students."

"More advanced than that? I think I'd have a heart attack, Kevvy."

Kevvy. That's what he used to call me. I felt something inside myself blooming so large that I didn't think I'd be able to contain it.

"You are kind of old," I teased. "Maybe we'd have to start at the intermediate level."

Tony started kissing his way down my body. "No time like the present."

After the encore, I looked at the time. It was 6:00. I had to meet Freddy at 10:00 at Sexbar. Just then, my phone rang. I picked up the receiver by my couch. (I couldn't bring myself to have sex with him in the bed where my mother had been sleeping.) Caller ID told me it was the very woman who had forced me into the living room. I had learned not to skip her calls.

"I have to take this," I said to him.

"Mmm," he said drowsily. "S'OK."

I sat up on the couch and pressed talk. "What's up, Mom?"

"Darling, it's your mother."

"Yes, I know that," I said. "What's up?"

"I just wanted to tell you I'd be home late. I'm going to Hannah Rosenberg's house to play canasta."

This was the best news I'd ever heard. "Great. Have fun." Tony's hand crept around to my lap.

Her voice dropped to a conspiratorial whisper. "All the girls in the shop today were talking about that bitch Dottie Kubacki's encounter with a Peeping Tom last night. Most of them thought she'd made it up on the grounds that who would want to peep at Dottie Kubacki?"

Tony was pulling me back into bed. "That's nice, Mom," I said.

"Will you be OK for dinner without me?" she asked.

Tony put my hand on his reawakening erection.

"Don't worry," I told her. "I have what to eat."

After the second encore (is there a word for that?) Tony and I realized we were starving. Not surprising, considering the amount of calories we must have burned off. Luckily, the fridge was stocked with the leftovers of several nights of my mother's home cooking. We sat naked at the kitchen table and pigged out on pot roast and gravy sandwiches.

"I have to tell you something," Tony said. "Something I didn't tell you before because I didn't want to, well . . . "

"Wait," I interrupted. "You didn't want to get my hopes up, right?"

Tony grinned. "Yeah, that."

"Listen," I said. "How about I take responsibility for my hopes, and you take responsibility for being honest, OK?"

Tony's eyes widened a little. "When did you get to be so smart? OK, well, remember when we first met? How I told you I was married and that our relationship was so great? Well, that wasn't exactly the truth."

"You're not married."

"We're separated. Six months now. I don't think we're getting back together."

"You don't think?"

"I'm being honest here."

Fair enough. "So, did this afternoon tilt the scales either way?" I regretted asking the question the minute the words left my mouth.

Tony looked down. Took a minute to answer. "I'm trying to keep things separate, if that makes sense. Not let one thing decide another. I think I owe that to her. To myself, too. Can you understand that?"

"Sure," I said quietly.

"But this afternoon was great. And," he said licking his lips, "this pot roast is pretty great, too."

"So, think we might do this again?" I asked hopefully.

"Mmm." Tony took another huge bite of his sandwich. "Will there be more pot roast?"

"It's possible," I said.

Tony leaned over the table and kissed me. "Then you got me."

After we finished eating, Tony and I, still naked, went back into the living room and jumped into the sofa bed. I rested my head on his chest. His slow breathing was a narcotic. He asked if he could stay the night. I had to explain that I was meeting Freddy at 10:00.

"Sexbar?" he asked. "Isn't that like some gay sex club or something?"

I nodded.

"You're going to a sex club after the day we had together? Are you that insatiable?" He slapped me on the head.

"It's work," I told him. I explained that once a month, Freddy and I went there to hand out condoms and brochures about safer sex. It was a volunteer thing we did for the agency Freddy worked for.

I didn't tell Tony that we did it in our underwear.

"OK," Tony said, "then you have permission." He kissed me on the forehead. "I think it's great that you do this kind of thing. You have a big heart to do volunteer work."

I stood up and took a playful bow. "Thank you."

Tony stood, too, and put his arms around me. "But I don't really understand about your day job," he said. "What exactly is it that you do?"

Uh-oh. "I'm a man of mystery."

Tony pulled me closer. "No, seriously, what do you do?"

I had just told Tony that he needed to be honest in our relationship. Could I be any less?

But he was a cop. And a man. An Italian man. Was there a chance he'd be able to accept how I made a living?

"Well," I began, not sure what I was going to say.

Just then, the door opened. "Darling," my mother called. "I'm home!"

Great, I thought. Last night, I spied on Dottie Kubacki naked and now my mother walks in on me and Tony in the buff.

Karma's a bitch.

"Oh!" she cried. "Excuse me!" She covered her eyes. "I didn't see a thing!"

"Hello, Mrs. Connor," Tony muttered.

"Tony?" my mother asked. I saw her spread her fingers apart as she peeked through them.

"Yes," he groaned.

"I thought you were married?" she said.

"He's separated," I said.

"Oh, well, that explains it, then." She put her hands up to her eyes like blinders. "I'm just going to scoot into my bedroom (her bedroom!) and give you two a chance to, um, finish up. Nice seeing you," she said to Tony. She took another peek at his naked butt. "*Really* nice."

"Uh, bye, Mrs. Connor," Tony said.

As soon as she closed the door, Tony pulled away and hurriedly got dressed. "Still want to spend the night?" I asked.

"I forgot she was staying here," Tony said. "What are you doing about that?"

"I'm working on it," I said.

Tony put his hand on his gun. "My offer still stands."

"Thanks, but I think I'll save that as a last resort."

"Suit yourself," he said, strapping on his holster. He pulled me against him. I liked the way my naked body felt against his clothed one.

"Aren't you going to get dressed?" he asked me.

"I'm going to grab a shower before I head over to meet Freddy," I said.

"I could use one, too" he said. "Although maybe I'll go to bed with your scent still on me."

Inside, I swooned.

"This was great," Tony said. "Thank you. I'll call you tomorrow, OK?"

"You better," I said.

"OK." He kissed me again. "I guess I'll be going now."

"OK," I said, kissing him back. We inched lip-locked toward the door.

"Bye," Tony said, still kissing me.

"So long," I said, not stopping.

"See ya later." He smiled through our kiss.

"Alligator," I completed the rhyme.

After a few more minutes, I had to push him away.

"OK, OK, I get the hint," he said.

I opened the door. "Talk to you tomorrow," I said.

"I . . . ," Tony began. "Thank you."

I thought he was going to say something else.

I closed the door.

I realized that I had forgotten. Forgotten what it was to be purely and totally joyful. To be happy and hopeful and ready for love.

I felt my frozen heart thawing faster than the polar icecaps in an Al Gore movie.

Oh Lord, was I smitten.

I looked down at my feet. Yep, they were still on the ground.

But it didn't feel that way, did it?

I felt like shouting, dancing, and running down the street naked after him. I felt like singing "Don't Let the Parade Pass Me By" from the back of a steamer ship.

Tony fucking Rinaldi!

I was trying to play it cool. To keep my feelings and expectations low. But now that I had lain in his arms again, now that I thought we might really have the chance to get back together, I had to admit it: *Damn,* I loved that boy!

A knock at the door.

He was back!

I was just about to open the door when I realized the knock was coming from inside the apartment.

From my mother's room.

My room, damn it!

"Is it safe to come out?" she asked.

"One minute!" I yelled. I kicked my underwear into the closet, hid the lube, and threw a towel around my waist. "OK."

My mother came out in a red velour robe with matching slippers and a turban. Cleopatra of Long Island. "I hope I didn't interrupt anything," she said.

"He was just leaving."

"Naked?"

"Well, he was getting ready to leave."

My mother made her way into the kitchen. "I need some tea.

I am telling you, you could use Hannah Rosenberg's bean dip for cement."

"Uh-huh," I said. All I could think was: Tony Rinaldi!

"And her cookies! They could deflect bullets!"

"Yeah." His hair was even softer than I remembered. It felt like strands of silk when his head traveled down my belly.

"So, you're really crazy about him, no?"

"Hmmm, interesting." His biceps were like coiled steel covered with rubber and when he came he made the most sensual . . .

My mother walked over to me and yanked my hair.

"Ow! What'd you do that for?" I said, rubbing my head.

"You haven't been listening to a word I said."

Had she been talking? "That's no reason to make me bald."

"You think I didn't see that same look in your eyes whenever Tony came around the house? From the time you were eleven, twelve years old? I should have told you that you were gay then and saved you the soul-searching."

She took my face in her hands. "Baby. That kind of love, it's not always a good thing, you know? We all think, 'wow, love.'" She widened her eyes comically.

"The movies tell us love is such a great thing that we can't have too much. But you know what? You can. You really can love some-one too much. That kind of love can kill you, you know?"

I nodded.

"I saw what you went through the first time with Tony. How you suffered. Oh, I saw it all. You think a mother doesn't know?"

She put her hand on her heart. "A mother *knows,* Kevin. What-ever pain you've felt in your life, I've felt double-triple.

"I don't want to see you hurt that way again."

That makes two of us, I thought. "I know, Mom. I'll be careful."

"You'll be a lot of things," my mother said, "but you won't be careful.

"You see, I know you think I'm a crazy lady. But why do you think I'm here? Because I love that old man I've been married to for forty years so much that I refuse—refuse!—to share him with anyone else.

"When he wooed me—oy, he was the most romantic man I'd ever known. At night, after my parents had gone to bed, he'd throw pebbles at the window to wake me. Then he'd sing to me, love songs, and I'd yell down 'shhh!' but he wouldn't listen. Finally, we'd see the lights go on in my parents' room, and he'd run away, and I'd be standing there by the open window thinking I wished I could just go down and run off with him.

"I know what it is to love too much, Kevin. I've been careful with my money and careful with my children, but I've never been careful with my heart.

"Not even once.

"And I think, maybe in that way, you're a little more like your mother than you know."

I don't think that I've ever heard my mother talk so honestly. If I weren't so fucking happy at that moment, it might even have sunk in. But as it was, her words fell on me like rain on hot pavement, there for just a moment before evaporating into the air.

I kissed her on the cheek. "Thanks for caring, Mom. I love you. But I have to go. Freddy's waiting for me."

"There's another one waiting?" she asked.

"You know Freddy," I said. "We've been friends forever. There's nothing between us." Well, nothing worth mentioning, I added to myself.

"Whatever. Just mark my words—don't let that Tony Rinaldi break your heart. Although," she added mischievously, "he does have a great tush."

CHAPTER 17

A Surprising Discovery at the Sex Club

I TOOK A quick shower, threw on my cutest underwear (black N2N square cut with a generous pouch), cargo shorts, a white tank top, and high-top sneakers and grabbed a cab to a nondescript building in the meat packing district by Greenwich Village. The building had no sign but those-in-the-know knew it as Sexbar. I was twenty minutes late.

I was still so strung out on Tony-loving that I felt I could have flown there. Which was probably why I was singing "Oh My Man I Love Him So" to myself the whole cab ride down there and why I tipped the driver ten dollars.

"Hello!" Freddy cried as I got out of the car. "Tardy much?" He hoisted his bag of flyers and condoms over his shoulder and walked towards me. "You know how many men have missed out on some quality AIDS education while you were off doing who knows what?"

"Sorry," I said, trying to keep the silly smile off my face.

"Aw, don't worry about it." Freddy waved his hand. "This place won't get busy till about midnight anyway."

"I wore cute underwear."

"Thattaboy," Freddy winked and gave me thumbs up.

Then he cocked his head and squinted his eyes. "Are you OK?"

"I'm fine," I told him. "Let's go in."

He put a hand on my chest. "No, wait a minute." He looked me up and down quizzically. "There's something different. You seem a little strange."

I tried to walk past him, but Freddy's arm was solid like a tree trunk.

"What is it?" he said, more to himself than to me.

"It's nothing. Come on, you said it yourself, we have work to do."

"Not so fast, Junior." He brought his face close enough to mine that I could feel his breath on my cheeks. "You look . . ." he blinked twice. "You look happy!"

I couldn't hold it in. "I am happy!" I shouted. I grabbed him in a bear hug and, even though he had fifty pounds of muscle on me, I spun him around. I stepped back and pointed to my face. "Look! This is me! Happy!" I gave a little jump.

Freddy laughed. "I take it you got laid?"

"Royally."

"Tony?"

"Finally."

Freddy smiled with just a touch of sadness in his eyes. "Good for you," he said. Then, seriously, "I just hope you're careful."

Why was everyone telling me that?

"So," he whispered conspiratorially, "how was it?"

"It was," I said, "worth waiting for."

"You haven't exactly been waiting." Freddy grinned.

I smiled back and forgave him for not knowing what I myself hadn't realized until just hours ago: I really had been.

And now the waiting was over.

By 1:00 in the morning, my ass had been patted about a hundred times, my nipples pinched half that much, and my crotch groped by a handful of especially stoned or brazen customers of Sexbar.

Which, by the way, was not a bar at all but a series of hallways with some large carpeted rooms, a few smaller ones with seating, and about fifty small cubicles with doors that ended two feet above the floor like the doors of a men's changing room, where two (or three, if they were small or limber enough) interested parties could retire for what passed for privacy.

There was also a snack room that served soft drinks but no alcohol, which is where Freddy and I stood in our underwear giving out safer-sex materials. Since we were young and cute and scantily clad, it wasn't hard to get a guy's attention.

"We're almost out of goodies," Freddy said, handing me the last of his bag's contents. "After this we can get out of here." An especially handsome young man in a jockstrap walked by. "Or not."

I handed them back. "Can you get this? If I don't go pee right now, I'm going to wet myself."

"Naw, that will just get the golden shower lovers rushing over, and you know how they are—they'll never stop buying us sodas."

"OK," I said, "I'll be right back."

Freddy and I had been doing these volunteer nights once a month for almost a year, so I knew my way around. The bathroom was just past the video lounge, through a row of cubbies, and behind the orgy room. I got there quickly, peed voluminously, shook myself for twice as long as I needed to (when you're just wearing underwear, you have to watch out for spotting), and headed back to the snack room.

A young guy of about my height stood outside the door. He was dead sexy and built like a swimmer, shaved or naturally hairless (it was hard to tell in the dim light), and wearing the exact pair of underwear I had on. "I've been waiting for you to take a break," he said. He winked one periwinkle blue eye and flashed a killer smirk.

He was delicious, but I was pretty sexed-out.

"Sorry," I said. "I have to get back to my friend."

"Aw, come on." He pointed to a cubicle two feet away. "Why should they have all the fun?"

I turned to see what he was pointing at and, sure enough, whoever was getting it on in there seemed to be having an exceptionally good time. The groans and grunts of the guy with his dress pants pooled around his Prada shoes were twice as loud as those of every other happy bottom in the place. Combined.

"He does seem like he's having a good time," I observed.

"I could make you drown him out," The Swimmer promised.

"Tempting," I said. "Maybe another time."

Only a loser lingers over rejection at a sex club, and this guy was no loser. "I'll keep an eye out for you," he said, walking away.

I looked one more time at the rocking cubby and thought that it was nice that I wasn't the only one who had a really good day. Good for you, lucky stranger, although you probably don't need luck if you can actually afford this season's Prada shoes.

Shoes I'd never even seen outside of a magazine except for . . . oh, no. It couldn't be.

I got closer to the cubby. Listened harder. Yes, there was a distinctively nasal whine to the moans.

Impossible, I thought. But still . . .

I had to know. I knocked on the door. "Hey, you guys sound hot. Got room for a third in there?"

"Go away," the guy in back shouted.

"I'm really good," I answered.

"Not interested."

"Um, can I just watch?"

"Get the fuck out of here!"

OK, that wasn't going to work.

I opened the cubby next door and walked in on two other guys just starting to make out. "Sorry!" I said.

I tried the cubicle on the other side. Empty. I went in and checked out the floor. Seeing no obvious puddles or stains, I grimaced, dropped to my knees, and peered under the partition. No good. From this angle I couldn't see their faces.

The only way to tell who was inside was to look over the partition, which was about two feet over my head. Not a problem. I jumped up, grabbed hold of the wall, and hauled myself up.

I was grateful for all those pull-ups at gym. Straightening my arms, I was able to suspend myself over the wall and see . . . the tops of their heads. That didn't do any good. I held my position for a few minutes, hoping the guy in the Prada shoes would throw his head back in ecstasy, but it never happened.

"Oh, yeah," he moaned. "Make it hurt, man!"

Bad dialogue aside, I wanted to get this over with. Not only were my arms getting tired, but the wall wasn't feeling too secure. I figured my best bet would be to get down and wait outside until they emerged.

Just then, I felt something slipping and the view started to shift. Was I sliding down?

No, it was the wall of the cubby, giving way under my weight.

As it began to lean down towards the couple next door, the metal objected with a terrible loud groaning. That made the guys look up.

"Holy shit," Prada shoes said, "the place is falling in on us!"

Oh great, I thought, now I got his attention.

Then his eyes met mine. "You!"

Yup, I thought, and I know you, too.

Paul Harrington. Allen's married son.

I had seen the guy he was with earlier that evening. He was actually pretty hot. Tall, dark hair, nice body. A couple of tattoos and a nipple ring kept his prep school good looks from being too boring.

Paul had good taste.

The door to their cubby flew open and the guys tumbled out, still attached at the crotch.

I would have laughed if the bolts holding the wall up didn't suddenly pull out from their supports, bringing the wall's slow controlled descent to a sudden loud collapse.

"Gah!" I yelled as the floor rushed up to greet me.

And then everything went dark.

Twenty minutes later I was sitting in Sexbar's office with an icepack on my forehead and Freddy at my side. I had only lost consciousness for a moment, by which time Freddy had already run over.

"Somehow, when I heard the crashing and shouting, I knew you'd be in the middle of it," he offered by way of support.

I explained to the manager that I was making out with a guy in the room when he got a little rough and playfully pushed me against the wall. "After that, I don't know *what* happened," I told him.

"That must have been some push," the manager said.

"Well, I like 'em big," I said.

The manager, pleased that I wasn't going to sue them for a hazardous condition, wasn't interested in pursuing the matter any further. He left me and Freddy to talk, telling me to take all the time I needed.

"Let me guess, Mr. I'm-So-In-Love-with-Tony," Freddy said, the moment the manager left. "There was no guy who pushed you against the wall, was there? I bet you . . . climbed up the wall to get a look at the guys in the next cubby!"

I touched my finger to my nose. "Got it in one."

"Damn," Freddy sighed, "they must have been *hot* if you were scaling walls to see them!"

"It wasn't like that." I explained about the shoes, which I recognized from the reading of Allen's will.

"I told you he seemed a little light in the loafers," Freddy said.

"Actually, they were Oxfords."

"You know what I mean. I guess this makes both brothers suspects."

"Both?" I asked. "Why? We know that Michael hates gay people and his father was gay. It makes sense that he'd want Allen dead.

But Paul turns out to be gay himself—well, at least we know he has sex with men. What's his motive?"

"Paul has a secret," Freddy leaned in. "Sometimes, people with secrets will do anything to keep them. Maybe daddy found out about him and threatened to tell his wife. Or his brother."

"Allen wouldn't do that."

"No, probably not. Try this: Paul is gay but he hates himself for it. Marries a woman, talks homophobic shit, the whole works. When all he really wants is to take it up the butt . . ."

"You make it sound so lovely."

"Yeah, yeah. So, when he thinks of his father, it makes him mad. He sees in his father all the parts of himself he wishes he could . . . wait for it . . . throw over the railing. But, he decides to throw his father over, instead."

I thought about it for a moment. "Possible."

"Paul sounds like one of those poor slobs who went to his brother's seminar," Freddy observed. "Only for him, 'the cure' didn't take."

"It doesn't take for most of them," I told him. "It makes them shameful and self-hating, but you can only keep your true nature suppressed for so long."

"How's your head?" Freddy pushed back my bangs.

"Not too bad," I said. "How does it look?"

"A little black and blue, but your hair mostly covers it. Here, let me give it a little kiss."

Freddy leaned over, rested his hands on my thighs, and put his incredibly hot and soft lips against my forehead. Even though I'd done nothing but have sex all day, I still got a little turned on remembering how good those lips had once made certain parts of my anatomy feel.

But those days with Freddy were past, and now I was with Tony.

Wasn't I?

Freddy leaned back. "Better?"

I stood up. No dizziness, no nausea. "I think I'm fine."

"OK, but why don't I cab it home with you and make sure you get there safe and sound?"

"You're the best," I said. "Thanks."

CHAPTER 18

A Dangerous Date

I DIDN'T GET home until after 2:00 A.M. I must have been exhausted because I slept though my mother's departure for work. A phone call woke me at 9:30.

Caller ID told me it was Mrs. Cherry. "My darling," she said when I picked up. "How is my most delicious boy?"

"Tired," I told her.

"You sound it, dearest. Are you still in bed?"

"Actually, on the couch," I said.

"Are you sleeping nude, pet? Or wearing tighty-whitey's? Or are you letting it all hang loose in boxers and no shirt, or maybe . . . oh, I mustn't, or your dear Auntie Cherry will become too, too aroused!"

I smiled at her flirting. "You know I charge for a phone session," I told her. "What's up?"

"My angel, I was wondering if you might be available for a little morning thing. An out-of-towner from Boston. You were recommended by name."

I was so tired, but I opened up my calendar and saw the day was open. "I don't know. What's he looking for?"

"You're gonna love this . . . he just wants you to wear a bathing suit while he smells your wet hair. That's it! Although he might be doing unspeakable things to himself during the process, it's not a bad way to make a buck. If you're up for it."

Truth was, it was about all I was up to today. Other than the guy who wanted to play "salesman," it was probably the easiest money I'd earn all week.

"Fine," I said, "where and when?"

She told me the guy's first name and where to meet him. I told her to let him know I could be there at 11:00.

Seconds after I hung up with Mrs. Cherry, the phone rang again. This time, the caller ID made me happy.

"Good morning," I said.

"Hey you," Tony answered. "You got a minute?"

"More than that. I'm still in bed. Well, the couch. You know what I mean."

"You are? Lucky dog."

"Yeah, and it's nice and cozy in here. A little lonely, though."

"Mmmm . . . what are you wearing?" Tony whispered

I'd only been awake ten minutes. Was I going to keep having the same conversation all day?

Of course, this one could take a different direction.

"My favorite underwear. Black boxer briefs with a nice pouch. They're really comfortable, especially when I get, well, you know. They're not too tight, so there's room to grow."

"Uh-huh," Tony said quietly. "Go on."

"And I love the way they hug my ass. The material's really smooth, so it feels good when I rub my hand over it. Mmmm . . . that's nice."

"Shit."

"I'm rubbing my belly now, right by the waistband of my shorts. It feels really nice. I wish this were your hand, rubbing me, touching me. Want me to put my hand lower?"

Tony said something I couldn't hear.

"What's that?"

"Yeah," Tony whispered.

"OK, I'm slipping my hand under the waistband. Just touching the top of my pubes. Rubbing my hand in little circles above my—hey, why are you whispering? Are you at work?"

"Yeah. Keep talking."

"You want me to talk dirty to you while you're at your desk?"

Tony growled. "Yeah."

"At police headquarters?"

"Yeah."

"Do me a favor," I said.

"What?"

"Stand up."

Tony laughed. "I don't think so."

"Why not?" I teased.

"Let's just say I don't carry a Billy club in my pants, so that excuse wouldn't work."

This time it was my turn to laugh. "I miss your Billy club," I said.

"That's what I was calling about. How about I drop by later?"

"How about now?" I asked. Then, I remembered the appointment I'd just made with Mrs. Cherry. "Scratch that. How about you come around one? My mom will still be at work."

Boy, did saying that make me feel like a teenager again. Then again, so did being with Tony.

"You got it. Now, go back to what you were telling me before."

I checked the clock. I was going to have to hustle, pardon the expression, to make my meeting on time.

"I'll save it till I can show you."

"You better."

"I will and—oh!" I said, remembering, "I have to tell you who I saw at Sexbar last night!"

"Who?"

"I'll save that too," I said. "See you at one."

I took a quick shower, shaved everything that needed shaving, and washed down my medication with a protein shake. My client was a businessman staying at a nice hotel, so I got dressed in chinos and a white button-down shirt. I was just ready to leave my apartment when I remembered my client's special request.

"Shit!" I rummaged through my drawers until I found an old blue Speedo. I took off the chinos, replaced my underwear with the bathing suit, and put the pants back on. I was just about to put on my shoes when I heard my instant messenger chime.

I looked at the computer screen and saw an IM from Marc Wilgus. "U there?"

I ran over to the computer. "Just heading out."

"Got the results of the data mining program I was telling u about," Marc typed back.

I looked at the clock. "I wanna hear it, but I gotta run. I'll call you later."

"K" Marc signed off.

I arrived at 11:00 at The Astor, the same hotel where I'd been working the night of Allen's death. I tried not to take that as a bad sign.

I checked my iPhone. I was going to room 813. I avoided the front desk. Nosy desk clerks sometimes enjoyed making me as uncomfortable as possible. Occupational hazard.

I took the elevator to the eighth floor. I knocked on the door of 813, but there was no answer. Strange. Usually, my clients wait anxiously by the door.

I knocked again. This time, the door swung open.

I stepped inside."Hello," I called out. "Hello!"

No answer. Weird. I was just about to look in the bedroom when I was grabbed from behind. "What the . . ." I started to say, and then a hand gloved in smooth leather was covering my mouth. One finger slid briefly into my mouth before I closed it. It tasted like a new car smells.

My first reaction was to panic and start screaming. But I'd taken enough self-defense classes to know that was exactly the wrong thing to do.

Focus Kevin, focus.

What do you know?

I could tell the guy was big, at least bigger than me. The chest against which he was holding me felt muscular. His arms were thick, too. He was strong enough to hold both my arms with one of his.

A weird client on an S&M kick. He wasn't the first one I've come across, but he was the most aggressive.

Thing was, there was no way to know how this was going to go down. He might just be playing with me, or he might be genuinely dangerous.

Unfortunately, with his hand over my mouth, I wasn't in a position to inquire.

Sorry, but there was no time to be subtle. If he was just playing, this wasn't going to earn me much of a tip, but I couldn't take the chance.

When your opponent is anticipating a right, my Krav Maga teacher used to say, throw a left. With that in mind, I let my body go limp, as if I fainted.

My client, expecting me to struggle, loosened his grip. That was all I needed.

I drove my elbows back with all my might. Hit him right in the solar plexus.

"Ooof," he exhaled. Thinking that I was trying to push away, he took his hand off my mouth so that he could hold me with both arms.

Big mistake. In Krav Maga, we learn to hit with the hardest parts of our bodies. That's why I led with my elbows. Now that my head was free, I had another weapon. I screamed, "Ah-yah!" threw my head back, and hit him on the chin.

A skull is very hard.

That sent him stepping backwards, giving me enough room to slip out of his grasp.

I spun around to confront him, ready to use another hard body part, my knee, where it would do the most good. We little guys fight dirty.

But by the time I pivoted, he was ready, too. He threw a punch that connected with my cheek. The pain was blinding. I tasted coppery blood in my mouth.

I stumbled back and got my first look at him. It was all going down so fast, I couldn't take in much detail, except for the fact that he was wearing all black, including a black leather slave hood that had zippers over the eyes and the mouth.

The zippers over the eyes were open, but the zipper over his mouth was closed.

OK, I thought, this guy is weirder than I thought.

He advanced again, and I stepped back. He was big enough that I didn't have a chance if he got too close. Unfortunately, he was blocking the door, and if I ran further into the room, he'd have me cornered.

He reached into his pocket and pulled out a knife. OK, he was now officially the world's worst client.

"Don fuffin moo," he said, his voice muffled by the mask.

I cocked my head. "What?" I asked .

"Doan fuffin moof!"

"I don't understand what you're . . ." oh wait, I got it! "Don't fucking move?"

"Rie!" he answered.

If I weren't so creeped out, it'd be laughable.

But this was no laughing matter. That punch he gave me hurt. And now he had a knife.

"Hey," I said to him, "if this is just a joke, or some freaky SM thing, you better let me know right now."

This time, the muffled sound that came from his mask was laughter. He started to head towards me.

Time for the oldest trick in the book.

"Fire!" I screamed at the top of my lungs. "There's a fire in here!"

The Masked Marvel turned around to look at the door. I knew he was trying to remember: In his haste to grab me, had he remembered to close it?

He had. But in the moment he turned away, I had time to reach into my pocket, too. When he turned back to face me, I took a step closer and raised my arm.

A stream of Mace squirted from the small canister I always carried with me and hit him in the face. Told you we little guys fight dirty.

He jumped back quickly. I imagined the mask he was wearing protected him from the worst of it, but enough got into his eyes to get his attention.

"Fuffer," he said through his mask. Then he turned and ran out of the room. By the time I followed him into the hallway, he had disappeared down the stairs.

I went back to the room, and, after deadbolting the door, sank down to the floor, exhausted. Now that the emergency was over, all the adrenaline drained from my body. A wave of nausea passed over me.

I also really, really needed to pee.

I used the bathroom and checked myself out in the mirror. Yup, there was a nice dark bruise along my cheekbone. By tomorrow, I might have a black eye. I spit into the sink. Traces of blood, but not too bad.

I looked around the room. Although Mrs. Cherry told me the client was from out of town, you'd never know it from the hotel room. There were no bags, no clothing, no personal belongings at all.

The client wasn't staying at that hotel.

What to do next? I could call hotel security and tell them . . . what? That I was a hustler whose trick had just gone mad? I'd probably be the one who got arrested.

Instead, I called Mrs. Cherry. I told her what happened.

"My poor, poor, darling. He sounded so nice on the phone."

I asked her for his full name: Albert Foley. It sounded familiar, but I wasn't sure from where.

"Are you all right?" Mrs. Cherry asked. "Do you need me to come get you?"

"No, I'm fine. But you're going to have to cancel my appointments for the next few days. I got a nasty black and blue on my face."

"Do you want Auntie Cherry to kiss it all better?"

I demurred.

"Darling, I want you to know this is entirely my fault. I should be checking out your clients better than this. But when he said you came recommended by Allen Harrington, I thought he was safe."

Thanks a lot, Allen.

"No problem," I said.

"Now listen, my dove, I insist on paying you for the next few days. Think of it as sick time. I'll send a messenger over with some cash when you're feeling better."

"OK," I said. Well, at least I'd have some time off.

"And, darling, I hate to be indelicate, but you have to know that you can't be in the business I'm in without dealing with some, let's just say, questionable partners. Now, it's nothing you need to know about, but rest assured that I *will* be following up with Mr. Foley."

"Thanks," I said. "I'll call you when I'm presentable again."

I had some time to kill, and a lot of nervous energy to burn off, so I decided to walk for awhile before hailing a cab home.

I supposed I was lucky that after a few years of hustling, this was the worst I had to show for it. But maybe it was a sign. With the money from Allen's will, I didn't have to do this anymore. I could go back to school and live off his bequest until I graduated.

Besides, I thought, I didn't think Tony would approve.

But then again, who was he to judge? He was *married*, for Christ's sake. If I could overlook that, surely, he could accept my *job*.

Tony. I'd be seeing him again in less than an hour. My body flushed with pleasure and I got a stupid grin on my face.

And, in the pit of my stomach, the wonderful/terrible squishy feeling that meant I was in deep.

But something still bothered me. *Albert Foley*. Why did that name seem so familiar? I had a feeling that it was important I remembered.

I thought about the names I had heard or said recently. Had I read it somewhere? Saw it on television? Was it someone I met?

Focus, Kevin, focus.

Then, it came to me.

It was a name I read to Marc Wilgus..

I pulled the list Tony gave me from my wallet.

There it was: Albert Foley.

He committed suicide two weeks ago.

Suddenly, I didn't feel very safe at all anymore. The squishy feeling in my stomach was replaced by the dull ache of anxiety.

Assuming Albert hadn't resurrected himself to bash me, someone was setting me up. Someone who felt free to use Albert's name, which meant he probably knew Albert was dead. He used Allen's name, too.

Was there a connection after all?

But who would want to see me hurt . . . or worse? Was it Michael

Harrington? The guy in the hotel room looked to be about his size, but it all happened so fast, it was hard to say.

Michael knew I had gone by his business to snoop him out. He seemed like he wanted to hurt me the other night. Plus, he really hated gay people.

But he didn't seem like the type to wear a slave mask.

Then there was the younger brother, Paul. What was it Freddy said?

"Sometimes, people with secrets are willing to kill to protect them."

Would Paul kill to keep *his* secret safe? It seemed suspiciously coincidental that I had just seen him at a sex club last night.

Of course, I didn't know that the guy in the hotel room wanted to kill me. He might have just been sending me a message: Back off.

As if.

Everything had gone down so quickly I couldn't tell if the guy was closer in size to Michael or Paul. Or it could have been neither of them. Maybe it was someone they hired to rough me up. Maybe like Mrs. Cherry, the Harrington brothers knew some "questionable" people.

How come everyone seemed to have criminal friends except for me?

Then I realized that, given my profession, I *was* a criminal.

I really needed to rethink my life. Which, given the fact that I just chased off a knife-wielding assailant, wasn't looking too long.

It might be time to get some help.

When I arrived at my building, Tony was once again standing outside. He looked so good that I forgot how bad I must have looked, until I saw his look of concern.

"What happened?" he asked, reaching out to gently touch my swollen cheek. "Are you OK?"

"I'm fine," I said. "It's a long story."

"Did you get mugged? Did you call it in?"

"No and no. Come upstairs and I'll tell you."

As soon as we got into my apartment, I gave Tony a nice, long kiss. He tried to push me away.

"Kevin, I'm serious. Tell me what happened. What can I do?"

"Two more minutes of this, just to flush the bad stuff away," I said. "Then, I'll tell you everything."

After a while, I felt his body start to respond. His breathing quickened, his hands moved down to my ass, cupping, kneading. Then he pushed me away again.

"That's it," he said sternly. "Sit. Talk."

So I did.

I wanted Tony to reach his own conclusions, so I started with the visit Freddy and I paid to Michael Harrington at The Center for Creative Empowerment Therapy. Then I told him about running into Paul at Sexbar.

"So, you hurt your cheek when the wall fell down?" Paul asked, pulling me closer on the couch to him. "Poor baby." He kissed my neck. I cuddled closer.

Then he smacked me on the head. "But what are you playing at? I told you, all the evidence points towards your friend's death being a suicide. Putting yourself in front of Michael like that was dangerous."

"If he didn't have anything to do with Allen's death," I asked, "why was it dangerous?"

"Because he sounds *crazy*," Tony said. "They all do!"

"That's my point exactly. With that many nuts running around, one of them's bound to be a killer."

"This is New York City!" Tony yelled. "Half the fucking population belongs in a straightjacket."

"There's more," I said.

"What more could there be?"
"I think someone might be trying to kill me."
"You haven't told me everything, have you?"
"Not yet." I sat up. "Here comes the hard part."

CHAPTER 19

Everything Falls Apart

WELL, I THOUGHT, an hour later, sitting alone in my apartment, that could have gone better.

There was no way to explain what had happened this morning without telling Tony why I had gone to that hotel room. Which meant I had to tell him how I made a living. So, I started with that.

"I don't understand," Tony said. "What do you mean you 'hustle?' You mean drugs?" He looked appalled.

"No," I said, "of course not! I mean, I date guys for money."

"You're a prossy?"

"Not exactly. More like an escort."

Tony stood up from the couch where we both had been sitting. "Let me get this straight. You have sex with guys for money?"

"I wouldn't call it sex. It's fooling around. It's nothing. One guy likes to spank me." I watched the color drain from Tony's face. "But very, very gently. Another just wants to measure my inseam. Then there's the guy who wants me to wrap him up in cellophane and . . ."

"Wait!" Tony put his hand up. "I have to sit down." He plopped down on the couch again.

"You mean, you never have sex with these guys?"

"Well, maybe sometimes, but it's not really 'sex.' It's just business."

Tony's eyes narrowed. "I can't believe I was starting to . . . what *happened* to you?"

"Nothing 'happened,'" I said. "I found out that I could get five hundred dollars for squeezing some guy's crotch in a fancy restaurant. Plus, I get a nice dinner! I told you, it's no big deal!"

"I just . . ." Tony was at a loss for words. He put his head in his hands.

I slid over and put an arm around him. "It doesn't mean anything. It has nothing to do with this. With you."

Tony pushed me away, angrily. "Don't touch me!"

"Tony . . ."

"No, I'm serious; I can't believe you're a prostitute! I arrest people like you!"

Now he was pissing me off. OK, maybe I had an unconventional line of work, but no one got hurt. Well, not until today.

"And I get paid by people like you!" I answered.

"What 'people like me?'"

"Supposedly straight guys who marry a woman and then screw around with boys on the side!"

"Oh, that's just great." Tony threw his arms in the air.

"Listen, I'm just saying that I don't judge the choices you've made for your life. I don't understand why you're judging mine."

"Because what you're doing is *illegal*!"

"There are places where *any* sex between two men is illegal. Does that make it wrong?"

"You know this is different," Tony hissed.

"I don't do anything that injures anyone," I said. "I probably save more marriages than I hurt."

"Great! You're Doctor Fucking Phil of the Whores!"

That was it. "Fuck you," I said. "I don't have to defend myself to you."

"No," Tony said, looking at me with contempt, "save your defense for when you go to court."

He got up and headed to the door.

"Here's a news flash." I shouted. "Things get tough and Tony Rinaldi gets going. Are you going to walk out on me again?"

Tony's stare was ice. "I never should have walked back in. This was a mistake."

As angry as I was, sadness started to seep in. There he was, at another doorway that was about to separate us again.

This time, I figured, for the last time.

How beautiful he looked standing there, nostrils flaring, eyes narrowed, his body tense and ready for action.

My eyes welled with tears.

"Wait," I said. "What if you don't leave right now? What if we just sit here for a minute?"

Tony looked like he wanted to hit me. But kind of like he wanted to kiss me, too. "A minute's not going to change anything, Kevin."

I tried to smile but my lips were trembling. "Five minutes, then."

Tony's expression didn't waver, but I thought I saw a trace of sorrow in his eyes.

"This isn't going to work, Kevin. I'm a cop, for Christ's sake! What you're doing is dangerous and wrong."

"I'm bringing some joy into people's lives," I said. "How is that wrong? We're all consenting adults."

"Well, maybe I don't want to be with someone who would consent to something like that."

What could I say? "Maybe you don't."

Tony sighed and his shoulders relaxed. "I'm sorry, Kevin. This just isn't something I can wrap my head around. It . . . disgusts me."

Now a tear did drop down my face. "I disgust you?"

"Yes. No. I don't know, Kevin. I just . . . what we did yesterday, was that just business to you, too?"

I felt like yelling but could only croak. "No, Tony, no." I reached a hand out to his face. "Tony, my whole life, no one else has ever touched me here." I put my hand on my heart.

Tony brushed the tear from my cheek with his thumb. "But a lot of people have touched you everywhere else, though. Right?"

His gesture was kind but his words were cruel.

Was that how it was always going to be with Tony? Was he always going to be coming and going? Straight but gay? Loving yet hurtful?

After Tony dumped me, I spent seven years closing off my heart. Yet, when he came back into my life, I was only too ready to reopen it for him.

Maybe I was right the first time.

There's this heartbreaking scene in *The Prince of Tides* where Barbra encounters Nick Nolte after he's made the decision to dump her and return to his wife. Even though she sees him from across the street, she takes one look at him and realizes that he's lost to her. She breaks into tears and they share a final embrace.

She doesn't beg, she doesn't plead.

She lets him go.

Let's see if I could be as classy as she was.

I threw my arms around Tony and squeezed him tight. He didn't hug back, but he didn't pull away, either.

I wished he didn't feel so fucking good, but there you have it.

I released him and opened the door. He looked surprised.

No more talking. The door is open, Tony. What are you going to do?

He looked at me unblinkingly for one long moment. I saw every kind of regret in his eyes.

His lips parted. I thought he was going to kiss me.

He walked out.

I closed the door, slid down to the floor, and cried myself hoarse.

After I got that out of my system, I took a long shower, put on some clean clothing, and pressed some ice against my cheek.

Truth was, my relationship with Tony died a hundred years ago. He was right. We never should have gotten back together. It was a mistake.

You can't raise the dead.

You shouldn't love the dead, either.

Tony was dead to me.

So was Allen.

Was that my problem? That I couldn't let go?

If the police didn't think Allen was murdered, maybe I should just accept it and move on.

After all, what was the point of pursuing Allen's death? It had gotten me beaten up in a hotel room and cost me my one chance to reunite with the man who was probably the great love of my life.

That's it, I decided, I'm through with Tony *and* with the Harringtons.

It was time to let the dead stay dead.

The phone rang. *Tony*? I thought, hating myself for wishing it was.

But Caller ID told me it was another man who had been on my mind.

Paul Harrington was calling me.

CHAPTER 20

The Shocking Secrets of the Harrington Boys

"**TELL ME AGAIN** what you want me to do," Freddy asked when I called him one minute after I finished talking with Paul.

"Just be at the bar where I'm going to meet Paul and sit in the back. I don't want him to see you. Then just . . . watch. Just to make sure he doesn't try anything funny."

"Honey, I've seen Paul Harrington," Freddy said. "The only funny thing he'd try would be to give you a handjob under the table."

"No, I think one of the Harrington boys might want to have me hurt."

"Just because Michael looked like he wanted to eat you alive the other night? And I mean, like Hannibal Lecter wanted to eat Clarice," Freddy clarified.

"No," I answered. I told Freddy what happened at the hotel.

"What!" Freddy said. "Are you shitting me?"

"I wish I were."

"Have you told your cop boyfriend about it?"

"I was about to, but then he dumped me." I explained what just went down between me and Tony.

"Poor baby," Freddy said. "Honey, I'm so sorry."

Freddy loved me, but to tell you the truth, he didn't sound *that* sorry.

"Thanks, but I really don't want to focus on that right now. The point is, we're not going to get any help from him."

"Doesn't sound like. But why are you meeting Paul?"

"I don't know," I answered truthfully. "I guess I'm curious. He said he wanted to talk to me but he wouldn't say why. I was just about to give up on the Harringtons when he called. Maybe it's a sign."

"'Wet floor' is a sign, too, angel. One you're supposed to *avoid.* Like the Harringtons."

"I know, but if I don't do this, I'll just spend the rest of my life looking over my shoulder. Let me see what he has to say. I'll let him know that the warning I got today worked and that I'm backing off."

"Are you?"

"I was half an hour ago. Now, I don't know. Will you help me?"

"Honey," Freddy asked, "what are you, meshuggana? Of course I'll be there. But listen—how about you call me on your cell and leave it on the table while you and Paul talk. That way, I can listen, too."

"You're a genius," I told him. "Thanks, Freddy."

For our meeting, Paul picked a bar well known as a place where married men of means could meet in a dark and discrete setting. From its mahogany bar to its twenty dollar martinis, live piano player, and subdued track lighting, Intermission reeked of money and good taste.

Of course, the men who came here were rarely interested in meeting each other. The bar was filled with hustlers of the highest order, young men with gym toned bodies, fake tans, and higher educations. Anyone of lesser quality would be ignored or evicted by the imposing bouncer who sat by the door as imposing and immobile as a Rodin.

I knew boys who worked Intermission. They usually did very well. The clientele was well-off and conducted themselves as gentlemen. I avoided it because it sounded like a meat rack, albeit one with leather seating and stunningly handsome bartenders.

"I figured I'd pick a place you were used to frequenting," Paul

Harrington said, in lieu of "hello," as I settled myself into the booth he had chosen, as far back and as dark as it was possible to find.

"Actually, I've never been here before," I said. "How about you?"

"Not really."

Just then, a waiter who could have been cast as "handsome college student #2" in a soap opera came to our table.

"Good to see you again, sir," he said to Paul in a deep baritone. "The usual?"

While Paul cringed and ordered, I took my cell phone from my pocket, discretely pressed the speed dial number for Freddy, and put it face down on the table. I saw him at the bar, with his back to us, and his Bluetooth headset firmly planted in his ear. He pressed the "answer" button and nodded. I knew he could hear our conversation. Good.

Studly McWaiter turned to me. "And you, sir?" His voice was respectful, but the look he gave me was condescending.

I ordered a bottled water.

"Very good then." He turned away, revealing an ass as perfect as the rest of him.

Please Freddy, I thought, don't get too distracted tonight.

Paul put his hands on the table. "If you don't mind, I'll be direct."

"I'd appreciate it," I said.

"How much?"

Huh? Was this a math problem that I missed the first half of? "How much what?"

"I thought we were going to be direct with each other," Paul said. "How much do you want?"

Paul looked very handsome tonight in his expensive suit and expertly knotted tie. His light brown hair was swept back in a slickly plastered down helmet not seen since the movie *Wall Street*, but it looked good on him. He might not have the expansively muscular build of his brother, but his shoulders were wide and his chest was broad.

His light blue eyes were very attractive, but I thought I saw a little redness there, too.

Had he been working late nights? Crying? Or was there still a little Mace left in them?

There was no way to know—at least not yet. I had to admit, though, Paul Harrington was a man who got better looking the more you saw him. I could totally see how he hooked up with that hot guy at Sexbar.

But still, ewwww. The fact that he wanted to have sex with me when he thought I had slept with his father was just totally icky.

"This bar is full of boys you can hire, Paul. I'm not one of them."

"I'm not talking about *that*," Paul grimaced. "I'm talking about buying your silence."

"My silence?"

"Look, you caught me in a very compromising position," Paul said. "I assume you're planning on using that information against me. Just as you used my father to get what you wanted."

"Paul, I didn't 'use' your father. We were friends. And I'm not going to blackmail you, if that's what you're worried about."

"Let's not use the word 'blackmail,'" Paul said. "Let's just say I'd like to reward your discretion."

The waiter brought our drinks over.

I picked up my bottle. "OK then, how about the drinks are on you? There, you've bought my silence."

Paul looked at me with disbelief. "That's it?"

"I don't know who or what you think I am," I said, "but I'm not a scam artist and I'm not interested in causing you any trouble. I loved your father too much to hurt his children."

"You loved my father?"

"Of course, I loved your father. He was a great man."

Paul's carefully composed expression of skepticism collapsed. He looked suddenly stricken, as if a great pain had descended upon him. "I loved him, too, you know. I just never . . . never . . . ."

He let out a great sob, then immediately brought his hands to his mouth to contain the noise. He wept silently into them.

Two minutes ago, Paul was a cocky son of bitch who was trying to buy me off. Now, he was a sobbing mess. People who have mood swings like that always make me nervous. Was he mentally ill?

Paul took a silk handkerchief from his pocket, squinted hard, and wiped his face. He took a few deep breaths and continued.

"Do you know how long it's been since I told my own father that I loved him? That's why I was going there that night."

Randy told me Allen was meeting one of his sons the night of his death. Now, I knew it was Paul. Another mystery solved. I was good at this detective stuff!

Out of the corner of my eye, I saw Freddy giving me a thumbs up.

"I've made so many mistakes," Paul said quietly. "My own father." He blinked away more tears.

"Allen told me you hadn't talked in years," I said.

"It's true. But you have to understand what my mother did to me and Michael. She blamed my father bitterly for leaving us. She made it clear we'd be betraying her if we didn't feel that way, too.

"She always told us that the life he'd 'chosen' was destructive and sick. That he picked it over his own children. What we didn't know was that he was reaching out to us all during our childhood, but my mother wouldn't let him near us. It wasn't his homosexuality that wrecked my family, it was her hostility.

"By the time Michael and I were old enough to make our own decisions about contact with our father, we had been brainwashed into seeing him as the enemy. We were just kids, we didn't know any better.

"She forced us to choose between them, and we chose her."

I nodded. "But it must have been especially hard for you," I said, "what with, you know, liking guys and all."

Paul reached across the table and grabbed my hands. "You *do* understand," he said. "It was hell. I was so confused, my whole life. I knew what I wanted, what I *was*, but it was the very thing I had been taught ruined my family's lives. That it was shameful and sick and wrong.

"I hated myself for so long." More tears rolled down his cheek. He took his hands from mine and wiped his eyes.

I felt a lump in my throat, too. Even if he were nuts, I felt his pain.

"Is that why your brother does what he does?" I asked. "This whole thing he has about making gay people straight?"

"Michael's a very complicated man," Paul said. "But yes, I'm sure that's a part of it."

"Complicated how?" I asked him.

Paul shuddered. "I don't want to get into that right now."

I tried a different track. "You were going to see your father the night of his death?"

"Yes," Paul said. "I was going to tell him about myself. I was going to ask him to forgive me for all those years of neglect. I wanted to explain things."

"What happened?"

"I'd thought of calling my father for years. I never had the courage or the strength. But I started therapy recently, and I was really starting to see things differently. My mother moved to Florida, and so I didn't have to hear her constant critiques of my father. And with Michael's work getting more demanding, I was seeing a lot less of him, too.

"Michael has a lot of influence over me. A lot of control, you might say."

Again, he gave a little shudder. There was something going on between him and Michael that troubled him.

Or scared him.

"I finally called him the evening of his death. It was so hard. But the moment he heard it was me, I couldn't believe how easy it was to talk to him. How kind he was, how forgiving. I told him how sorry I was, what an idiot I had been, but he wouldn't even hear it. He said I was his son and always would be."

Paul stopped for a moment to compose himself.

"He told me to come right over. I got there as soon as I could. But when I arrived, I saw the body on the ground. I stopped for a moment like the rest of the crowd did. Typical NY rubbernecking. I didn't know who it was. Not until you arrived. What to hear something funny?"

I nodded.

"When I first saw you, I thought to myself 'what a cute kid. I wonder if I could bag him?' Of course, this was before I knew you were sleeping with my father."

"Listen," I said, "I never slept with your father."

Paul tilted his head in disbelief.

"OK, let me just clear this up once and for all." I told Paul the true story of how Allen and I met. I explained how we became friends. How I loved him like a father, not a lover. How I thought some of the attention and guidance he gave me was because he was denied the opportunity to give it to his own children.

Paul sighed. "That makes me so sad," he said. "But I see now that you gave him a lot of happiness." He took my hands again. "Thank you for being there when I was too stupid to be a good son."

"You were telling me about the night you went to meet your father."

"Right. When you said my father's name, that's when I knew it was him. I ran away and headed right over to Michael's house. I told him what happened and totally broke down.

"Michael called Alana, my wife, and she came over. They sat with me for hours. First, they told me that I should never have called my father. That he was an evil man and that I had brought this pain upon myself. Then, they told me this was our father's ultimate 'fuck you' to me. That he jumped knowing I was coming over, knowing that I'd see him, just to mess me up even further."

"And you believed them?"

"You have to understand, Michael has a way with me. Maybe he has it with a lot of people. When he says things, they just make sense. He's very persuasive."

I'd seen that for myself at The Center. He had that crowd in the palm of his hand. And later, in the hallway, he almost convinced me to go with him to his office, despite the fact that I was afraid of him.

"The things he told me were the things I had heard my entire life. He made me hate my father again. That's why I was so awful at the reading of his will. I thought he killed himself just to hurt me."

"Paul," I said gently, "I know you didn't know him, but I did. I don't believe that he killed himself. Not for a minute."

"I don't think so, either," Paul said. "I've been replaying our conversation in my head ever since that night. He was looking forward to seeing me. I *know* that. Why would he take his own life? Why then, of all times?"

"So, if he didn't kill himself, what *do* you think happened?" I was sure now that Michael was the killer, but I wanted Paul to be the one who said it.

"I don't know."

"You don't know?"

"Maybe it was an accident?"

"What kind of accident?"

Paul looked like the child he had been when his father left them. "I don't know," he whined. "Maybe he fell."

"Doing what? Practicing his balance beam on the ledge?"

"I don't know!" He banged his fist on the table, causing his gin and tonic to soak the cuff of his shirt. He didn't seem to notice.

Out of the corner of my eye, I saw Freddy turn around to face us. He started to get up from his stool.

"Everything's fine," I said to Paul, but really to Freddy, who I knew could hear us on his headset. Freddy nodded and turned back.

Tears came back to Paul's eyes. "It's not fine! Nothing's fine!"

I thought I'd give it another go. "Paul, what *do* you think happened to your father?"

"He killed him!" Paul's eyes were wide and bulging, the muscles in his neck strained.

"Who killed him?"

"I don't know." The whine was back.

"You said 'he.'"

"I meant 'whoever.' Maybe another guy he was seeing." He gestured around the room. "Or another hustler. I don't know."

"No, Paul. He didn't have anyone else over that night. He was waiting for you." I told him about what Randy Bostinick had said.

Paul's face crumpled. He really did look a child again. He bit his lip. "I don't know," he cried. "I don't know, I don't know, I don't know." He put his hands on his temples and rubbed furiously.

It was as if Paul was cycling through personalities before my eyes. Confident businessman, sorrowful son, petulant teenager, lost child.

But given everything he had gone through in the last few weeks, could I blame him? In a short time he had accepted his own sexual orientation, let go of the hate and anger he'd been indoctrinated with, finally reached out to his father, and then lost him—Paul Harrington had been through a lot of changes. I regretted that what I was going to say might push him further along the edge.

"Paul," I said gently. This time, I took his hands. He looked off into space with a steady fixed stare. "Paul. Look at me."

His head weighed a hundred pounds. He turned it slowly. His eyes met mine, but they were blank and unfocused.

"Paul: Do you think your brother could have killed your father?"

"Michael wouldn't hurt anyone." His voice had a hollow, robotic ring.

"Is that true?" I asked.

"Michael wouldn't hurt anyone." The exact same intonation.

"He hurt me, Paul." I pointed to the bruise on my face. Actually, I didn't know for sure that it had been Michael in the hotel room, but I had to break through Paul's withdrawal.

"Oh Lord," Paul pulled his hands from mine and buried his face in them. "He told me never again, never again."

"Never again?"

"Not another boy."

"Did he hurt another boy, Paul?"

"He hurt *me*!" This time, Paul was loud enough that several heads turned. He didn't notice.

"He *liked* hurting me," Paul continued. "Sometimes it would start as tickling, or wrestling, you know. He told me all brothers did it. But he'd always carry it too far. He'd make me cry, and then make me beg him to stop. The more I'd beg, the more excited he'd get."

"Excited?"

"Once I saw it," Paul whispered fiercely. "He was hard. He was hard from hurting me. I was so *ashamed*!"

"You didn't do anything to be ashamed of," I told him.

"I liked it!" he cried. "Don't you get it? He'd hurt me and I'd like it. I liked the closeness, how strong he was, that I was the one getting his attention. It was so fucking . . . sick!"

"You were kids," I said.

Paul winced. "It didn't stop until he went to college."

Oh.

"Did you have sex?" I asked him.

"No. It wasn't about sex. Well, not normal sex. It was about power. And I think Michael always knew I was gay and he was punishing me. And, God help me, I wanted to be punished."

We sat quietly for a moment. I didn't know what to say. I looked up to see Freddy once again looking at me.

"Holy shit!" he mouthed.

I wanted to know as much about Michael's psychology as I could. "Did you ever talk about it with him?"

Paul sat up a little straighter. He looked up at me again.

"When he came back for his summer home after his freshman year at college. He told me that he had taken psychology courses in school, and that it helped him understand that what we were doing was wrong. That my wanting to be hurt was a sickness, and that he should never have gone along with it. That he'd never hurt anyone again.

"He made it sound like it all happened because of me. But it was OK, he told me. It was all my father's fault. Of course I was neurotic. He said he could help me. We'd spend hours in my room. Just talking. He'd learned hypnosis from a professor of his, and he'd put me under. He told me he was freeing me from my self destructive patterns."

"He'd hypnotize you?"

Paul nodded.

"Did it work?"

"Did it make me straight? Did it make me stop wanting men? No. Did it make me hate myself for what I was feeling? Yes."

Paul's face was a portrait of anguish.

I leaned forward. "Paul, I'm so, so sorry that he did that to you. But he's doing it to other men, too. Every day. That's what his whole practice is about. He's using the same techniques he used on you to make hundreds of other men miserable."

Paul nodded. "I know."

"It's wrong."

"I know."

"Do you think he's still hypnotizing you?" I asked.

"No, we haven't done that for years."

"But you said he has a lot of control over you."

Paul was silent.

"A lot of influence." I reminded him of his own words.

Paul looked down at the table again.

"Are there ever occasions when you're with him and you can't remember what happened? Or there's missing time?"

Paul gave the tiniest nod. I would have missed it if I weren't looking so hard.

He didn't look up. He could have been talking to the table. He said, "And you know what? When that happens, when I think that I've just zoned out and I find him staring at me . . . the look on his face?

"It scares me."

"Holy mother of Christmas," Freddy said when I walked back into the bar after having made sure that Paul got safely into his cab. By the time we had finished talking, Paul was a wreck, and I didn't trust him to make it home in one piece.

"I know," I agreed.

"That story had everything in it but the bloodhounds snappin' at his rear end."

"I know."

Freddy peered into my eyes. "Are you OK?"

"I think I need to sit down." It had been a long day.

Freddy got off his stool and steered me into it.

"And maybe a drink."

Freddy handed me his beer. I downed it in seconds.

Freddy put his arms around me. The hug made me feel better than the beer had.

"That good?"

I nodded. "Thanks. You always seem to know what to do."

"That's what sisters are for," Freddy said.

"Let's go somewhere a little less creepy."

This being New York City, the nearest coffee house was eighteen steps away. We sat in comfortable chairs and had some kind of frozen blended coffee chocolate thing with whipped cream and caramel.

We both got the largest possible size.

"So, what do you think?" I asked him.

"I think my headset almost melted in my ear," he said. "That was a hot story."

"Freddy!"

"Well it was," Freddy said. "The hunky older guy who holds you down and tickles you until you can't catch your breath? Hello! You've seen that Michael Harrington—you got to admit you could do worse than being straddled by that stallion."

I shook my head. "That's gross. They were brothers."

"OK," Freddy admitted. "That part was kind of gross. But still, Michael Harrington. He's like Christian Bale in *American Psycho*. The yummiest sadist in town."

"Do you think he could have killed his father?"

"My guess? He's capable of anything."

"That's what I think, too."

Just then, a dead-sexy guy in running shorts and tank top came in to order something. Freddy looked at him like a vulture spies a particularly delectable carcass.

"Could you excuse me a second?" Freddy went to the counter right behind the guy. Somehow, he started a conversation with him. I heard them both laughing and I turned away.

Two minutes later, Freddy returned with a scone and the guy's card.

"What was that all about," I asked.

"The runner? An old friend of my mother. I was just sending her regards. But back to business: Why do you think Michael is still hypnotizing his brother?"

"It's all about domination. That's what he gets off on. His whole business, his whole life, is based on his fetish for control. Plus, when Paul's in a trance, who knows what Michael does to him?"

We sat for a moment. Just when I thought Freddy was going to make another allusion to *Charlie's Angels*, he surprised me.

"You want to talk about what happened with Tony?"

"Wow," I said. "Do you know that Paul's revelations were so shocking that I haven't thought about Tony all night? Well, not until you just brought him up, that is. Thanks."

"Sorry," Freddy said, looking concerned.

"Naw, it's all right. I think I'm fine. If there were more time to think about it, maybe I'd be more upset.

Freddy gave me one more sympathetic look. "So, let's not think about it," he said, brightly. "Tell me how you left things with Paul when you took him to the cab."

"Nowhere, really. I think he felt better after he got all that off his chest, though. He told me he was thinking of coming out to his wife and getting on with his life. He said he thinks that's what his father would have wanted. He sounded optimistic."

"So, maybe he'll have a happy ending after all. As opposed to just having a 'happy ending,' which I think you probably spoiled for him when you brought the walls of Jericho down on him at Sexbar."

"I suggested he avoid Michael for a while, though. That guy really does scare me."

"Let me ask you a question," Freddy said. "If Michael is doing crazy shit to his own brother when he's got him hypnotized, what do you think he's doing to his clients?"

I got a shiver. "I don't know," I answered truthfully.

"I bet it's nothing good," Freddy said.

"We have to stop him."

"I agree. But how?"

"I don't know," I said. "But I'm going to figure it out."

CHAPTER 21

Romeos at the Balcony

ON THE WAY home, I had the cab drop me off at the corner deli so I could grab some milk and a box of cookies. I figured if I were going to take a few days off, I could afford to gain a percent or two of body fat. Besides, I'd been beaten up and dumped today. I deserved to pig out.

Fuck it, I thought, standing in front of the Ben and Jerry's assortment in the freezer case. I might as well go whole hog.

I was trying to decide on which flavor of ice cream I wanted when my iPhone rang. I put the Bluetooth receiver in my ear and picked up.

"Hello," came the high, thin voice of Melvin Cuttlebeck. "We had a phone session scheduled for tonight?"

Melvin, my favorite wannabe S&M top. He was right. I had completely forgotten to put it in my calendar. Oh well, he finished so fast we'd probably be done before I choose my dessert.

"Yes sir," I said. "I'm ready."

"Thank you," he said. "I mean, 'good boy.'"

He proceeded to rattle off a fantasy about restraining and torturing me. Of course, his version of torture ran along the lines of "I'm spanking your bottom now (but don't worry, not too hard)," and "how would you like it if I gave you a really dirty look?"

Why couldn't all sadists be like Melvin? He's so sweet that he taught me how to escape his own bondage devices. He indulges his fantasies without really hurting anyone. Unlike a certain Harrington boy, I thought.

I left my microphone on mute, every once in a while coming back on to give Melvin an encouraging "oh yes, sir, spank this bad boy's tush," or "oh, thank you sir, that hurts so good."

I finally settled on *Cherry Garcia* and turned around to see the chubby but cute goateed young clerk was listening to my every word. He stared at me open-mouthed, his hands in his front pockets. I shrugged. He gave me a leering nod.

Sure enough, Melvin noisily reached his fulfillment within five minutes. "Thank you very much," he said formally. "Sometimes after we talk, I can go a whole day or two without feeling ill whenever I see my boss."

"Glad to help," I said. We disconnected.

"Wow," said the clerk as he rang up my junk food orgy. "That sounded like . . . something."

His forehead was beaded with sweat and his jeans made his excitement clear.

"It's a living," I answered.

"You into that stuff in real life?" he asked, looking at the bruise on my cheek.

"No," I said, hoping he'd give me my change really quickly.

He leaned over the counter and whispered, "I am." He pulled the collar of his shirt down to show me that he was wearing a dog collar. "Woof!"

I nodded appreciatively. "Good for you." I almost added, "Fido," but thought better of it.

"Maybe one day we could get together," he said.

I put my hand out for the change. He handed it to me, his fingers lingering in my palm for a second too long.

"I'm kind of seeing someone right now," I lied.

"Me, too," he said. "But I think my mistress would like you, too."

"Let me get back to you," I said, thinking, *doesn't anyone have straight sex anymore?*

I opened the door to my apartment, noticing that the lights and radio were on. "I'm home," I shouted.

My mother emerged from her—my!—bedroom. "Bubbie," she said, "how was your day?" Then she looked at my cheek and gasped, "What happened?"

"Oh," I said. "Would you believe a crazy man on the street just ran up to me and did that?" I took my wallet out of my pocket. "He didn't even want my money. Just hit me and ran off."

"Poor baby," my mother said, taking my shopping bag from me. "Oh, look—ice cream!"

She never did suffer from an overabundance of maternal concern.

"Oh," she said as we sat at the kitchen table eating ourselves into oblivion. "I think that bitch Dottie Kubacki had one of her friends call here tonight."

"What do you mean?" I mumbled though a mouthful of chocolate.

"I picked up the phone and this deep voice said, 'Tell the whore to stay away from us or someone's going to get hurt.' Can you imagine her calling me a 'whore' when she's the one fooling around with my husband? What a bitch."

I was pretty sure the call wasn't meant for her.

"It was probably just a wrong number," I told her. "Or a prank call. It doesn't sound like Dottie's style."

"The woman almost shot you to death!"

"Yeah, but to be honest, she didn't know it was me. And I was peeping into her window at the time."

"I still say that woman is capable of anything," my mother grumbled.

Just then, a crashing noise came from the window. We both turned to look.

Gunshots!

"Get down!" I shouted at my mother.

"What?"

I threw myself in her lap, knocking both of us to the floor. "Someone's shooting at us!" I cried.

Apparently, Michael Harrington wasn't going to be satisfied with a warning delivered by phone.

"Ow!" my mother screamed.

"Mom!" I would never forgive myself if my mother got hurt because of my involvement with the Harringtons.

"My hip!" she moaned. "Ow!"

Shit, she'd been shot!

I looked at her. "I'll call the cops," I told her. I was about to crawl to the phone when I looked at her again. "I don't see any blood."

"Of course there's no blood," she said, standing up. "You just almost broke my hip with that meshuggana move you pulled. Are you trying to kill me?"

"Get back down!" I shouted, pointing at the window where more bullets struck the glass. "Someone's shooting at us!"

"Those aren't gunshots," my mother said.

They weren't?

I listened again.

The sound was more of a tapping then a blasting.

Ooops. OK, maybe I did overreact. Had I taken my medicine today?

"Someone's throwing something at the window," she said. "Rocks or . . . pebbles. I haven't heard that sound since . . ."

Hip hurting or not, she ran to the window like a schoolgirl. She flung it open and we heard him outside: "Don't sit under the apple tree, with anyone else but me, anyone else but me, anyone else but me . . ."

My father's singing voice was legendarily bad, but my mother's face glowed as if she was listening to Sinatra.

I joined her at the window. My father was standing on the street in a white tuxedo and tails. He held a bouquet of blood red roses. A white limousine was parked on the street behind him, the driver holding the door open.

A small crowd gathered behind my father. More street theater. These are the moments New Yorkers live for.

"Rapunzel, Rapunzel, let down your golden hair," my father called.

My mother blushed and waved him away.

"Come on," a guy who looked like a construction worker (and was actually pretty hot) called out to her. "Give da guy a break."

"Come, fair lady, upon my glorious steed." My father gestured towards the limo.

My mother blushed and put her hands on her cheeks.

A fifty-something African-American woman shouted at us, "Honey, if you don't get your ass down here, I'm going with him!" The crowd laughed.

My mother turned to me. "What do I do?"

"Well," I said, "you could hop on the fire escape and climb down, but since you're wearing white slacks, I'd probably take the elevator."

"Should I forgive him?"

"I don't think you have anything to forgive him for, Mom. He never laid a finger on Dottie Kubacki and you know it."

My mother smiled wisely. "You see, what he's doing now? I think this is what I needed."

My father began singing again "Daisy, Daisy, give me your answer, do . . ."

My mother leaned out the window. "If I come down, will you promise to stop singing?"

The crowd laughed.

"You call this singing?" my father asked. More laughter.

"What I call it," my mother said, "is very sweet."

This time, the crowed "awwwed."

"I'll be right down!" my mother shouted and she skipped—actually skipped!—to the door. "I might not be back tonight!" she trilled to me.

"You better not be back!" I called back to her.

"I love you," she said.

"Love you too, Mom."

I watched for a minute as my mother emerged from the lobby door and ran into my father's arms. Given that she had at least thirty pounds on him, most of it in the bosom, I was surprised he didn't fall over.

The crowd cheered. So did I.

And not just because I had my apartment back.

My father watched as the limo driver guided her into the backseat. When he closed her door, my father turned to me. "Not bad for an old man, huh?"

"I'm proud of you Dad," I said, my eyes for some reason filling with tears. Must have been relief.

"Your old man, you have to admit, he's still got it," my father said. "Now, you won't miss her too much, will you?"

"I'll survive."

"You're a good boy. Thanks for looking after her."

"Thanks for taking her back!"

My father climbed into his seat and the limo took off. The crowd dispersed, except for Construction Guy who stayed looking at me. I looked back. I'd guess he was maybe twenty-eight or twenty-nine. Dark skin and dark eyes. Italian or Latino. Built like a tank.

"Hey," he said.

"Hi," I answered.

"Pretty crazy family you got dere." His accent was pure Brooklyn.

I laughed. "Yeah, well, they're the only one I have."

"So tell me, cutie," he yelled up. "Think I could get you to throw down your golden locks, too?"

It was tempting. God knows I deserved something fun after the day I had. "It's not a good time," I said.

He pointed to my cheek. "I can see that."

I chuckled. "Believe it or not, that's the least of my problems."

"Sounds like you could use a good massage." He winked, grinning at the obvious lasciviousness of his suggestion.

That sounded good. "Some other time?"

"Really?" he said. He grinned ear to ear. Damn, he was cute.

I realized I spent the past few years waiting for Tony or having sex for money.

It had been a long time since I dated an attractive boy just for the sake of a date.

"Sure," I said, reassuring him as much as me. "I'd like that."

"One second," he said. With a great leap, he jumped up and launched himself onto the railing of the fire escape. He pulled himself up to the first floor landing. "I'll be right dere."

Monkey-like, he climbed the metal structure, displaying a natural grace and limberness that belied his muscular build. In a minute, he was standing by my window.

"Hi," he said.

"Hi." Up close, he was a total snack. "That was pretty slick."

"Well." He cocked his head, "I'm a pretty slick guy."

"I'm Kevin," I said.

"Romeo," he put out his hand.

"You're kidding."

"What?"

"You just climbed onto my 'balcony' and your name is 'Romeo?'"

He shrugged. "That's what they called me. Romeo Raul Romero."

I bit my tongue. "That's quite a name."

"Yeah, my parents really had a hard-on for de letter R, huh?"

I smiled. "It's a very handsome name, Romeo. It fits you."

"Ya think?" He leaned in closer.

"Uh-huh." I leaned in a little, too.

Romeo planted one on my lips.

In the movie *Norma Rae,* Sally Fields is being pursued by an unattractive but intriguingly-Semitic liberal activist played by Ron Leibman. Just in case his every characteristic and frequent use of Yiddish wasn't enough to let you know he was Jewish, they saddled him with the name Reuben Warshowsky.

In any case, at one point Rueben expresses his sexual interest in her. She kisses him, explaining that if the kiss is good, the rest will follow.

If she was right, then Romeo was really, really good.

I know, it seems crazy that after the day I'd just had I'd be standing by my window under a full moon being kissed by a beautiful stranger who scaled my fire escape. But on the other hand, would I ever get a better excuse for acting a little crazy?

You know what they say: When God closes a door, he opens a window.

I just happened to be kissing a dark-skinned boy with biceps the size of my thighs through that window right now.

I pulled away. "That was nice."

Romeo raised his eyebrows. "It gets better."

"I bet. One second." I got a pad and pencil. "Can I have your number?"

He wrote it down for me.

"OK, Romeo," I said, "I have to crash."

"If you don't call," he warned, "I'm gonna be back out here in a white suit with flowers and a limo. And I'm gonna sing. If that's what it takes."

"How's your singing?"

"My kissing's better."

I smiled. "Next time. Maybe I'll even let you use the front door."

His face grew serious. He put his hand on my cheek. "Did a guy do this to you? Cause I'll fuck him up if you want me to."

"No." I told him the lie about the stranger on the street.

"A cute little guy like you needs some protection," Romeo told me. "I wouldn't mind looking out for you. If you wanted me to, dat is."

"I take pretty good care of myself," I said. "But I can always use a friend."

Romeo extended his hand. "Friends, then. At least to start."

"Friends." We shook hands.

"OK," I said, pushing him back. "I'll call you."

Romeo leapt up, grabbing a rung on the fire escape above me. He showed off with an effortless pull-up.

"I'll be waiting," he said. He dropped back down, and ran down the fire escape, jumping off the last landing and landing cat-like on the pavement.

"Good night, cute Kevin," he called.

I waved goodbye and closed the window.

I called Freddy and told him about my parents' reconciliation and my flirtation with Romeo.

"Wow," said Freddy. "That could be two times in one month you get laid without getting paid."

"Ha ha," I said, thinking that counting my last encounter with Marc Wilgus, it would actually be three.

"No, I think that's great. You have to wash that cop right out of your hair, darling. Ow! Watch the teeth!"

"I'm sorry?"

"Nothing, I was just saying that you've already gotten over Tony once. Just move on."

"That's exactly what I'm going to do," I said more confidently than I felt.

"That's my boy. I'm very proud of—hey, what did I tell you about those teeth?"

"Umm, do you by any chance have someone there?"

"The boy from the coffee shop tonight," Freddy said. "I think he's part vampire." I heard a muffled defense in the background.

"No, dear, those aren't 'love bites,'" Freddy said to his guest. "Love bites don't break the skin. And it's too hot to wear a turtleneck, so watch the hickeys, too. Mmm, that's better." To me: "So, what's your next move."

"Why don't we talk tomorrow?" I said. "I don't want to interrupt."

"Darling, don't be silly. You know you always come first." I heard the muffled voice again.

"Fine," Freddy said to his guest. "Yes, you did get to come first. Now, be a good boy and get me a glass of water and maybe I'll let you come third, too."

I heard Trick Boy walking away. "Is he any good?"

Freddy whispered, "Not bad. A little quick on the trigger, but I bet he's got a lot more left in him. What I don't understand is, if you finally got rid of your mother, why didn't you have Hamlet . . ."

"Romeo."

"Whatever. Why didn't you have Romeo in for some hot man on man action? Most guys have to spend a few hours on an Internet chat line to have a sexy construction worker show up at their window. And then he turns out to be a skinny accountant wearing brand new boots and a toy tool belt. As if that was going to fool me—I mean, someone. You had the real thing in the all-too-present flesh."

"I'm thinking of maybe going out on a date with him first."

"Kevin Connor on a date!" Freddy shouted. "Oy, hold on, I think the earth just started spinning in the opposite direction."

"Yeah, well, don't get too excited," I said. "I'm just thinking about it."

"Well, it's a good start. What about Michael Harrington? Any thoughts?"

"No, I'm waiting to hear from that computer guy I was telling you about, Marc Wilgus. Hey, wait a minute, he IMed me this morning on my way out the door. Let me call him."

"Go for it, Nancy Drew. Call me in the morning."

I called Marc. "Can you come over?" he asked. "I'd like to tell you in person what I found out."

I was incredibly tired. "Is it important?"

"Crucial."

"Sure," I said. "Give me twenty minutes."

Fifteen minutes later, the doorman let me in. I took the elevator to Marc's expansive penthouse apartment.

"Hey," he said, opening the door. Then, "what happened?" He touched my cheek, gently.

I went in and lied again about the stranger in the street.

"That's not true, is it?"

"What makes you say that?" I asked.

"Because I think you've gotten yourself involved in something very dangerous."

I told him about the guy in the hotel. "I thought it might be related to the Harringtons, but I didn't want to be paranoid."

"I don't think you can be too paranoid right now," he said. "Let me show you."

He brought me to his office. It was like walking into a super high-tech computer store. LCD screens hung from the walls and were perched on tables, where their displays were constantly flashing and updating. He took me to a large desk where three widescreen displays flanked an ergonomic keyboard. It was all very *Minority Report.*

"So, what do you run," I asked, trying to sound smart, "Windows or Mac?"

Marc looked at me as if I'd asked if he slept with sheep.

"I run my own operating system," he said. "Wrote it in high school."

"Natch."

Marc directed me to sit in the futuristic desk chair that seemed to mold itself to my body. He stood behind me, using a wireless mouse to run the computer.

"I ran that data mining program I told you about. It basically looked for connections between the information you gave me that other investigations may have missed. Look at this."

On the screen furthest to the left, he called up the list of gay suicide victims that Tony had given me.

"You know who these are, right?" he asked. I nodded.

On the right hand screen he brought up what looked like the internal databases of The Center for Creative Empowerment Therapy. He pulled up a file titled "Clientbase."

"You got into their system?" I asked.

"I've gotten into the Pentagon," Marc said. "This was nothing. Watch."

He pressed a button and the information from the two side screens seemed to melt and merge into the middle screen. In a few seconds, the names of the suicide victims were on the middle screen, flashing in red, with the word "match" listed next to each one.

"What does this mean?" I asked.

"All of the men who committed suicide were clients of Michael Harrington's."

Holy shit.

"So," I said, "not only doesn't his 'reparative' therapy work, but it drives his clients to kill themselves."

"It may be worse than that." Michael pressed more buttons. On the left screen a New York State Office of Taxation Web site popped up. Something about the Office of Probate. On the right, the financial records of The Center for Creative Empowerment Therapy appeared.

Again, the two side screens overlapped on the middle screen. When they were done, the same names were listed on the middle screen, but this time, for all but one of the men, the word "match" was replaced by numbers: 150,000; 75,000; 225,000; 50,000; etc.

"What are those numbers?" I asked?

"Bequests," Michael answered.

"To who?"

"To The Center for Creative Empowerment Therapy. Almost all of the men who killed themselves left sizable donations to the Center in their wills."

A wave of dizziness passed over me.

"He's killing them," I whispered.

"I thought they killed themselves," Marc said.

"Yes but no," I said. "I think he's directing them to do it. Think about it—his 'therapy' involves intensive hypnosis. It teaches his clients to hate their own sexuality. It makes them feel ashamed and sick.

"That might be enough to make some of them suicidal. Michael sees this. But if the client is sufficiently well off, and maybe if he's someone with no friends or family who are likely to ask too many questions, Michael doesn't do anything to help him. Instead, maybe Michael gives him hypnotic suggestions that he needs to provide more support for the Center. Maybe even provide for it after his death. Then, if the client offs himself, well, who's the wiser?

"Or maybe Michael even encourages the client to kill himself once he updates his will. Who knows how much control over his clients he has?"

Marc looked even paler than usual. "He's programming them."

"Yes."

Marc looked around the office. "But people aren't computers. You can't control them to that extent."

"Maybe he doesn't have to. Maybe he's tried it with fifty clients, but it's only worked with these. That would still be enough to put . . ." I scanned the list, "over a million dollars into his bank account."

Marc sat down. "Wow. This is heavy."

He wasn't used to the real world intruding on his virtual existence.

"Yeah," I said. "It is."

Marc said, "I could forward all this to the authorities. I could do it anonymously. When they see what he's doing . . ."

"It would mean nothing," I said. "There's no proof. Michael could make the case that of course some of his clients kill themselves—they come to him because they're unhappy to begin with, right? He gives them help and they gratefully provide for the Center in their wills. Sadly, despite his best efforts, they still wind up killing themselves. Who's to say otherwise?"

"So, let's send it to the press instead."

"Same problem. They're not going to risk a libel case based on coincidences."

Marc's eyes narrowed. "Then, let's take him down ourselves. I can do it, you know. Erase his bank accounts. Foreclose on his house. I could download so much child pornography onto his computer that he'd be in jail for the next hundred years."

Now, that was tempting. I knew there was a reason I liked Marc.

"I'd need to prove it to myself, first," I said. "I could be wrong."

"How can you prove it?"

"I don't know," I said. "Not yet."

Marc put his hands on my shoulders. "Don't do anything crazy. And don't go near him again."

"I won't," I said. "I'm kind of scared now."

"You should be." Marc stroked the back of my neck.

Marc's touch was just reassuring enough to make me think how truly over my head I was. I gave a little shiver and then couldn't stop. All of a sudden, my teeth were chattering and I felt as if the temperature had dropped a hundred degrees. I started to shake.

"Hey," Marc said, dropping to his knees, "hey."

He put his arms around me and held me through my mini anxiety attack. "It's going to be OK," he said, "nothing's going to hurt you."

"It feels safe here," I told him, warming in his embrace.

"I know," said Marc, "why do you think I never leave?"

My hero, the agoraphobe.

CHAPTER 22

Lights Out for Kevin

I SPENT THE night with Marc. We didn't have sex. He just held me and I feel into a sleep deep enough to pass for a coma. I woke to the sound of him padding around the kitchen. The smell of baked goods got me out of bed. It was 10:00.

I was still wearing my clothing from the day before.

I peed, washed up, put some of his toothpaste on my finger and ran it over my teeth, then joined him. This time, there was only one cup from Starbucks waiting for me. Chai tea. I thought it was nice he remembered.

However, the counter was also home to every kind of bagel, croissant, muffin, and Danish known to man.

"Let me guess," I said, "you didn't know what I wanted."

"I figured you'd like a choice," he admitted.

I picked up a croissant. "Sorry I wigged out on you last night."

"No problem." He tousled my hair. "It was nice having you in my bed."

I pointed to the bruise on my cheek. "I couldn't bear to look in the mirror. How bad is it?"

Marc looked down and blushed. "You still look beautiful to me."

If Freddy was the sexiest man I knew, and Tony was the toughest, Marc was definitely the sweetest.

I kissed him on the cheek. "Thank you."

Just then, I heard my cell phone ring. I ran into the bedroom to get it. It was Tony.

Shit.

I didn't want to talk to him.

I desperately wanted to talk to him.

I turned off my phone and put in my pocket.

I went into the kitchen and took a long swig of my tea.

"Who was it?" Marc asked.

"Just someone I used to know."

"Are you OK?" he asked me.

"I'm better," I said. "I just got a little freaked out."

"What are you going to do?"

Good question.

"First, I'm going to finish this croissant, which, by the way, is delicious. Then, I'm going to go home, shower, and get into some clean clothing. I'll figure the rest out later."

"You can stay here if you want," Marc said. "I mean, if you don't want to be alone."

"I don't think I'm in any danger," I told him, remembering how I thought that the pebbles my father was throwing at the window were gunshots. "I don't think I need to be too paranoid."

"I don't know," Marc said. "You can't be too careful."

I was getting advice from a man too afraid to leave his apartment. Had it come to this? I kissed him on the cheek. "Thanks for taking care of me."

By the time I left Marc's apartment, it was almost noon. I grabbed a cab home and on the drive turned my phone back on. Three messages from Tony. I was debating whether or not to listen to them when the phone rang.

It was Freddy.

"Hey," I answered.

"Yo, bubbala," he said, "how are you holding up? Did you cast off your spinsterish ways and spend the night with Macbeth?"

"Romeo."

"Whatever."

"I spent the night with someone," I said. I explained what Marc had found out about Michael's customers.

"That evil fuck," Freddy said. "I knew he was bad news from the moment I laid eyes on him."

"You thought he was hot the moment you laid eyes on him," I reminded him.

"Well, that too," Freddy admitted. "What are you going to do?"

"That's the question everyone's asking me. What do you think I should do?"

"Call Tony. This needs to go to the cops now."

"He's been calling me," I said.

"See? It's *bershert*."

"What if he doesn't believe me?"

"What if he does?"

"What if he's calling because he wants to get back with me?" I asked. "What if I can't say 'no,' and then he breaks my heart again? How many times am I going to keep making the same mistake? I can't keep doing the same wrong things and expecting them to turn out right. It's been seven years now . . ."

Freddy interrupted. "You didn't take your medication today, did you?"

I admitted that I hadn't.

"OK, champ," he said. "Just take a breath and listen. What if the mistake is *not* taking that chance with Tony? You've waited seven years for him, Kevin. And, let's face it; you did lay a kind of heavy trip on him with the whole *Working Boy* thing. Maybe he just needed some time to work through it.

"He's calling *you,* Kevin. Isn't that what you wanted? What if you gave him one more chance?"

That's the thing about Freddy. A part of him would always be in love with me, just like a part of me was always drawn to him.

But in the end, what he wanted most for me was to be happy. Even if that meant I wound up with another man.

The cab was just pulling up to my apartment.

"I think I will return his call," I told him. "I love you, you know."

"Please, you know I detest cheap sentiment," he answered. "Now go call your man. And be sure you tell me all about it."

On my way up to my apartment, I thought about what Freddy had said. He was right; it was a big deal for me to tell Tony I was working as an escort. Of course he was upset. Not that he had a right to be, but I could understand it.

I was looking forward to a nice long shower and then a call to Tony. With any luck at all, he'd be moved to come right over and the makeup sex would be great.

But when I got to my door I discovered the worst news of the day—it was unlocked.

My mother was back.

Great, I thought, I guess the limo didn't work. Thanks a lot, Dad.

"Mom?" I said, opening the door.

The masked figure from the hotel room stepped out from the hallway. "Not quite, whore."

I had just enough time to see the flash of the Taser before the lights went out.

CHAPTER 23

Naked in the Belly of the Beast

DARKNESS.

I tried to open my eyes, but they weighed a million pounds.

Arms hurt.

Whole body hurt.

I slipped back into the darkness.

Huh?

Where am I?

Opened my eyes but everything's still black.

Must be night time.

So sleepy.

Woke up again. The good news was I wasn't dead.

That was pretty much it for good news.

Now for everything else.

I was blindfolded, so I couldn't tell anything about my surroundings.

I was standing with my arms tied above my head. My shoulders ached. The floor under my feet felt rough, like cement. The air was stale and smelled faintly of leather.

One arm hurt like it had been jabbed with something. My guess was an injection of some kind.

The last thing I remembered was coming home and someone shooting me with a stun gun. It knocked me out. Whoever did that must have drugged me and brought me here.

Wherever here was.

I felt cool air on my skin which made me realize something else.

I was naked.

This was *so* not good.

I would have expected that my heart would have been pounding out of my chest, but I felt strangely calm. Whatever my abductor knocked me out with must have still been in my system.

Good, I thought. Use that to your advantage.

Breathe. Relax. Listen.

Don't panic.

Focus, Kevin, focus

Boy, did I wish I'd taken my medication today.

I heard someone in the room with me. Breathing.

"Uh, hello?" I asked.

I felt something touch me on the belly. I jerked away. "Hey!"

"Shhhh . . ." someone said. Something—a finger—touched me again, right under my neck. The finger slowly trailed down my chest, between my nipples, over my abdomen, stopping at my pubic hair.

"Shhh . . ."

It was all very *Silence of the Lambs.*

I knew I was supposed to be screaming or something, but I couldn't muster the energy. The hand slipped down to my balls, rolling them between his fingers. Then around to my ass, tracing over my crack, lingering at my hole.

"Shhhh . . ."

I know it sounds weird, and it must have been the drugs, but my most prominent feeling at the moment was boredom. If he was going to kill me, I wished he'd get on with it.

"What are you doing, Michael?"

The hand smacked my ass. Hard.

"Ow!"

OK, maybe hoping he'd get on with it wasn't such a good idea.

"I'm not Michael," he answered.

And it wasn't.

I knew that voice.

It hadn't been Michael all along.

How had I gotten everything all wrong?

The brother I thought was the victim was really the killer.

"Paul," I said.

"I'm not Paul," he said.

Huh?

"Call me Stryker," he said.

OK, that was definitely Paul's voice.

This time, he slapped me on the balls.

"Oww!"

"I said 'call me Stryker!'"

"Fine, fine, you're Stryker!"

I felt my blindfold being pulled off. The room was dim, and it took a minute until my eyes adjusted.

Yep, it was Paul Harrington, all right.

He also was naked. Hmm, I thought absently, he really does get better looking the more you see him.

I looked around. I was in a real, honest-to-goodness dungeon. The windowless walls were padded with what I assumed was some kind of soundproofing material. Many had shackles hanging from them. There was a rack, stockades, and even a sling.

An open cabinet held a cache of chains, whips, and clamps. On a shelf was a collection of dildos that ranged from dwarfish to Kong-like.

Welcome to Pervert's Paradise.

I liked it better with the blindfold on.

Paul's face looked fierce. His lips were tight and pulled back into a menacing grimace. His nostrils flared with rage. His eyes were narrow and looked dead inside.

I thought he was unhinged when I met him at the bar, but just how crazy was he? Was this Stryker crap a pose or some kind of split personality?

Had he killed his father and those other men—the supposed suicides?

But why would he have had them leave their money to his brother?

And how had he controlled them?

Control.

That was the key.

I looked again at Paul's eyes.

They weren't dead, they were vacant. He wasn't controlling anyone. Not even himself.

Oh Paul, I'm so sorry.

Suddenly, I didn't feel quite so calm. I was angry.

"Michael, you son of bitch! Your own brother! What have you done to him?"

From behind me, I heard muffled applause. Then the deep, sensuous voice of Michael Harrington.

"Well done," he said. He came around to face me.

Michael was the Dark Lord of Scary Sex. His tall muscular body was clad in skintight black leather lace-up pants tucked into black boots. He was shirtless except for a black leather vest. He wore matching gloves with studs along the back. His huge pectorals flexed with each breath. His handsome face wore a condescending smirk.

He reached up and pinched my nipples. Hard. I denied him the pleasure of crying out.

"I'm impressed," he said. "I thought it would take you a lot longer than that to figure out what was happening. You're a smart little faggot, aren't you?"

"Fuck you."

Michael punched me in the gut. I saw it coming and relaxed into it, but it still hurt. Michael wasn't playing around.

"Unfortunately for you," he said, "I happen to like hurting pretty little boys. You don't want to make things worse for yourself by provoking me."

I looked at Paul to see how he was reacting. Now that Michael was on the scene, Paul stood motionless, his face a blank slate.

Michael had every advantage in this situation. I had to play him right.

"I know you're in control," I said. "Look at what you've done with Paul."

Michael laughed. "Oh, that? Paul has been mine since we were teenagers. Watch this."

Michael turned to his brother. "Stryker: Wake up."

Suddenly, Paul's entire demeanor changed. Awareness came back into his eyes. His body relaxed, then jerked even more upright. "What the hell—Michael who's that?" He walked closer to me. "Kevin? You're naked." He looked down. "I'm naked! What the fu—."

"Paul: Stryker's back."

Bam: Just like that, the light went off for little brother. Once again, he stood alert but expressionless.

Michael spoke to him dismissively. "Now, just stand there and await your orders until you're called again."

Things weren't looking too good for me.

"Pretty cool, huh?" Michael winked at me. "It's one of my favorite tricks."

I figured my best bet was to keep him talking while I thought of a plan. "Who's 'Stryker?'" I asked.

"Oh that? Just a little alter ego I created for him when it worked to my advantage to have him rough someone up a little. It allows him an excuse to let his anger out. You know what they say, every bottom wants to be a top, and every top wants to be a bottom."

"Nice," I said. "So, I guess it was you who sent Paul to talk with me at the bar the other day."

"Oh no," Michael said. "That was Paul working on his own. I didn't approve of it at all. Of course, I had to punish him for that."

He looked at Paul. "Stryker: Turn around."

Paul pivoted. Rows of whip marks crisscrossed his lower back and his ass.

"I think he learned his lesson," Michael said. "But the damage he did—telling you about me, well, that's damage I have to undo."

He sighed. "Yes, I always have to clean up after my brother's messes."

"How are you doing this?" I asked Michael.

"Paul has always been my greatest achievement. He's the one who gave me my start, you might say.

"Even when we were kids, I knew he idolized me. It didn't take much encouragement to turn that into devotion. He would pretty much do whatever I said from the time he was twelve.

"But I wanted more. When I went to college, I sought out people who shared my . . . interests. First, it was just hypnosis. Standard stuff. I was good at it. Soon, I was putting my classmates under. They thought it was just for fun, but they didn't know that all the fun was mine.

"From my sophomore year on, I didn't have a roommate who wasn't under my control by October. I had boys who did my homework, boys who gave me their allowance. I had one boy who did my laundry every week for three years. He was trained to have an orgasm in his pants every time he handled my dirty boxer shorts.

"My only problem was keeping him from stealing them. That was a hard habit to break.

"And the girls—the girls! That's where my true passion lies, you know. I had more pussy in college than the entire football team put together."

"Classy," I offered.

Michael leered at me. "Well, you know what they say: Any slut in a storm." He flicked a finger towards my dick and I jerked back. He chuckled, then continued.

"In my senior year, though, that's when I really took it up a notch. I had a psychology professor who had worked for the CIA in the sixties. I did some research on him, and it turned out he was working on mind control experiments."

Michael started rubbing my chest and shoulders. His touch was gentle.

"Can you see why I believe I'm doing the Lord's work? What are the odds that, given my talents, I'd meet such a gifted mentor? It was meant to be.

"He taught me techniques that weren't documented anywhere. Of course, in exchange, I had to let him blow me every once in awhile. Yes, he was another little faggot." Michael gave me a surprised look. "There sure are a lot of you."

Michael's hand moved lower. He traced slow circles over my stomach.

"We're such simple beings. All of us driven by the desires to seek out pleasure and to avoid pain. Professor Standler taught me all about using those most basic of human drives to get even more control. To train people to condition themselves for you."

Michael's hand gently cupped my balls. "Pleasure." He squeezed. "Pain."

I doubled over as much as my restraints would allow. That one hurt.

He laughed. "It's so simple!"

He went over to the cabinet and took out a black box.

"Of course, over the years, it's gotten even simpler." He pulled out a long syringe.

"Better living through chemistry," he beamed. "An hour from now, you'll be no worry to me at all."

"You can't kill me. Too many people know I'm onto you."

"Oh, I don't need to kill you," Michael said. "I'm thinking I'll keep you around. For fun." He smacked my ass again. "Controlling boys like you is my definition of fun."

"You can't hypnotize someone against their will," I said.

"I'm afraid that old wives' tale is a little dated," Michael said. "And what I'm going to do goes far beyond what you know as 'hypnotism.'

"Today, for example, I'm going to give you a shot of this. It will make you very suggestible for a period of about twenty-four hours. In that time, I'm going to convince you that not only am I your friend, but that you find me irresistibly attractive."

He ran his hand over his huge pectoral muscle. "My guess is that won't be too much of a stretch for you."

Great, I thought. In addition to all his other bad traits, he's full of himself.

"Not only will you stop butting your nose into my business, but you'll find yourself compelled to come back here tomorrow. And the day after that. Within seven days, you'll be doing anything I say.

"Basically," Michael said, "you'll belong to me. Won't that be fun?"

Michael walked towards me with the needle. I had a plan. If I timed it just right, I should be able to pull up with my arms and get him with a good kick in the gut.

Unfortunately, that was pretty much it for the plan. After that, I'd still be tied up.

Unless I got him right on the nose. With the heel of my foot, at just the right angle, I could drive his nasal bone right into his brain. I've heard you can kill a man like that.

That worked for me.

Of course, my odds of pulling it off were pretty low, but it was the best plan I had.

He was getting closer.

I gripped the ropes that held me to ceiling, getting ready to pull up my knees.

He pulled the plunger back on the syringe.

Focus, I thought. I visualized the movement of my leg, the arc of my foot as it made contact with the middle of his face. Hit him with the heel, the hardest part, and follow through with all my strength.

I was ready.

He was almost within reach.

One more step.

Come on, you bastard.

If this didn't work, I was dead.

I was ready.

The phone rang. From upstairs came a distinctive ring tone. Darth Vader's theme song from *Star Wars.*

Michael lowered the syringe. "Ah," he said. "Talk about the proverbial saved by the bell. It's wifey, I'm afraid. But don't worry." He grabbed my cock and squeezed hard. I bit my lip to keep from crying out. "I'll be back soon."

What "wife?" I wondered. Michael wasn't married.

He went up the stairs two at a time and closed the door behind him.

This was my chance.

I looked at Paul, who stood ramrod straight awaiting further instructions.

"Paul," I hissed, "help me!"

He didn't move.

"Snap out of it!"

Nothing.

"Come on man," I implored, "wake up."

I might as well have been talking to the wall.

I tried to remember how Michael had directed him.

"Paul: Up!"

Zip.

"Paul: Untie!"

Nada.

"Paul: Wake!"

This wasn't going to work.

I pulled at my bonds. Nothing. I felt the ropes with my fingers.

Wait, I knew this knot. A standard double eight.

It had been taught to me by Melvin Cuttlebeck, my favorite would-be sadist.

He had also taught me how to get out of one.

I wiggled my fingers. Just enough slack for me to work the knot. I relaxed my mind, took a deep breath, and went to work.

Two minutes later, my first hand slipped free.

Please, I thought, please Michael keep talking to whatever woman you've blessed with a Darth Vader ring tone.

It was the work of a minute to free my second hand.

I dropped to the floor as quietly as I could. I was free!

Now that the ropes were untied, blood flowed back into my fingers in a painful rush. I shook it off. I tried to stand up, but my knees were too shaky and my head was too dizzy.

Keep moving. I crawled over to Paul. "Wake up, man, we've got to get out of here." I shook his shoulders.

Still, nothing.

All right, no help there.

I looked around for another exit, but the only way out was through the door that Michael had gone through.

A weapon? If my clothes were down here, I could grab my Mace and try to spray him. I looked around. There, behind me, was what I had been wearing.

Even better, I saw the Taser that had zapped me.

Time for Michael get the shocking surprise, I thought.

"Aren't you the tricky one?"

Michael's voice boomed from the bottom of the stairs. I was so focused on grabbing the Taser that I hadn't heard him come down. There was no way I could get to it before he reached me.

"Oh," he said, descending the steps, "breaking you is going to be even more fun than I thought."

CHAPTER 24

The Final Showdown

I RAN THROUGH my options. The Taser was too far away for me to make a grab for it. I didn't think I could take him in a fight, either. I had no weapon, no ally, and nowhere to go. I was naked, totally vulnerable, and at his mercy.

I had nothing. Here I was facing my death and what had I accomplished? I spent the last five years of my life making men's sexual fantasies come true. What fucking good could that do me in a situation like this?

Hmmmm, I thought. I looked at Michael in his carefully assembled leather daddy drag. Wasn't he just another trick playing dress up? He wanted to be the big man? The master?

Lucky for me, I had a lot of experience knowing how to exploit a man's desires.

You think you're in charge, Michael? Well, you're about to learn that there are all kinds of control, motherfucker.

I was scared. I was hurt. But I could do this.

Focus, Kevin, focus.

"Please sir," I said, falling to my knees again. "Please, before you give me that needle, just one thing."

Michael regarded me from where he stood by the stairs.

"Just let me service you," I said. "Just once. As I am. Let me remember this.

"Look at you," I said. "Look at those muscles. Those arms. That chest. Do you know how much I've wanted to be here, like this? On my knees before you?

"Give me the shot sir," I said. "Make me your slave. I want to be yours. Why do you think I went to see you at The Center? Why do you think I met with Paul that night?"

Michael took a step forward. His mouth was slightly open and his breathing grew ragged.

"When Paul told me about what you had done to him, it made me so hot, Sir. I wished it could have been me you were controlling. So I could touch you. Please you. Serve you."

I started to crawl towards him, keeping my head turned up so he could see my pleading face.

"You're so fucking hot, sir. So big. So strong. So much in control."

Michael wasn't gay, or even truly bisexual, but this wasn't about sex. What had his brother told me? It was about power.

Michael was used to using all kinds of tricks to get that power, but had he ever been in a situation where he didn't have to? Here I was crawling towards him. Submissive, vulnerable, naked, willing. How would he handle that?

Michael's pants began to fill out.

Got you, fucker.

"Break me to your will, sir. Hurt me. Use me. I want it."

I was at his feet. I looked up at his bulging crotch. "Please let me taste you, Sir. Just once. Take it out. Please." I started licking the smooth surface of his boots.

That did it. With a groan, Michael frantically started unlacing his pants. His big fingers fumbled with the strings. He was shaking.

An eager slave. I could see how badly this was turning him on.

He finally got his pants open. He pulled out his cock and balls. Both were oversized, in direct proportion to the rest of his massive body.

Some guys have all the luck, I thought ruefully.

But not for long.

I looked up from his boots.

"You're so big, Sir. So strong."

I met his eyes and saw his naked lust.

"Thank you Sir," I said, remembering that time at the gym when Randy Bostinick straddled me on the bench and I accidentally sat up too fast. The force of that blow almost neutered him.

That's the bitch about history. It tends to repeat itself.

I pushed up off my hands with all my might, bringing the full weight of my head right up to where it would do Michael the least good. The impact sent his balls up somewhere into the vicinity of his lower colon.

"Fuck!" Michael cried, doubling over.

"You fucker!" I screamed, bringing my knee into his crotch. This time, his hands blocked some of the blow, but he still staggered backwards.

Bent over, his head was just about level with my arm. I pivoted back onto my left foot and brought my fist back for a right hook. The trick to a hook is not to hit with your hand, but to put your whole body into it. I twisted my hip and extended my arm.

"Ai-yee!" I cried.

This time, Michael was ready for me. As much pain as he was in, he managed to catch my arm in his left fist. Following through, he brought his right fist around and caught me on the chin.

Even though he was off balance, Michael's tremendous strength was enough to knock me to the floor.

In a flash, he was on top of me, sitting on my crotch. We were both panting with exertion.

"You really hurt me, boy," he snarled. "But you know what? I kind of like being hurt." He leaned over and licked my face, humping his still-exposed genitals over my stomach. He got hard again.

What had he said? *Every top wants to be a bottom*?

"Good," I said, "then you'll like it when I fuck your brains out."

Michael laughed; a deep throaty rumbled that scared me more than anything else yet.

"Oh, I don't like to be hurt by little boys like you, whore," he snarled. "No, I have something else in mind for you."

He brought his mouth to my neck and licked there, too. Then a playful nip. Then he sunk his teeth in and clamped down.

This time, screaming wasn't a pleasure I could deny him. "Aaah!" I cried.

He pulled back. I felt blood dripping down my neck. I thought I would vomit from the pain.

I could still get out of this. I just had to play along again until he let me up.

"Yes," I said, "hurt me, let me . . ."

Michael put his finger to his lips. "No more games. No more words."

"I could make you feel so good," I said, "if you'd just let me . . ."

Michael put both his hands around my neck. "Maybe it would be better if you never said anything again."

He leaned into his hands, cutting off my air. I felt myself panic as I struggled to breathe.

He took his hands away. "You like that, whore?"

I gulped in some air. "Are you going to kill me? Like you did your father?"

"You little idiot," Michael laughed again. "I didn't kill my father."

I coughed. "Made him kill himself, then."

Michael leaned over and kissed me on the lips. I clenched my teeth. "You stupid little whore. Is that really what you think? I haven't spoken to my father since I was a child. I had nothing to do with his death."

He laughed again. "Oh, maybe I convinced a couple of other guys that life wasn't quite worth living. Well, not until they changed their wills, of course." He chuckled. This was all a game to him.

"But not my father. No, I think that old queen killed himself, you little idiot. But don't worry—you'll get the chance to ask him soon enough."

So, Michael hadn't killed Allen either? I really was the worst detective ever.

I bucked my hips wildly, but there was no way I was going to get him off me.

No one to help me either.

"Paul!" I screamed out one more time.

"No more of that," Michael said. He brought his hands back to my neck. They tightened around me. I couldn't breathe.

"Stryker," I tried to scream, "help me!"

But with Michael's huge hands on my throat I could barely be heard.

"Shhh," Michael said. "Shhh." He leaned in more.

"Tony!" I cried, but by now, only in my mind. "I love you!"

I felt a huge rush of heat as adrenaline surged through me, but there was nowhere for it to go.

The lights in the room flickered and dimmed until I realized it wasn't the lights at all.

It was my life that was going out.

Michael's face started to float away.

Blackness descended.

This was it.

Good-bye, world.

What a shitty way to go.

From a hundred miles away, I heard a sizzle and then a thud.

Michael's arms relaxed and released.

I turned onto my side and gasped for breath. Michael's body rolled off me and slumped to the floor. It was a minute before I could look up.

Paul Harrington stood there, naked, holding the Taser limply in his hands. Tears rolled down his cheeks and his shoulders shook. "You bastard," he said, looking at Michael's unconscious body. "You bastard, you bastard, you bastard, you bastard . . ."

I pulled myself up and put an arm around Paul. "It's OK," I told him. "It's over. It's over now." He dropped the stun gun. He put his arms around me and sobbed into my shoulder. "It's over."

There was a loud bang and I felt Paul's arms go limp as he slumped to the floor. A bright red bloom of blood spread across his chest. What? I turned to the door.

I saw who Michael referred to as "wifey." Not his wife. His brother's.

Paul's wife, Alana Harrington, stood at the top of the stairs holding a small pistol. She wore a black business suit, black pillbox hat, and black leather boots.

Damn if she didn't look a little like Darth Vader.

"You boys," she said, descending the steps, "I can't turn my back on my own husband for a minute without finding him making out with some guy in my own house."

She shrugged. "Can you blame me for shooting him?"

I thought I had been in Michael's house this whole time, but really it was Paul's. Somehow, though, I knew this sick little playroom wasn't his. Looking at Alana, I understood who the real master around here was.

Or should I say "mistress?"

Alana walked over to Michael's inert body and kicked him absently. "Useless piece of shit. Fun to play with, and not without his talents, but, still, look at him."

She went over to the cabinet and took out a long whip. She transferred her gun to her left hand and held the whip with her right. She flicked it with an expertise not seen since Michelle Pfeiffer played Catwoman in *Batman Returns.* The tip landed with exact precision on Michael's exposed butt with enough snap to draw blood.

But not enough to rouse him.

"Useless!" Alana cried. She sneered at his backside. "Maybe if he could have kept it in his pants I wouldn't have to clean up this mess."

Michael had used almost the same words. Now that I had a chance to give his ass a good look, I saw that the lash mark Alana delivered today wasn't the first one to scar him. "So," I asked, "how long have you and Michael been having an affair?"

"Aren't you the clever one?" she asked. "Paul had always been of little interest to me, but he was rich, and trying so desperately to be straight. I knew I wouldn't have to put up with much sex from him so I figured 'what the hell.' We married, I had everything I ever wanted. Life was good.

"But, as you can imagine, things were a little boring. I had playmates, of course, men Paul knew nothing about. He was so busy with his own secrets he never suspected mine.

"When I met Michael, though, there was a challenge. It didn't take me long to figure out what was going on between him and Paul. When I confronted Michael, he thought I'd go to the police. Imagine that!

"I loved it! His control over Paul was amazing! Oh, together, the things we'd have poor Paul do! I'd be *dripping* with excitement. In the beginning, being with Michael was thrilling. Thrilling!"

She planted her stiletto heel in the small of his back and pressed down hard. No response.

"But after a while I understood what he really wanted. Isn't it what all men want?" She kneeled next to him and stroked his hair. "He wanted to be told what to do. He wanted to be punished."

She stood up and cracked the whip over his head.

"He wanted Mommy."

Every top wants to be a bottom.

Alana narrowed her eyes. "What do *you* want, Kevin?"

On her lips, my name sounded like a curse.

"Well," I said, "now that you ask, I would really, really like to leave." I walked towards my clothing. "And don't worry—your secrets are safe with me. You guys just keep on doing . . . whatever it is you're doing and I'll be on my way." I reached for my pants.

"Freeze, faggot," Alana thundered, pointing her pistol at me. I froze.

"Jesus!" she cried. "My husband, my lover, their father, you—I'm surrounded by faggots!

"Here's how I see this going down," she continued. "I shoot you now. When the big dummy wakes up," she gestured towards Michael, "we'll figure out some way to make it look like you and Paul killed each other in a lover's quarrel. I'll be the grieving widow and no one will ever be the wiser.

"A year or two from now, I'll marry Michael. With all the money he's been making at the Center, especially after I gave him some particularly brilliant suggestions on how to increase his revenue, I think I'll be pretty comfortable, don't you?"

Now, I was sure who was in charge. It wasn't Paul. It wasn't Michael. It was Alana who held the whip. Literally, as it turns out.

"It was your idea to have him make those men kill themselves?" I asked her.

Her grin was pure evil. "Guilty as charged!" she said cheerily. "But those weren't men," she added. "They were faggots, like you." She looked at Paul. His face was white as snow, but I could see his chest still rise and fall. He wasn't dead. At least not yet. "Like him. Trust me, they won't be missed."

Her hatred of gay men, her twisted relationships with the Harrington men . . . it was Alana who murdered my friend, wasn't it? I finally figured it out.

"You killed Allen, you psychotic little bitch!" I shouted at her. "And I miss him! And Paul misses him too!"

Alana looked at me quizzically. "Allen? Michael's father? I didn't kill Allen. Why would I kill Allen?"

Damn. Was I never going to get this right? Who did kill Allen?

She pointed the gun at me.

"You, however, should *not* have called me a bitch."

I had run of out tricks.

There was nothing left me to do, nowhere for me to go.

I wouldn't beg, though. Fuck her.

She pulled the trigger. A shot rang out. Blood exploded across my face and chest.

It didn't hurt, though.

That was weird.

Then I realized the blood wasn't mine.

Alana fell to the floor.

Twenty feet behind her, at the top of the stairs, Tony Rinaldi stood with his service revolver in both hands. "Police—freeze!" he shouted. Then, to me, "are you hurt?"

I've been happy to see that son of a bitch before in my life, but never with such good reason. If I wasn't already in love with him, I'm pretty sure I would have fallen right then and there.

"I'm fine," I answered.

He raced down the stairs, keeping an eye on Michael and Paul.

"I think they're out," I said.

Tony stood awkwardly in front of me.

"What the hell happened here?"

I pointed at Michael. "Bad guy." I pointed at Paul. "Good guy."

I pointed down at Alana, who laid moaning and cursing on the floor, holding her hand over her shoulder where Tony had shot her. "Total fucking bitch. Can you shoot her again?"

Tony laughed. He put an arm on my shoulder. "My little tough guy. Are you OK?"

As shaken as I was, I couldn't help but notice that Tony had called me "his" little guy.

I had held it together for a long time, but now that Tony was here, I didn't have to be strong anymore.

My lips quivered. “Paul really is innocent in all this. He needs an ambulance.”

Tony put his arms around me, keeping an eye on Michael at all times. “I’ve already called one,” he said. “And backup, too.”

I started to shake in his arms. I really didn’t want to cry in front of him again, but I wasn’t sure I could hold it in anymore.

“I’m so sorry,” Tony said gently.

“Sorry?” I sniffled. “You just saved my life.”

“No, for everything else,” he said, kissing me on the top of the head. “I love you, Kevvy.”

There was no holding back now. The tears came hot and fast as I sobbed in his arms. He kept kissing me, telling me shush, shush, it was all over, everything was going to be fine.

I finally was able to catch my breath for long enough to say what I’d been longing to say for seven years.

“I love you, too, Tony.”

He kissed me on the lips. Angels sang.

Alana muttered, “Everywhere I go, even the cops—fucking faggots!”

CHAPTER 25

Who Killed Allen Harrington?

I GOT DRESSED before the ambulances and police arrived.

They took me and Tony aside and asked us what happened. Since Tony was a fellow cop, they let him speak first. He explained how he had found me. He had called me several times with some important news. When I hadn't returned his calls, he went looking for me at my apartment.

When he found the door open, and I wasn't there, he got worried. Not knowing who any of my friends were, he took a chance and pressed redial on my home phone. It connected him with the last person I had dialed from it—Marc Wilgus.

Marc told Tony that he had reason to believe the Harringtons might have done me some harm. He gave Tony their home addresses (there wasn't any information Marc couldn't get within a minute), and Tony went by Michael's place before showing up at Paul's.

Just in time, it turned out.

Then Tony got to hear while I gave my statement to a grey-haired detective in his fifties with kind eyes and a sympathetic manner.

I told the detective how Michael and Alana had confessed their crimes to me. How they were responsible for the deaths of several men who had gone to Michael for help. I also explained how they had planned on getting rid of me and Paul. I left some of the story out, like the parts that involved Randy Bostinick and Mrs. Cherry, to protect my friends.

"You're a pretty brave kid," the detective who took my statement said. He looked at Tony. Although he didn't know what the relationship between us was, from the way Tony was looking at me, he could tell it ran deep. "You should be proud of him," he told Tony.

Tony nodded. "I am."

The detective turned back to me. "We're going to need you to come into the station at some point to give a formal statement, but I bet you're pretty beat."

I nodded.

"Do you want to go to the hospital? You've been through a lot—you should get yourself checked out."

"Please," I said. "I just want to go home."

He turned back to Tony. "Can I trust you to get him home safely and look after him?"

Tony nodded. "I'll take care of him." He looked at me. "I want to take care of him."

The detective nodded. "Alrighty, then." He handed Tony his card. "Have him call me tomorrow. You're free to go."

The minute we got into Tony's car, I started to ask him questions.

"Listen," Tony said, "why don't you just relax for a minute? Close your eyes. We'll talk when we get back to your place."

I looked around at the suburban neighborhood.

"Wait a minute," I said. "Where *are* we?"

"White Plains," Tony said. "Now, quiet."

Fine, I thought. I'll close my eyes for a minute.

Then I'll call Freddy and tell him all about what happened. I think my little adventure was even better than *Charlie's Angels.*

That was the last thing I remember thinking before falling into a sleep so deep that I didn't wake even when Tony carried me into my apartment.

I woke up an hour later in my bed. In Tony's arms.

Finally.

He had fallen asleep while holding me. I looked at his still, peaceful face. How beautiful he was with his strong cheekbones and silky black hair. Even his eyelashes were perfect as they fluttered in his slumber. Like butterflies, I thought.

Then they opened.

"Hi," he said.

"Hi, yourself," I answered.

"You OK?"

"Never better."

He pulled me onto his chest. "You sure? Maybe we should go to the hospital. Just to get you checked out."

I slipped my hand inside his shirt and felt his strong chest.

"I'm fine," I insisted. "There's just one thing I can't figure out."

"Shoot," Tony said.

I shuddered. "Don't use that word."

Tony chuckled. "Sorry."

"If it wasn't Paul, Michael, or Alana who killed Allen, who did? I still can't believe he killed himself."

Tony sat up. "That's what I was trying to call you about! You were right, Allen didn't kill himself. But it wasn't a Harrington, either."

"Who was it, then?"

"Remember those two women at the reading of the will? From the Association for the Acceptance of Lesbian and Gay Youth?"

I nodded.

"Turns out that one of them was embezzling contributions," Tony explained. "Allen was studying the financials and noticed the discrepancies. He called them the day of his death and explained that he was going to have someone look into it.

"What he didn't realize was that the one he talked to was the one who was doing the embezzlement. She was a quiet woman, but she had a quiet problem: an addiction to gambling. She panicked and went to see him. She was terrified that the exposure of her crimes would cause her partner to leave her. She's very shy and withdrawn and would have been lost without her girlfriend."

I remembered Lori, the woman I thought of as a "gentle giant."

"Anyway, she panicked and went to see him. She thought she could change his mind. When that didn't work, she totally lost it and hit him over the head with a marble paperweight he kept on his desk. It knocked him out cold.

"She didn't know what to do. Not only was he going to expose her as a fraud, not only would she find herself alone, but now he would have her arrested for assault. So, she threw him over the railing. Figured that would hide the fact that he'd been hit, and with his death, any chance of her charity scam being exposed would die with him. She had no idea her group was in his will, though."

"Holy shit," I said under my breath. I remembered bumping into Lori at The Stuff of Life and being struck by how powerful she was. I could see her tossing Allen's body as effortlessly as I'd toss a tin can. I shuddered.

"She knew that if Allen lived he'd tell the truth about her and that she'd probably end up in jail. Of course, she's going away for a lot longer now."

"How did you figure this all out?" I asked.

"I didn't," he said. "She was right—the fall from the balcony crushed the back of his skull so badly that we totally missed the trauma of her blow. But she confessed to her girlfriend, and the girlfriend convinced her to turn herself in. Apparently, she did it in a moment of madness and she's been unable to live with herself since. Plus, I think there's something a little off with her, too. Turns out there were a lot of victims in this case."

I remembered Lori's words to me when I met her at The Stuff of Life. Something about how you don't know what someone was capable of until they did it. The stricken look on her face when she said it. I wasn't surprised she confessed—I think she was giving us clues even then.

Then I remembered something I had seen when I went to Allen's apartment with Tony. The spreadsheets I saw on his desk with "call

T. S." written on them. They must have been the financial statements for the Association and T. S. was . . .

"Tamela Steel!" I shouted.

"Excuse me?"

"Tamela Steel, Allen's lawyer. I met her at the reading of his will." I reminded him about the note on Allen's desk. "That's who he was going to call about the embezzlement."

"Huh," said Tony.

"So that uncapped pen really *was* a clue," I bragged. "See, I'm not bad at this detective stuff." I couldn't wait to tell all this to Freddy.

"I gotta admit you got a lot of it right. Allen didn't kill himself. And if you hadn't looked into the Harringtons, we would never have found out about Michael and Alana's sick little game of murder by suicide. Who knows how many more people they would have convinced to kill themselves?

"Plus," Tony added, "there was that business with the brother, Paul. Maybe now he can get his life back together."

He tousled my hair. "You done good, Kevvy."

Kevvy. If he knew how giddy it made me every time he called me that, would he still say it?

"Those men," I said, leaning up on my elbows so I could look him in the eyes. "The ones who killed themselves. They only wound up going to Michael because they couldn't accept themselves."

"I know," Tony said.

"What about you?" I asked him. "Can you accept yourself? This? Me?"

Tony pulled me towards him. "I don't know. I think so. I want to find out."

I smiled.

"But I don't think I can accept what you do for a living, Kevvy. We're gonna have to talk about that one."

Ouch. "OK," I said.

"And I still have a wife. Let's not forget that."

I nodded.

"We have a long history, kid. It hasn't exactly been a great one, either."

History does tend to repeat itself, I thought for the second time that day.

"I guess I don't know. I just don't want . . . "

"You don't want to hurt me," I finished for him.

He rolled his eyes. "OK, you got me all figured out, don't you, Doctor IQ?"

I nodded.

"How about you?" he asked. "What do you want?"

What did I want? What did I need? Conflicted, complicated Tony who still made my heart race like no other man? Sexy, faithful Freddy who was always there for me? Brilliant, sweet Marc who needed me to rescue him? And what about Romeo at the balcony? He was a good reminder that there were a lot of possibilities left to be explored.

Tony was waiting for an answer. So was I.

I spent so much time trying to figure out what Tony was after, but what did *I* want?

That was the mystery I *really* needed to solve.

Have I mentioned recently how beautiful he was?

"I know what I want right now," I said, straddling him. His lips parted in anticipation of my kiss.

I figured it was a start.

Acknowledgments

My fondest gratitude goes to my wonderful, supportive agent, Matthew Carnicelli. Matthew, when you called to tell me you "laughed out loud" and wanted to represent my book, it was the highlight of a year's hard work. Thanks for pestering me to finish the first sequel, too. I'm working on it, I promise!

All of you at Alyson Books rock for publishing this. Thanks for taking a chance on a first-time author. I hope this sells tons of copies and we work together again.

A special shout-out to my first editor, Joseph Pittman. I miss you, man. And great big thanks to Richard Fumosa, for coming in at the end and taking me over the finish line.

Starting this book was easy—actually finishing it took more discipline than I had on my own. My sincerest thanks, then, to my life coach, Laurie Hubbs. If you, dear reader, are stuck on any of your life goals, shoot me an e-mail and I'll give you Laurie's number.

Thanks to Lis and Stephen, my beta testers. If you had hated the book, I wouldn't have had the courage to show it to another living soul. Your early encouragement meant the world to me.

Appreciation and apologies to any friends, relatives, exes, or other individuals who feel they were lampooned or misrepresented in these pages. Whichever character you feel is based on you probably isn't—unless you like the depiction, in which case—you're welcome!

Lastly, thanks to anyone who's reading this—especially if you paid for it. Kevin Connor is coming back soon. Till then, you can follow his adventures and mine at ScottSherman.typepad.com